THE
BABY-SITTERS
CLUB®

BOY-CRAZY STACEY

DON'T MISS THE OTHER BABY-SITTERS CLUB GRAPHIC NOVELS!

KRISTY'S GREAT IDEA

THE TRUTH ABOUT STACEY

MARY ANNE SAVES THE DAY

CLAUDIA AND MEAN JANINE

DAWN AND THE IMPOSSIBLE THREE

KRISTY'S BIG DAY

ANN M. MARTIN

THE BABY-SITTERS CLUB

BOY-CRAZY STACEY

A GRAPHIC NOVEL BY

GALE GALLIGAN

WITH COLOR BY BRADEN LAMB

An Imprint of
■ SCHOLASTIC

All rights reserved. Published by Graphix, an imprint of
Scholastic Inc., *Publishers since 1920.* SCHOLASTIC, GRAPHIX,
THE BABY-SITTERS CLUB, and associated logos are trademarks
and/or registered trademarks of Scholastic Inc.

The publisher does not have any control over and does not assume any
responsibility for author or third-party websites or their content.

Library of Congress Control Number: 2018953576

ISBN 978-1-338-30452-7 (hardcover)
ISBN 978-1-338-30451-0 (paperback)

10 9 8 7 6 5 4 3 2   19 20 21 22 23

Printed in the U.S.A.   40
First edition, September 2019

Edited by Cassandra Pelham Fulton and David Levithan
Book design by Phil Falco
Publisher: David Saylor

This book is for June and Ward Cleaver
(alias Noël and Steve) from the Beav

A. M. M.

For Mom, Dad, Lori, and all
our childhood beach adventures.

And for Patrick, who I forgive for pretending to be
a sea monster and grabbing my ankle that one time.

G. G.

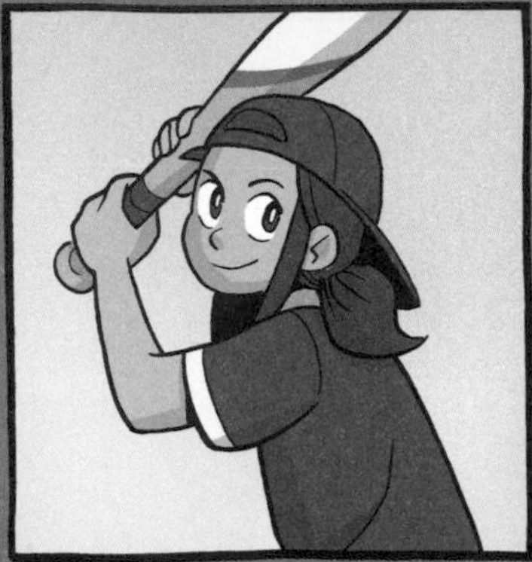

KRISTY THOMAS
PRESIDENT

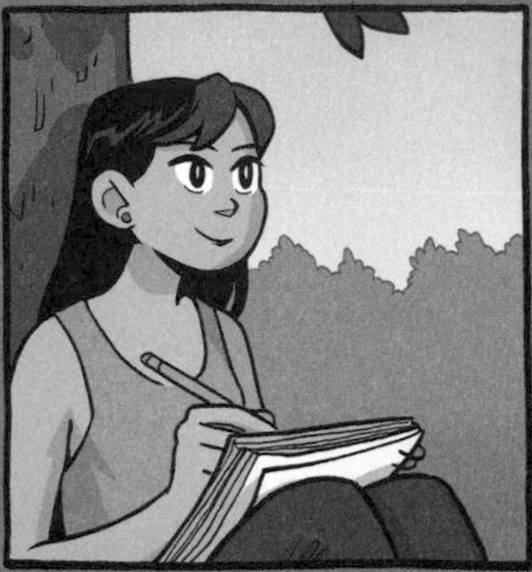

CLAUDIA KISHI
VICE PRESIDENT

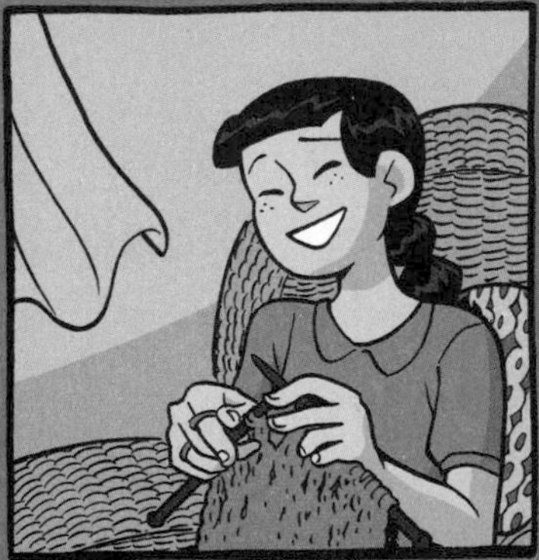

MARY ANNE SPIER
SECRETARY

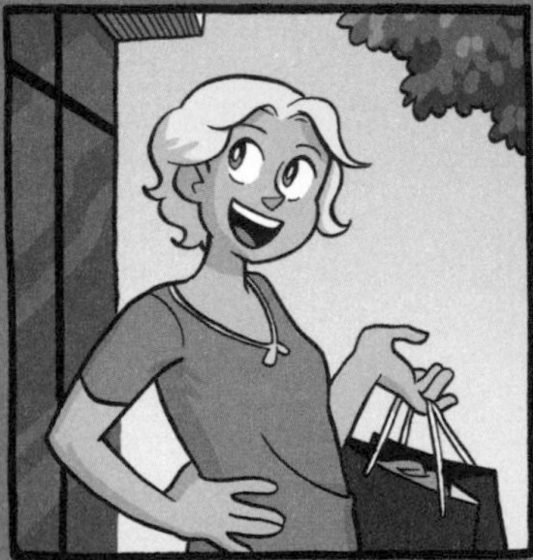

STACEY MCGILL
TREASURER

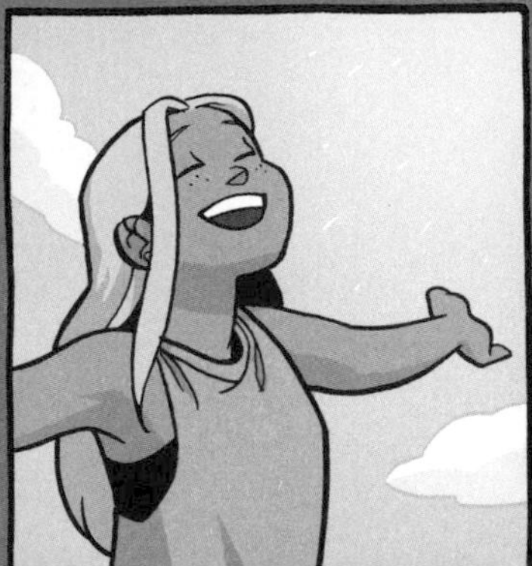

DAWN SCHAFER
ALTERNATE OFFICER

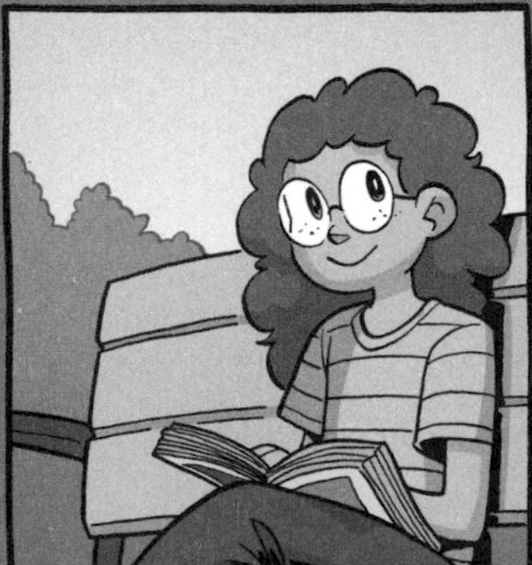

MALLORY PIKE
JUNIOR OFFICER

CHAPTER 1

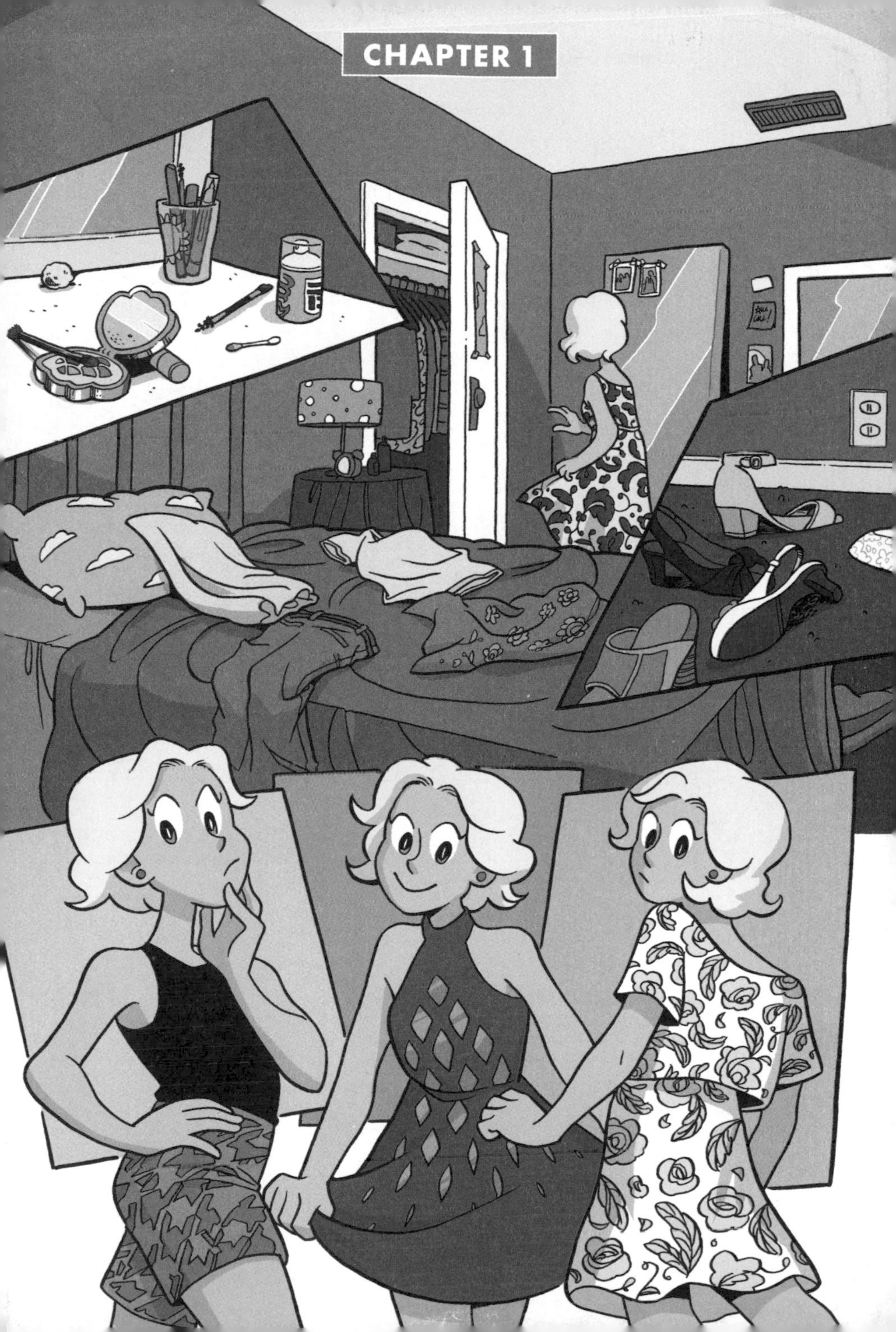

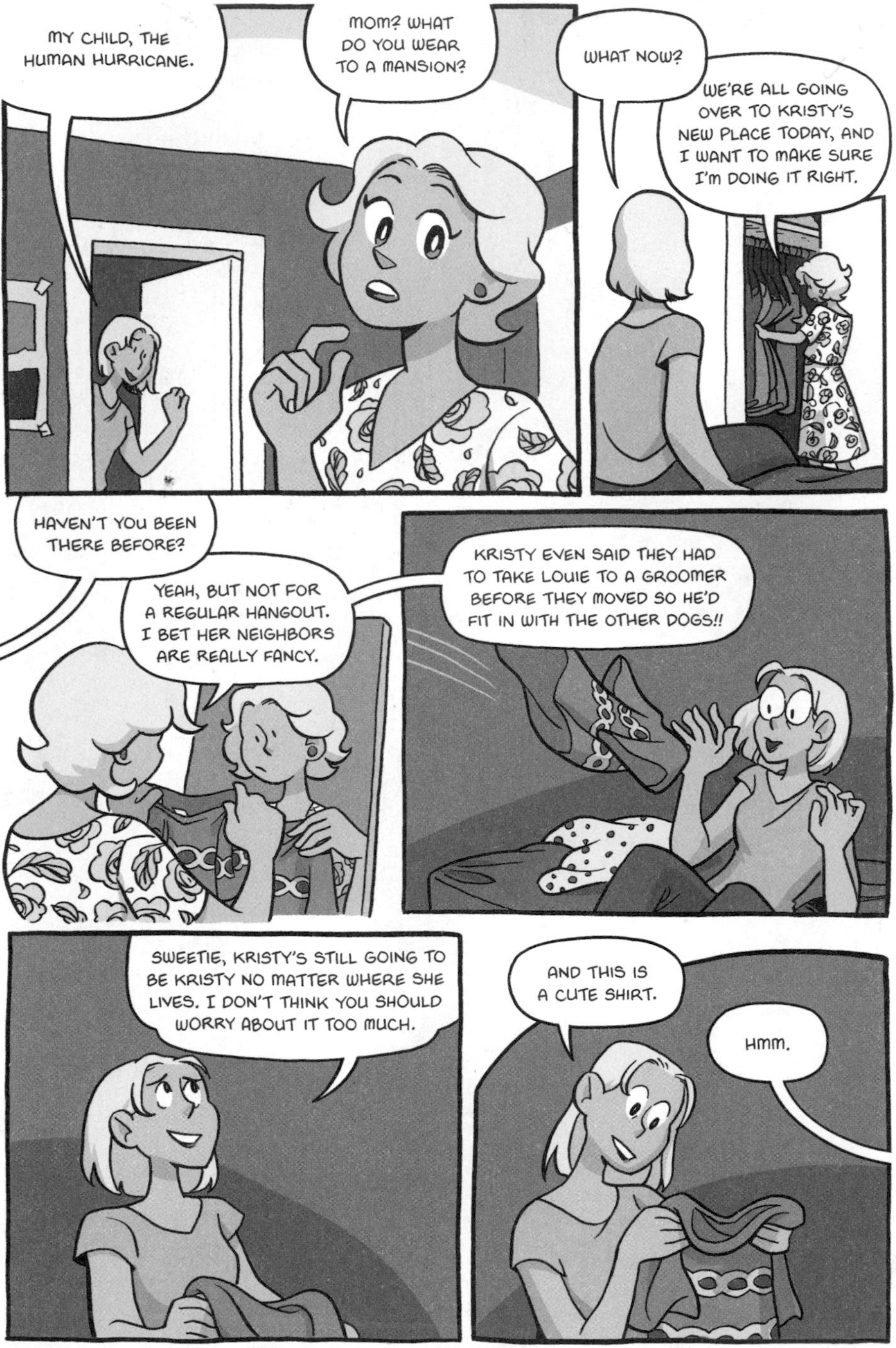
MY CHILD, THE HUMAN HURRICANE.
MOM? WHAT DO YOU WEAR TO A MANSION?
WHAT NOW?
WE'RE ALL GOING OVER TO KRISTY'S NEW PLACE TODAY, AND I WANT TO MAKE SURE I'M DOING IT RIGHT.
HAVEN'T YOU BEEN THERE BEFORE?
YEAH, BUT NOT FOR A REGULAR HANGOUT. I BET HER NEIGHBORS ARE REALLY FANCY.
KRISTY EVEN SAID THEY HAD TO TAKE LOUIE TO A GROOMER BEFORE THEY MOVED SO HE'D FIT IN WITH THE OTHER DOGS!!
SWEETIE, KRISTY'S STILL GOING TO BE KRISTY NO MATTER WHERE SHE LIVES. I DON'T THINK YOU SHOULD WORRY ABOUT IT TOO MUCH.
AND THIS IS A CUTE SHIRT.
HMM.

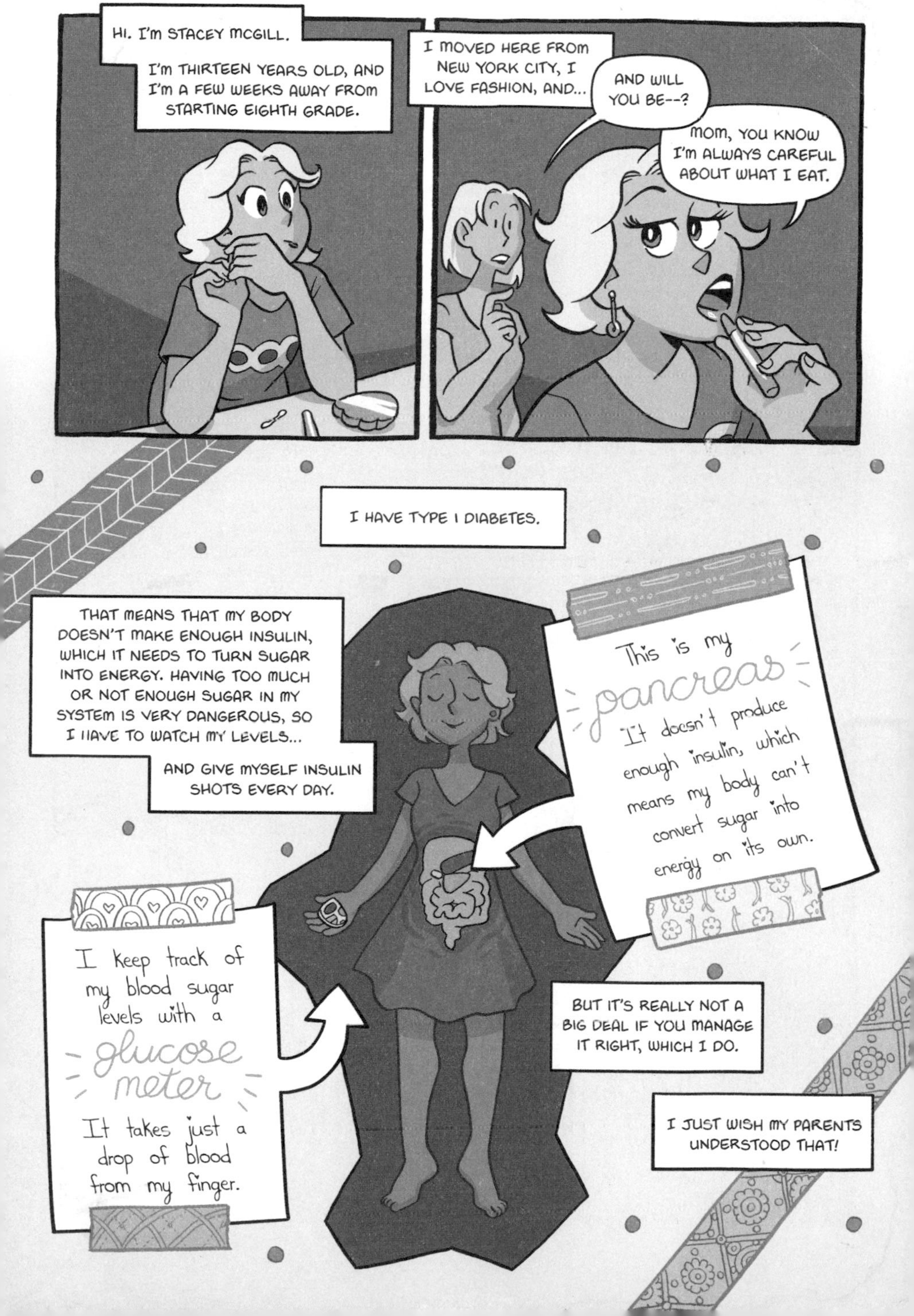
HI. I'M STACEY MCGILL.
I'M THIRTEEN YEARS OLD, AND I'M A FEW WEEKS AWAY FROM STARTING EIGHTH GRADE.
I MOVED HERE FROM NEW YORK CITY, I LOVE FASHION, AND...
AND WILL YOU BE--?
MOM, YOU KNOW I'M ALWAYS CAREFUL ABOUT WHAT I EAT.
I HAVE TYPE I DIABETES.
THAT MEANS THAT MY BODY DOESN'T MAKE ENOUGH INSULIN, WHICH IT NEEDS TO TURN SUGAR INTO ENERGY. HAVING TOO MUCH OR NOT ENOUGH SUGAR IN MY SYSTEM IS VERY DANGEROUS, SO I HAVE TO WATCH MY LEVELS...
AND GIVE MYSELF INSULIN SHOTS EVERY DAY.
This is my pancreas
It doesn't produce enough insulin, which means my body can't convert sugar into energy on its own.
I keep track of my blood sugar levels with a glucose meter
It takes just a drop of blood from my finger.
BUT IT'S REALLY NOT A BIG DEAL IF YOU MANAGE IT RIGHT, WHICH I DO.
I JUST WISH MY PARENTS UNDERSTOOD THAT!

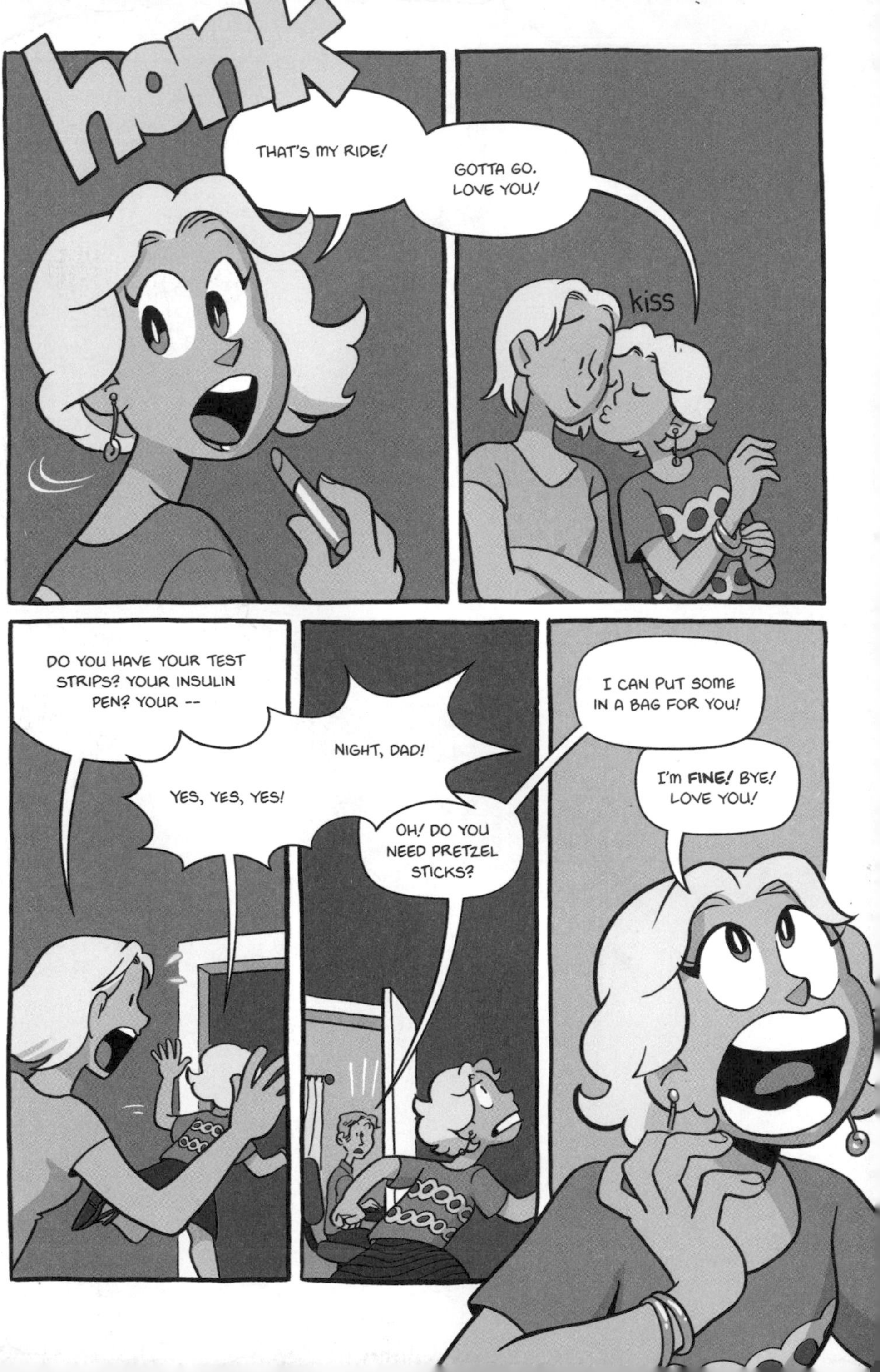

honk
THAT'S MY RIDE!
GOTTA GO. LOVE YOU!
kiss
DO YOU HAVE YOUR TEST STRIPS? YOUR INSULIN PEN? YOUR --
YES, YES, YES!
NIGHT, DAD!
OH! DO YOU NEED PRETZEL STICKS?
I CAN PUT SOME IN A BAG FOR YOU!
I'M **FINE!** BYE! LOVE YOU!

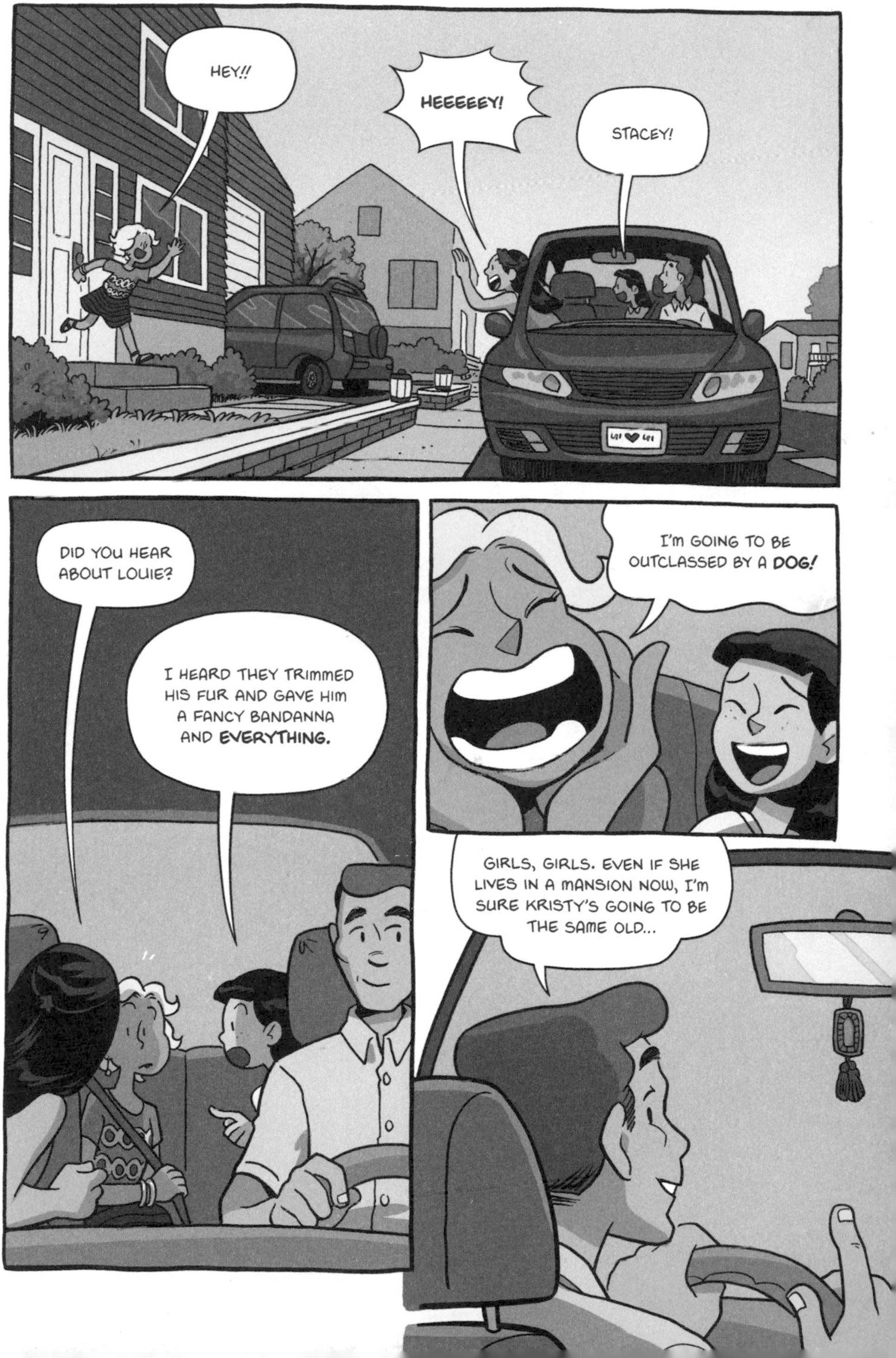
HEY!!
HEEEEEY!
STACEY!
DID YOU HEAR ABOUT LOUIE?
I HEARD THEY TRIMMED HIS FUR AND GAVE HIM A FANCY BANDANNA AND EVERYTHING.
I'M GOING TO BE OUTCLASSED BY A DOG!
GIRLS, GIRLS. EVEN IF SHE LIVES IN A MANSION NOW, I'M SURE KRISTY'S GOING TO BE THE SAME OLD...

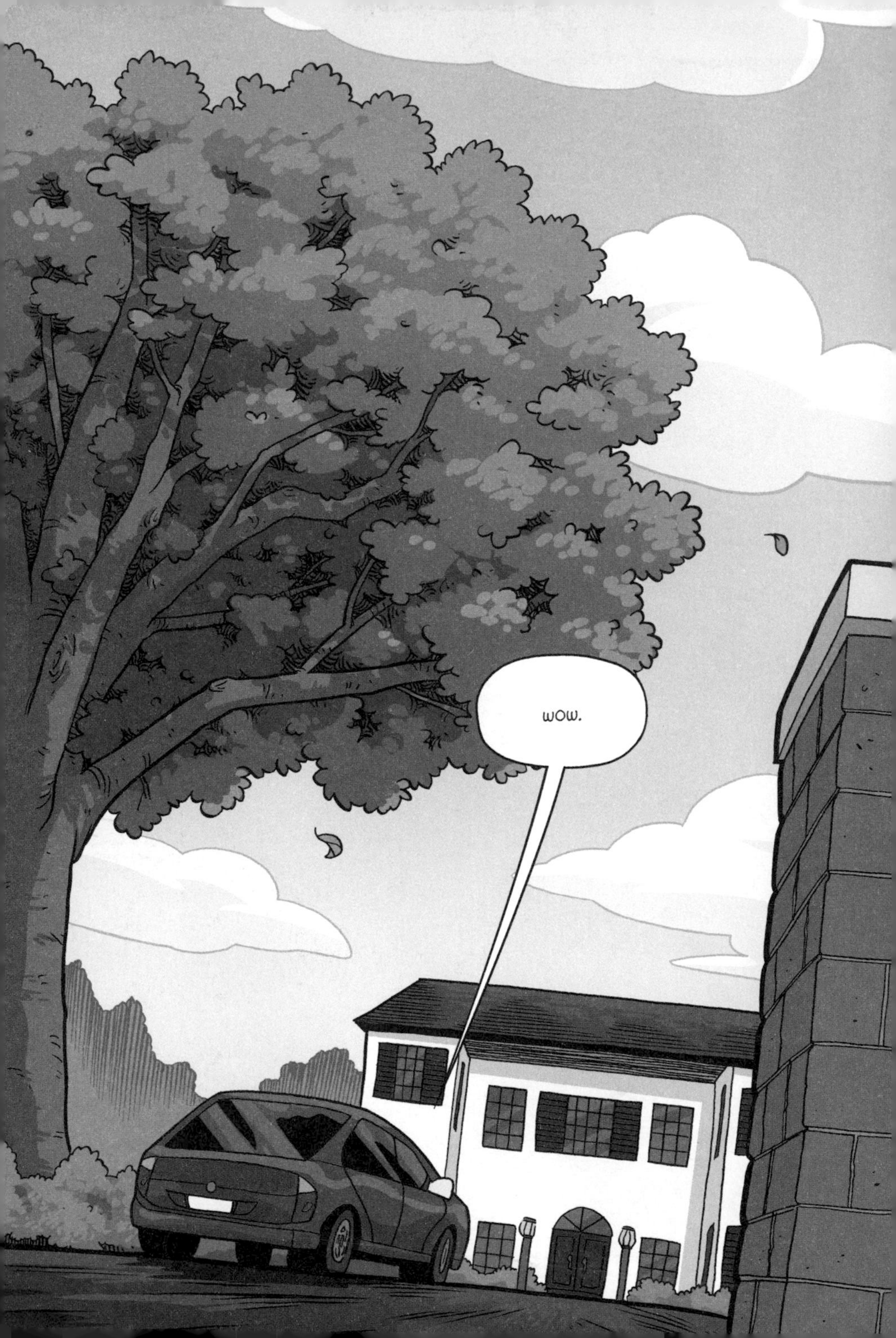
WOW.

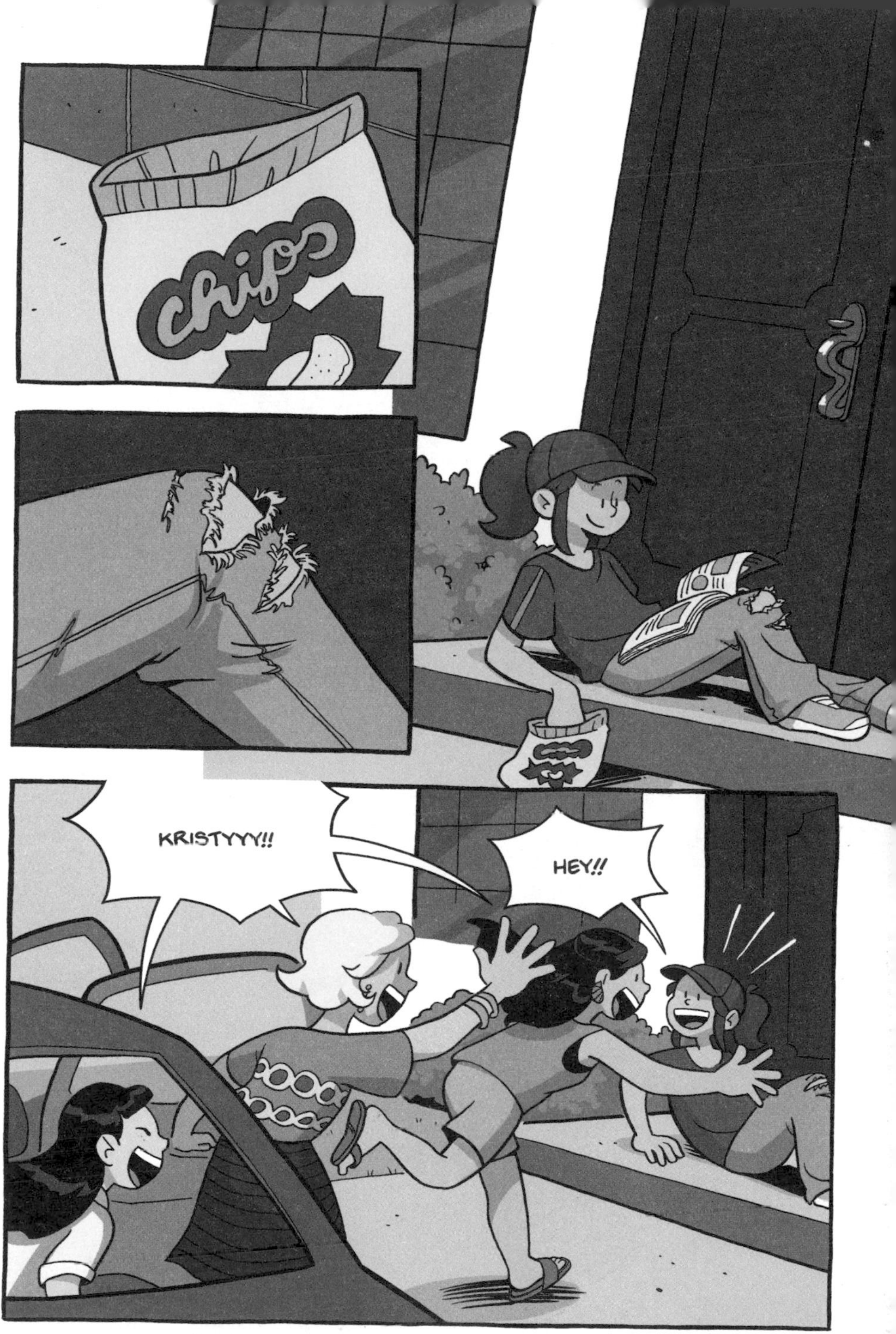
chips
KRISTYYY!!
HEY!!

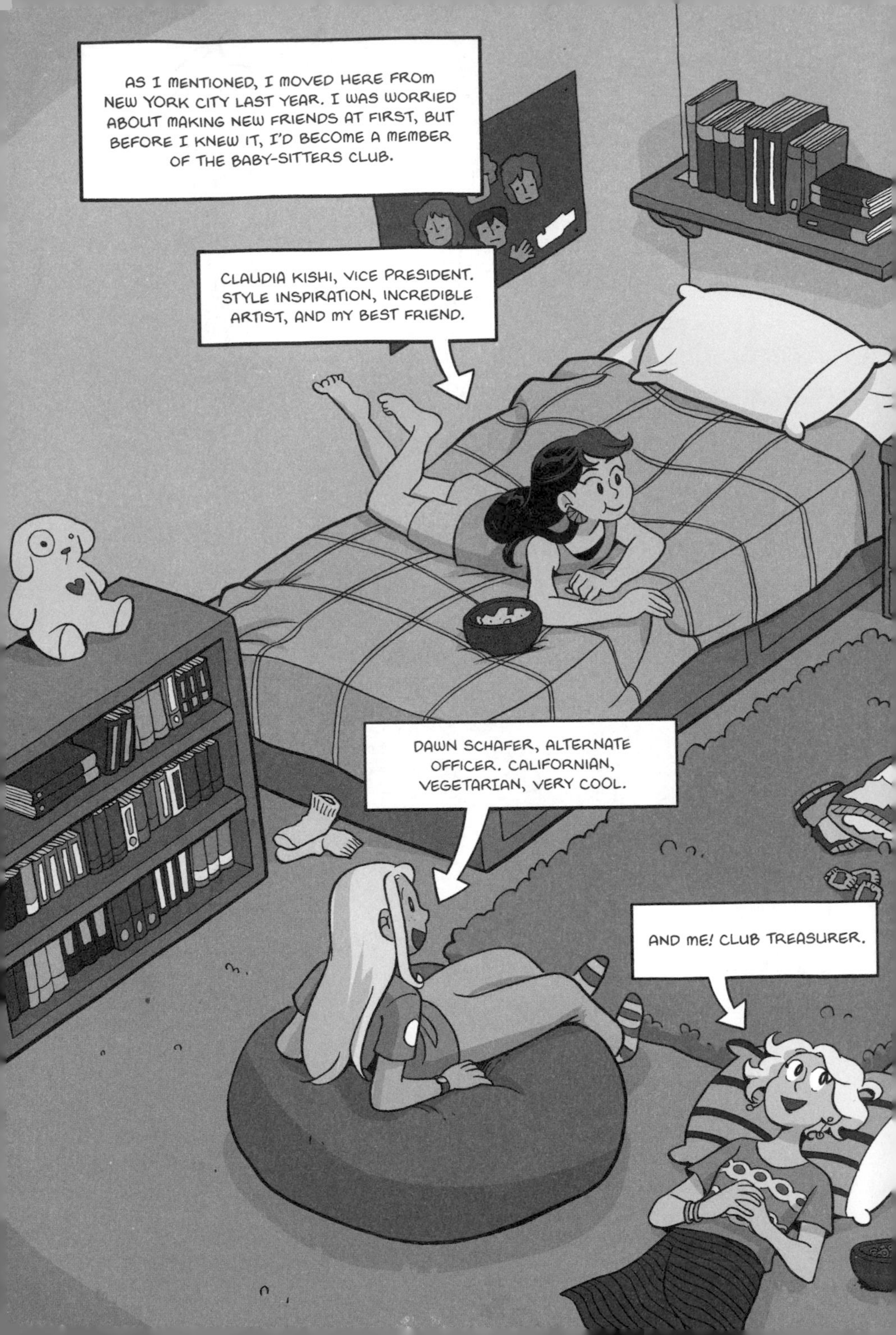
AS I MENTIONED, I MOVED HERE FROM NEW YORK CITY LAST YEAR. I WAS WORRIED ABOUT MAKING NEW FRIENDS AT FIRST, BUT BEFORE I KNEW IT, I'D BECOME A MEMBER OF THE BABY-SITTERS CLUB.
CLAUDIA KISHI, VICE PRESIDENT. STYLE INSPIRATION, INCREDIBLE ARTIST, AND MY BEST FRIEND.
DAWN SCHAFER, ALTERNATE OFFICER. CALIFORNIAN, VEGETARIAN, VERY COOL.
AND ME! CLUB TREASURER.

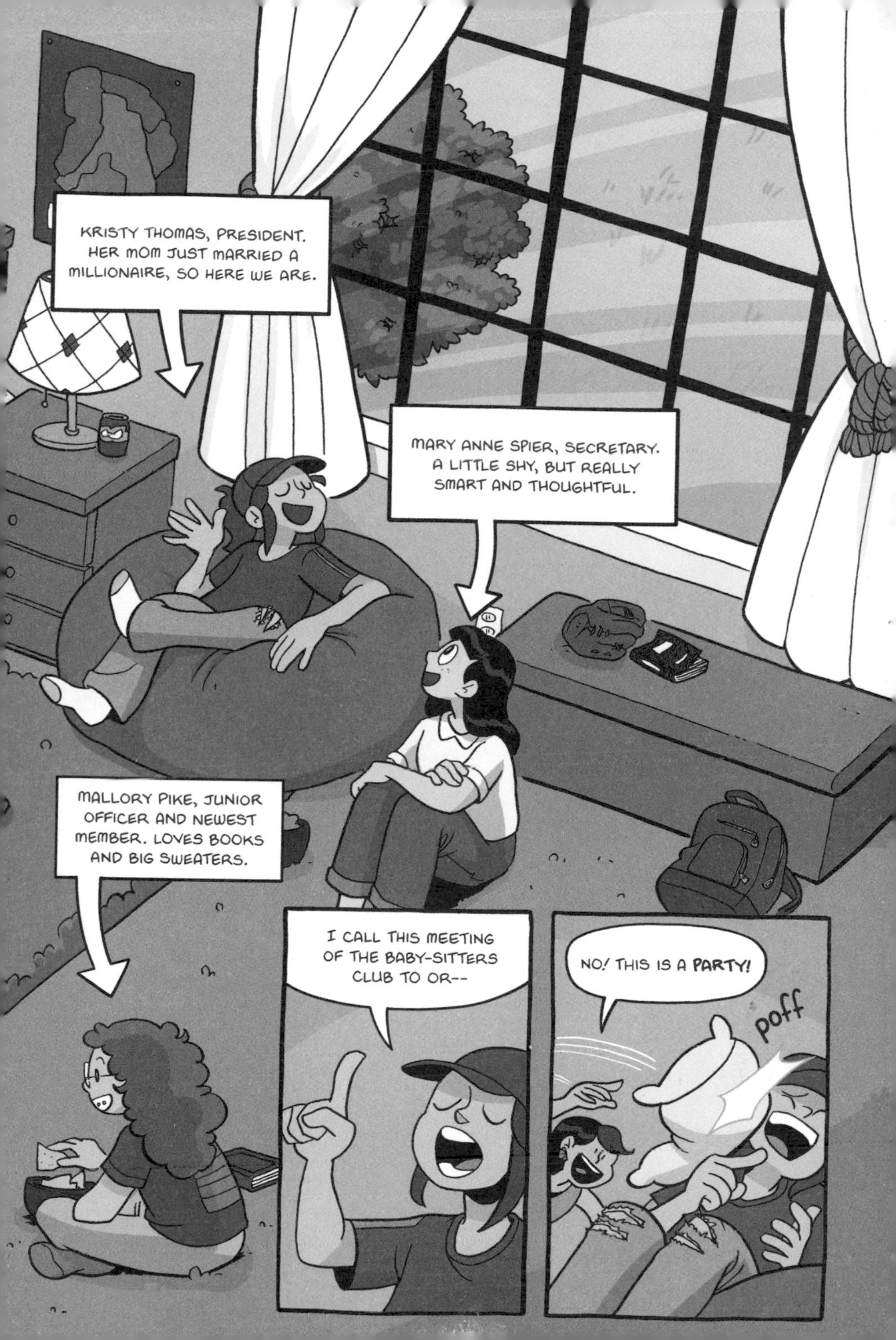
KRISTY THOMAS, PRESIDENT. HER MOM JUST MARRIED A MILLIONAIRE, SO HERE WE ARE.
MARY ANNE SPIER, SECRETARY. A LITTLE SHY, BUT REALLY SMART AND THOUGHTFUL.
MALLORY PIKE, JUNIOR OFFICER AND NEWEST MEMBER. LOVES BOOKS AND BIG SWEATERS.
I CALL THIS MEETING OF THE BABY-SITTERS CLUB TO OR--
NO! THIS IS A **PARTY!**
poff

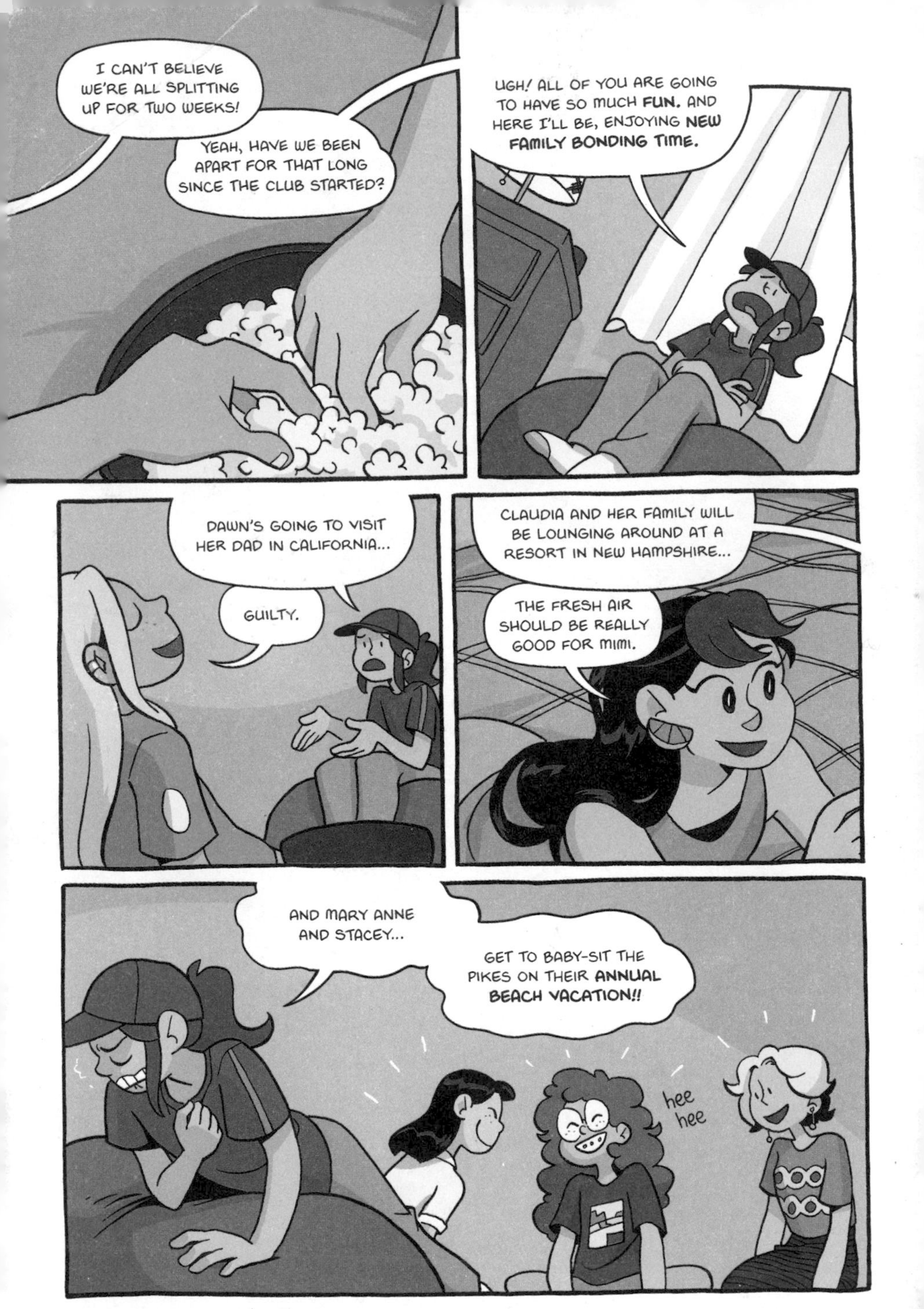
I CAN'T BELIEVE WE'RE ALL SPLITTING UP FOR TWO WEEKS!
YEAH, HAVE WE BEEN APART FOR THAT LONG SINCE THE CLUB STARTED?
UGH! ALL OF YOU ARE GOING TO HAVE SO MUCH **FUN.** AND HERE I'LL BE, ENJOYING **NEW FAMILY BONDING TIME.**
DAWN'S GOING TO VISIT HER DAD IN CALIFORNIA...
GUILTY.
CLAUDIA AND HER FAMILY WILL BE LOUNGING AROUND AT A RESORT IN NEW HAMPSHIRE...
THE FRESH AIR SHOULD BE REALLY GOOD FOR MIMI.
AND MARY ANNE AND STACEY...
GET TO BABY-SIT THE PIKES ON THEIR **ANNUAL BEACH VACATION!!**
hee hee

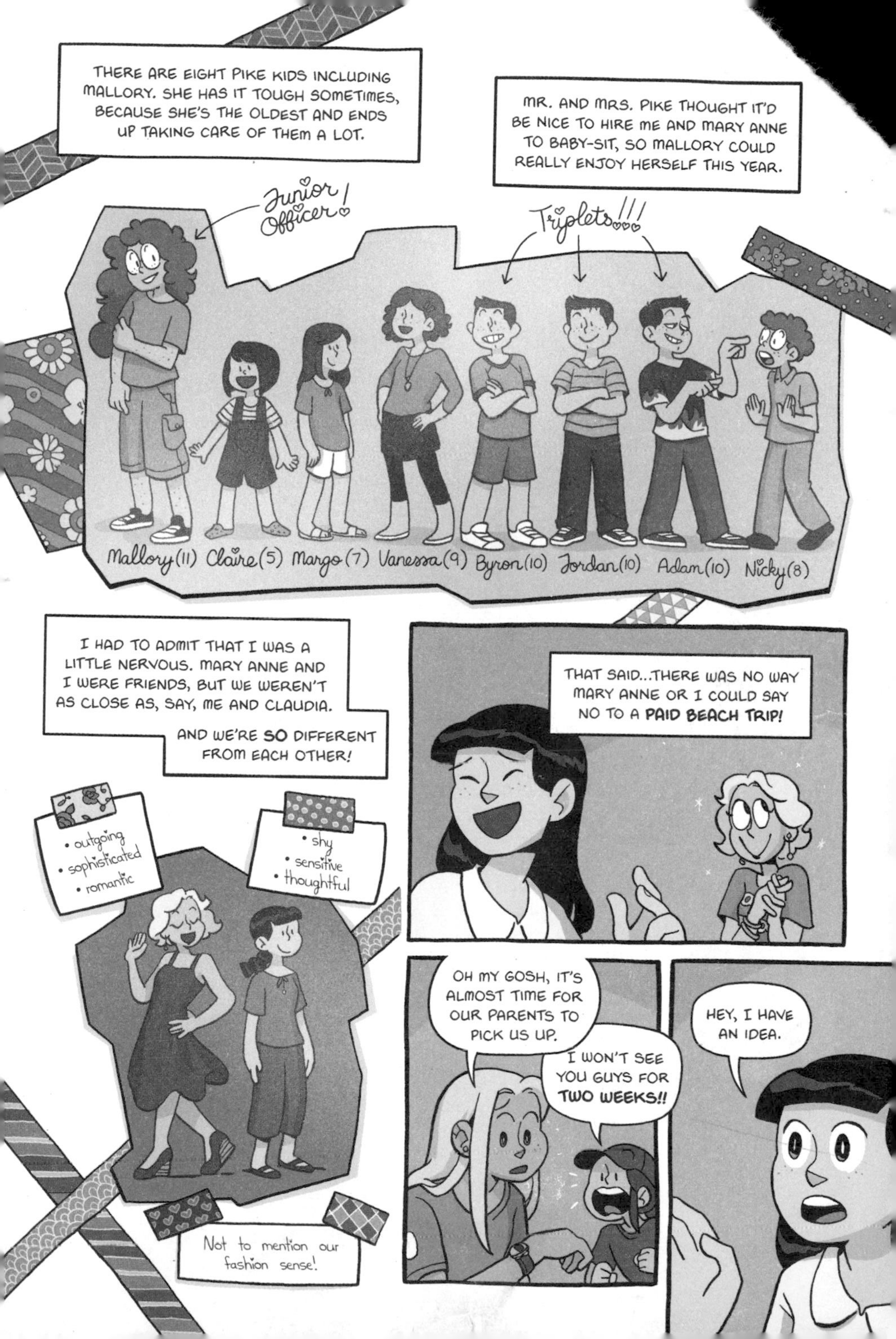

THERE ARE EIGHT PIKE KIDS INCLUDING MALLORY. SHE HAS IT TOUGH SOMETIMES, BECAUSE SHE'S THE OLDEST AND ENDS UP TAKING CARE OF THEM A LOT.
MR. AND MRS. PIKE THOUGHT IT'D BE NICE TO HIRE ME AND MARY ANNE TO BABY-SIT, SO MALLORY COULD REALLY ENJOY HERSELF THIS YEAR.
Junior Officer!
Triplets!!!
Mallory (11) Claire (5) Margo (7) Vanessa (9) Byron (10) Jordan (10) Adam (10) Nicky (8)
I HAD TO ADMIT THAT I WAS A LITTLE NERVOUS. MARY ANNE AND I WERE FRIENDS, BUT WE WEREN'T AS CLOSE AS, SAY, ME AND CLAUDIA.
AND WE'RE **SO** DIFFERENT FROM EACH OTHER!
• outgoing • sophisticated • romantic
• shy • sensitive • thoughtful
Not to mention our fashion sense!
THAT SAID...THERE WAS NO WAY MARY ANNE OR I COULD SAY NO TO A **PAID BEACH TRIP!**
OH MY GOSH, IT'S ALMOST TIME FOR OUR PARENTS TO PICK US UP.
I WON'T SEE YOU GUYS FOR **TWO WEEKS!!**
HEY, I HAVE AN IDEA.

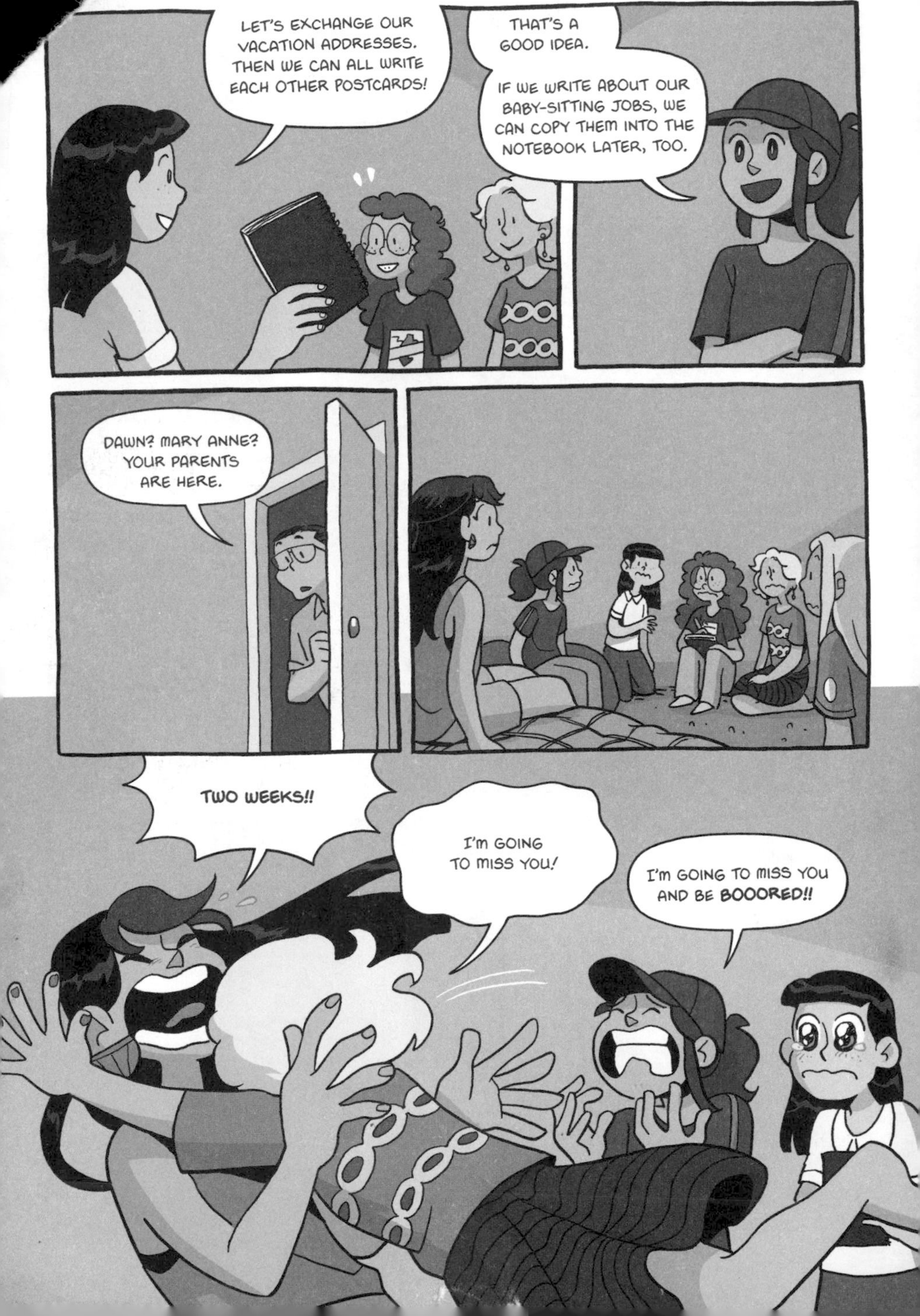
LET'S EXCHANGE OUR VACATION ADDRESSES. THEN WE CAN ALL WRITE EACH OTHER POSTCARDS!
THAT'S A GOOD IDEA.
IF WE WRITE ABOUT OUR BABY-SITTING JOBS, WE CAN COPY THEM INTO THE NOTEBOOK LATER, TOO.
DAWN? MARY ANNE? YOUR PARENTS ARE HERE.
TWO WEEKS!!
I'M GOING TO MISS YOU!
I'M GOING TO MISS YOU AND BE BOOORED!!

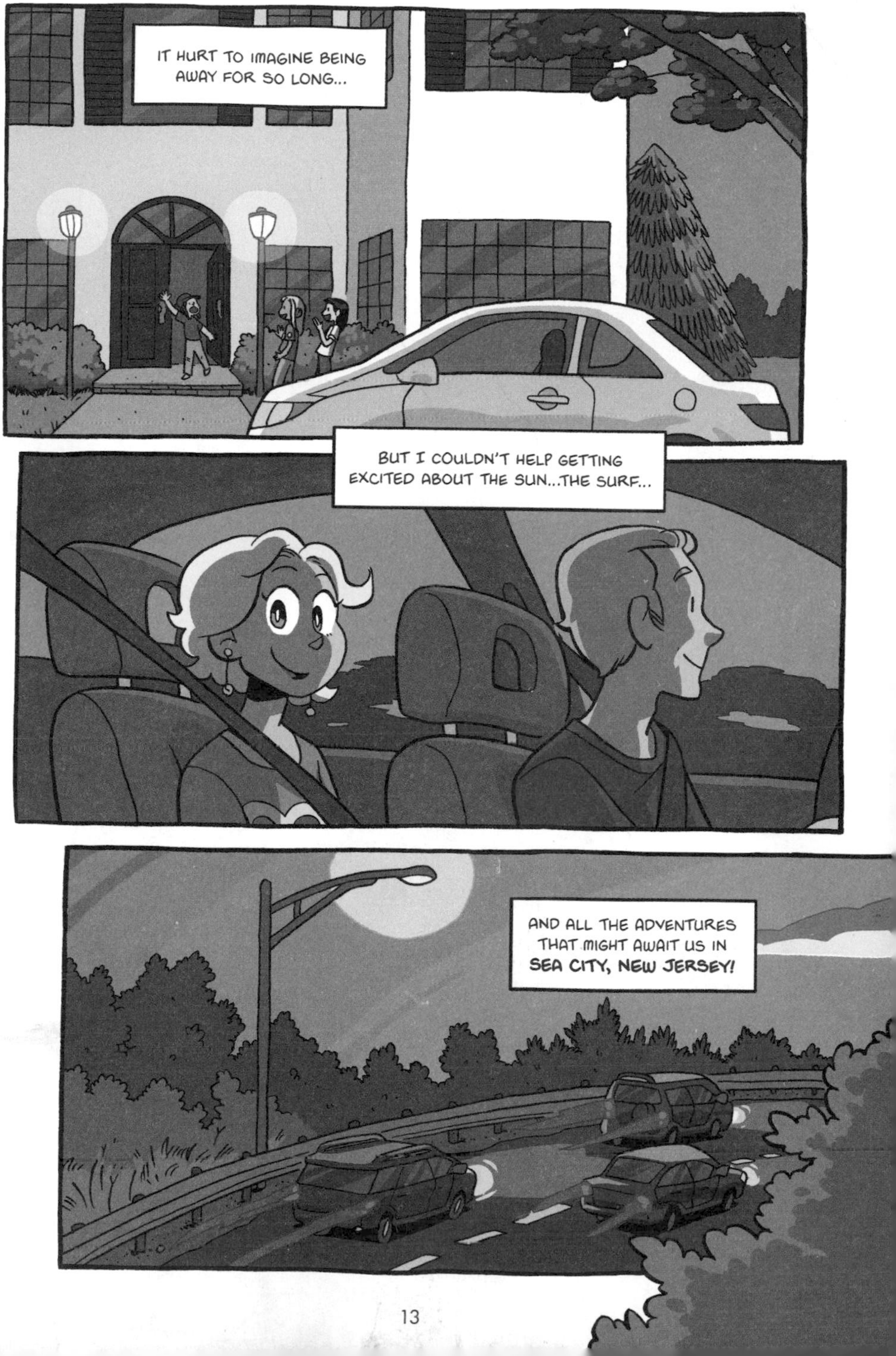
IT HURT TO IMAGINE BEING AWAY FOR SO LONG...
BUT I COULDN'T HELP GETTING EXCITED ABOUT THE SUN...THE SURF...
AND ALL THE ADVENTURES THAT MIGHT AWAIT US IN SEA CITY, NEW JERSEY!

CHAPTER 2

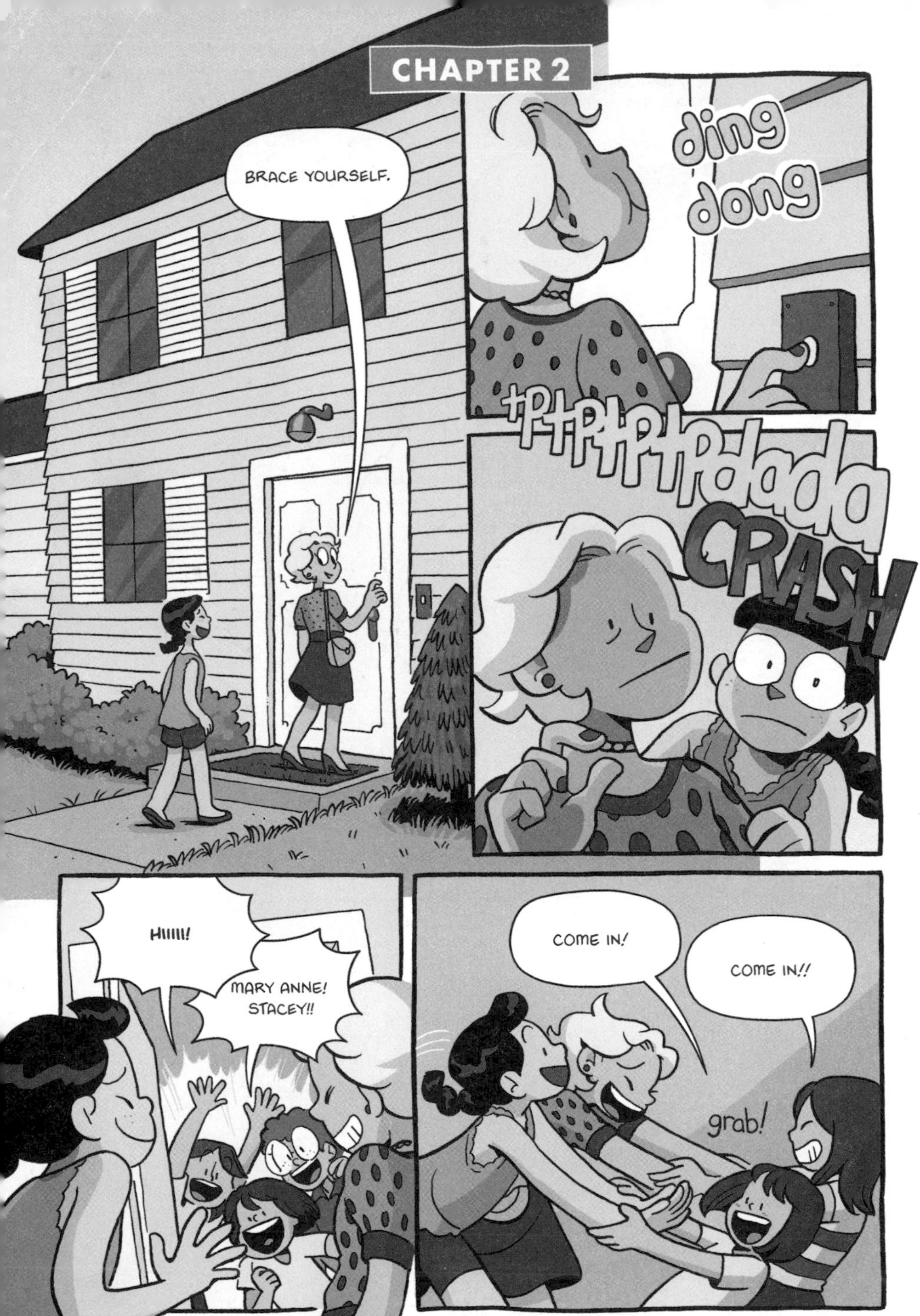
BRACE YOURSELF.
ding dong
tPtPtPtPdada
CRASH
HIIIII!
MARY ANNE! STACEY!!
COME IN!
COME IN!!
grab!

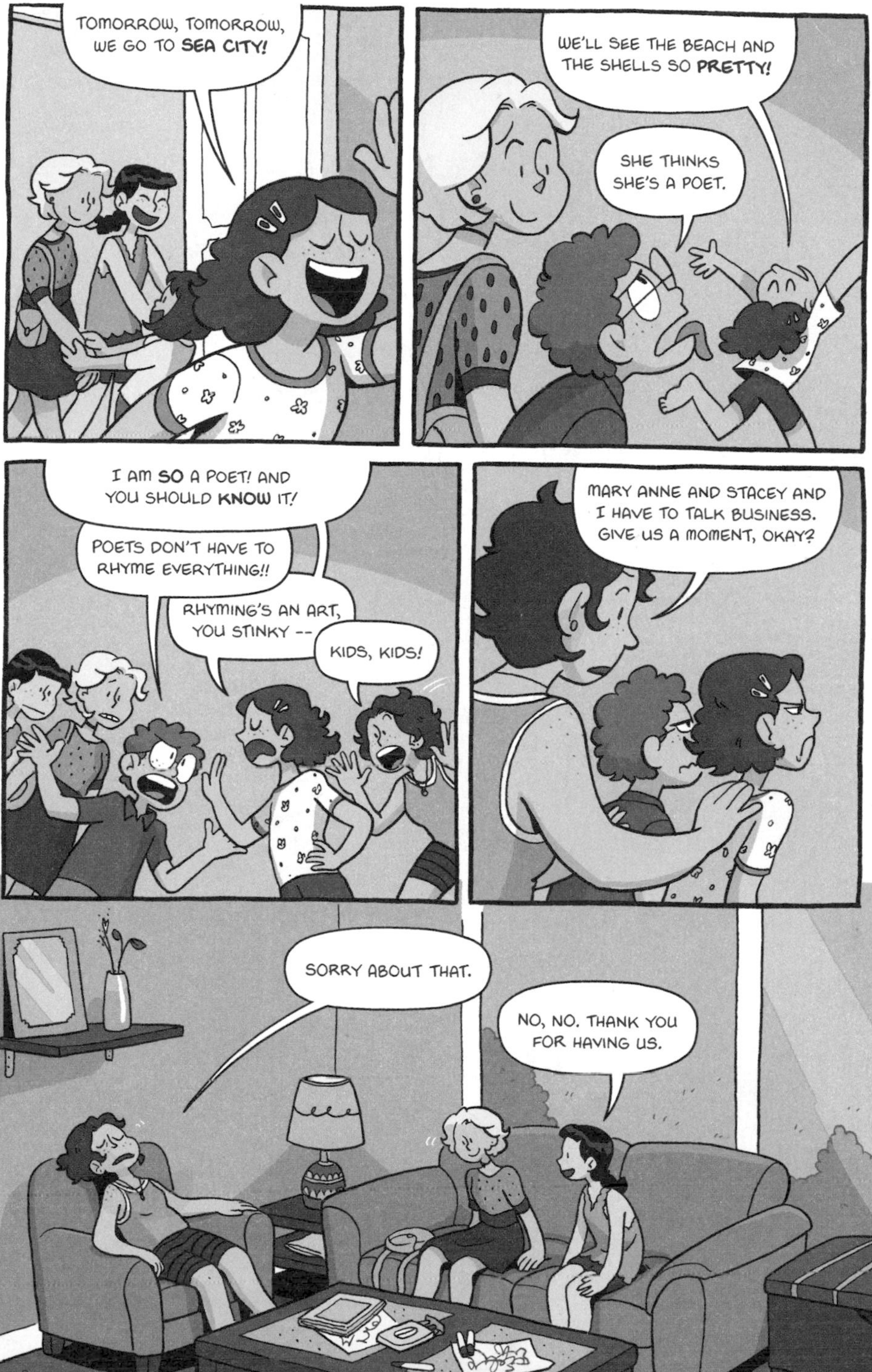
TOMORROW, TOMORROW, WE GO TO **SEA CITY!**
WE'LL SEE THE BEACH AND THE SHELLS SO **PRETTY!**
SHE THINKS SHE'S A POET.
I AM **SO** A POET! AND YOU SHOULD **KNOW** IT!
POETS DON'T HAVE TO RHYME EVERYTHING!!
RHYMING'S AN ART, YOU STINKY --
KIDS, KIDS!
MARY ANNE AND STACEY AND I HAVE TO TALK BUSINESS. GIVE US A MOMENT, OKAY?
SORRY ABOUT THAT.
NO, NO. THANK YOU FOR HAVING US.

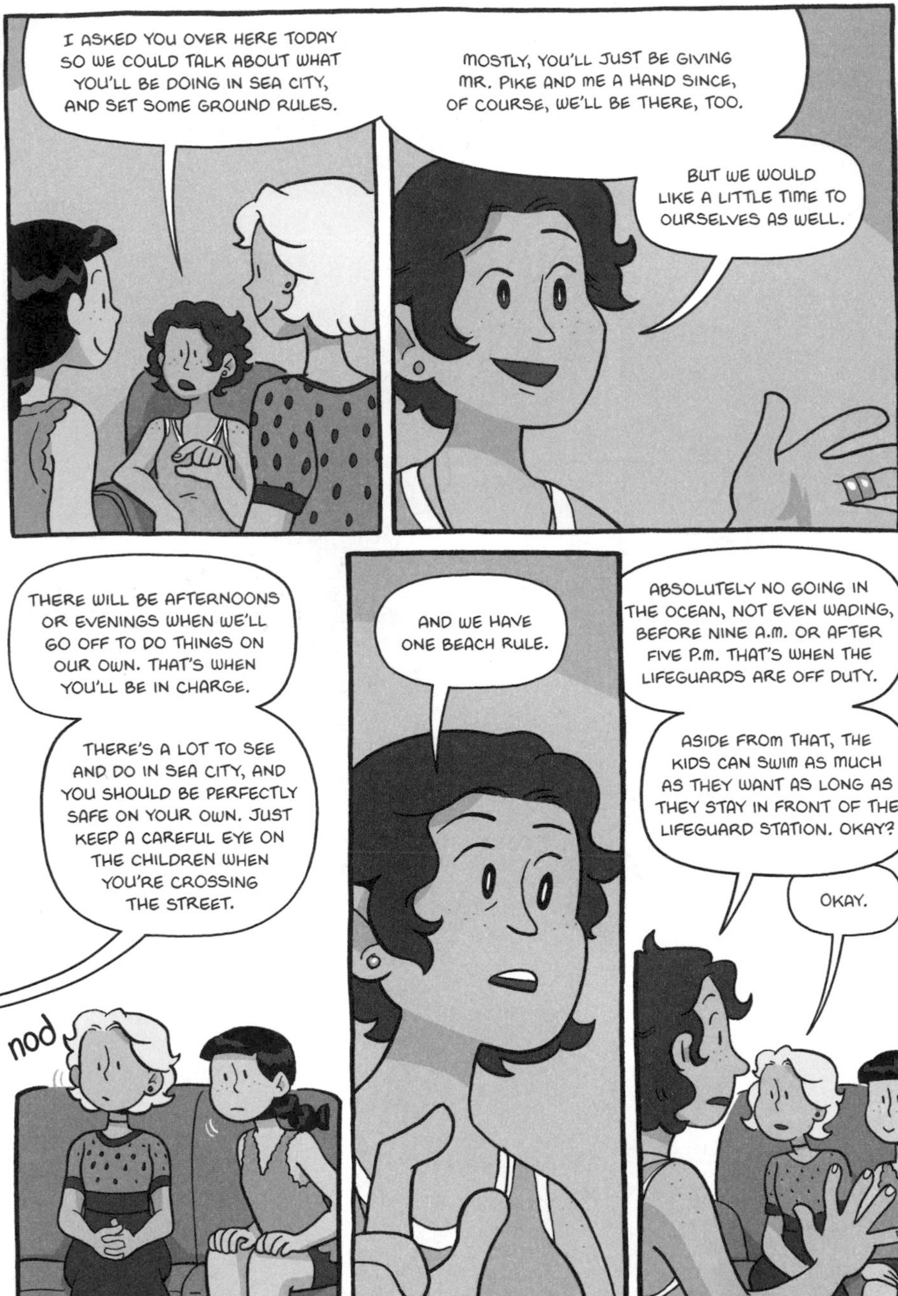
I ASKED YOU OVER HERE TODAY SO WE COULD TALK ABOUT WHAT YOU'LL BE DOING IN SEA CITY, AND SET SOME GROUND RULES.
MOSTLY, YOU'LL JUST BE GIVING MR. PIKE AND ME A HAND SINCE, OF COURSE, WE'LL BE THERE, TOO.
BUT WE WOULD LIKE A LITTLE TIME TO OURSELVES AS WELL.
THERE WILL BE AFTERNOONS OR EVENINGS WHEN WE'LL GO OFF TO DO THINGS ON OUR OWN. THAT'S WHEN YOU'LL BE IN CHARGE.
THERE'S A LOT TO SEE AND DO IN SEA CITY, AND YOU SHOULD BE PERFECTLY SAFE ON YOUR OWN. JUST KEEP A CAREFUL EYE ON THE CHILDREN WHEN YOU'RE CROSSING THE STREET.
nod
AND WE HAVE ONE BEACH RULE.
ABSOLUTELY NO GOING IN THE OCEAN, NOT EVEN WADING, BEFORE NINE A.M. OR AFTER FIVE P.M. THAT'S WHEN THE LIFEGUARDS ARE OFF DUTY.
ASIDE FROM THAT, THE KIDS CAN SWIM AS MUCH AS THEY WANT AS LONG AS THEY STAY IN FRONT OF THE LIFEGUARD STATION. OKAY?
OKAY.

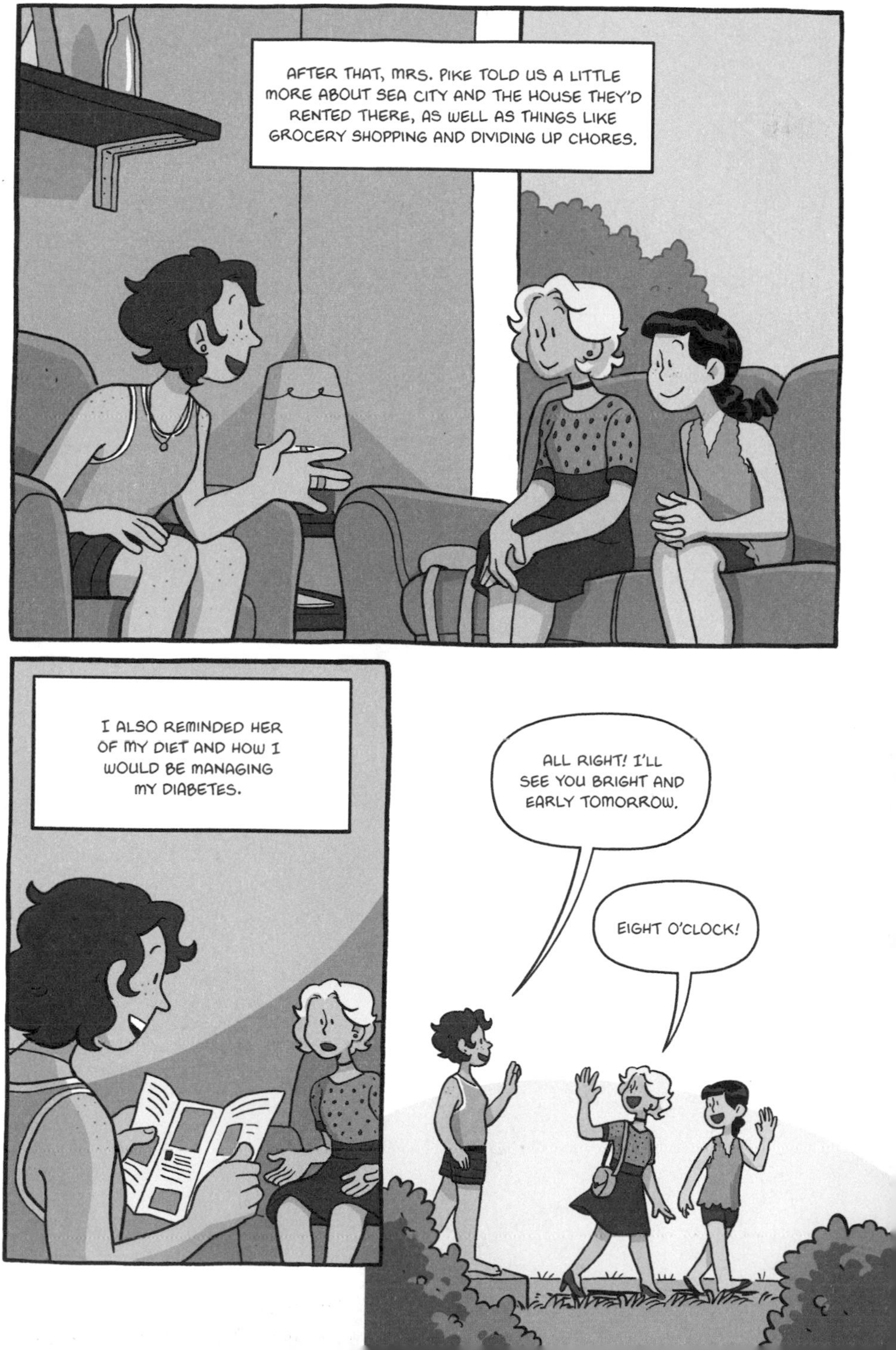
AFTER THAT, MRS. PIKE TOLD US A LITTLE MORE ABOUT SEA CITY AND THE HOUSE THEY'D RENTED THERE, AS WELL AS THINGS LIKE GROCERY SHOPPING AND DIVIDING UP CHORES.
I ALSO REMINDED HER OF MY DIET AND HOW I WOULD BE MANAGING MY DIABETES.
ALL RIGHT! I'LL SEE YOU BRIGHT AND EARLY TOMORROW.
EIGHT O'CLOCK!

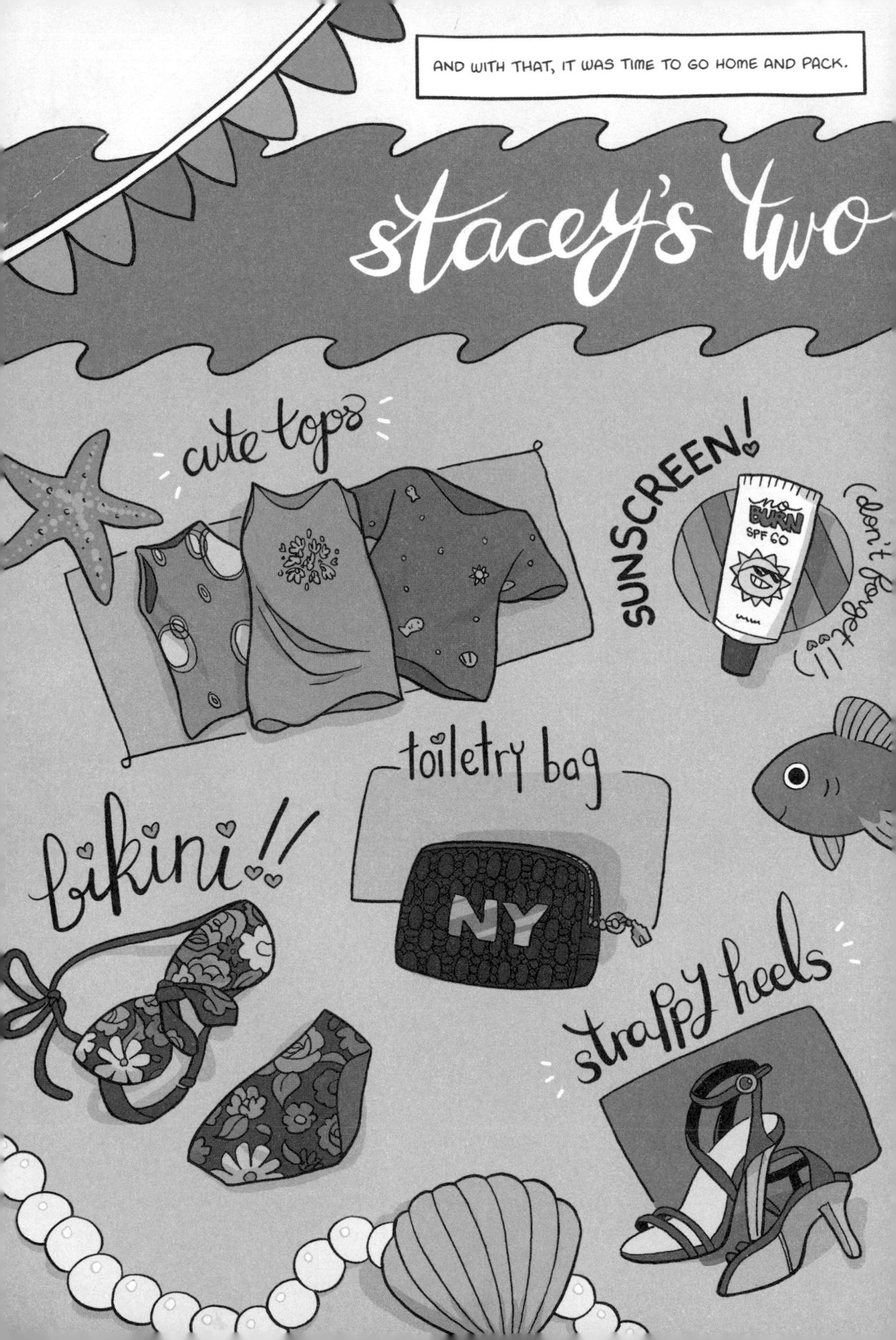
AND WITH THAT, IT WAS TIME TO GO HOME AND PACK.
stacey's two
cute tops
SUNSCREEN!
NO BURN
SPF 60
(don't forget!!)
toiletry bag
NY
bikini!!
strappy heels

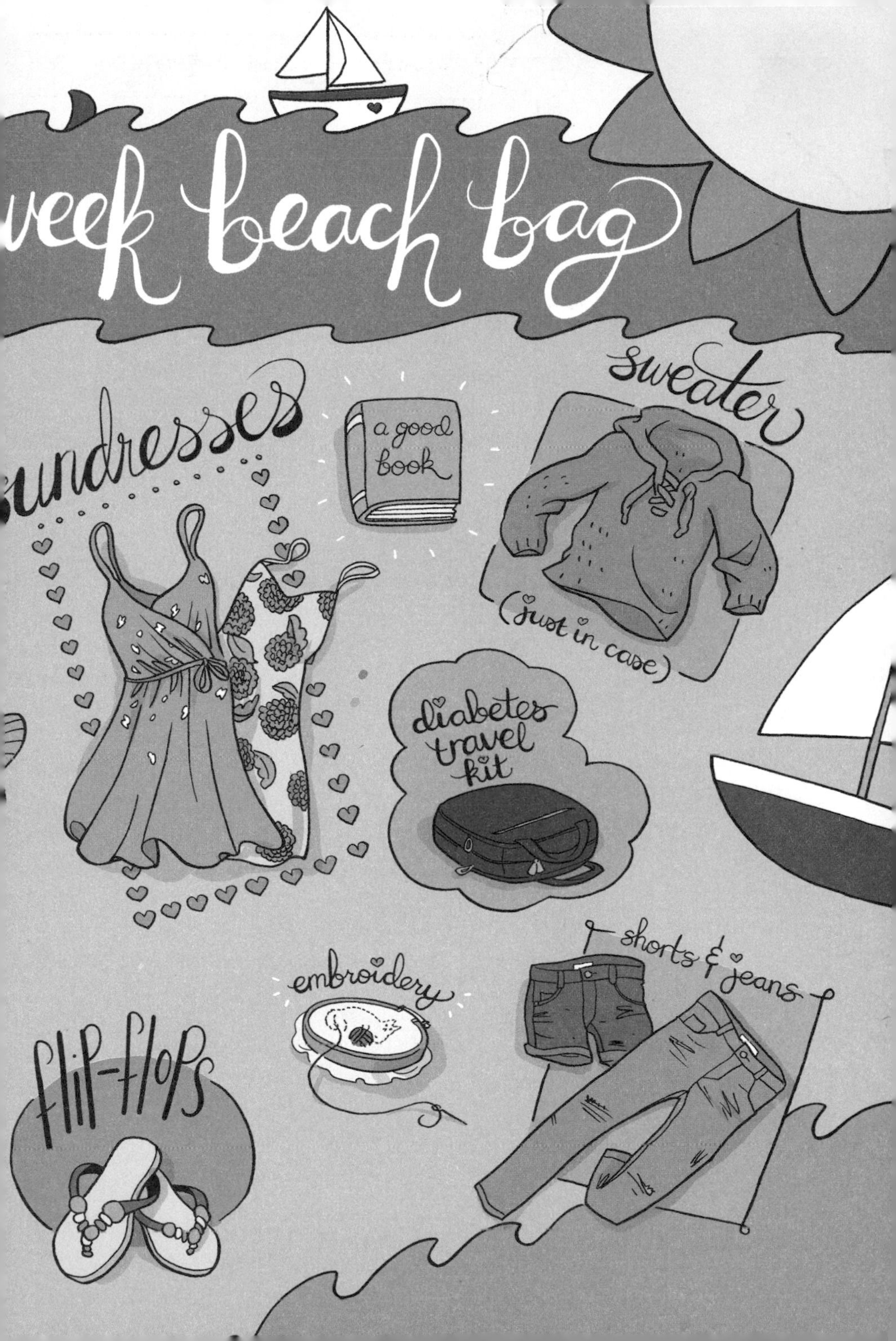

week beach bag
sundresses
a good book
sweater
(just in case)
diabetes travel kit
shorts & jeans
embroidery
flip-flops

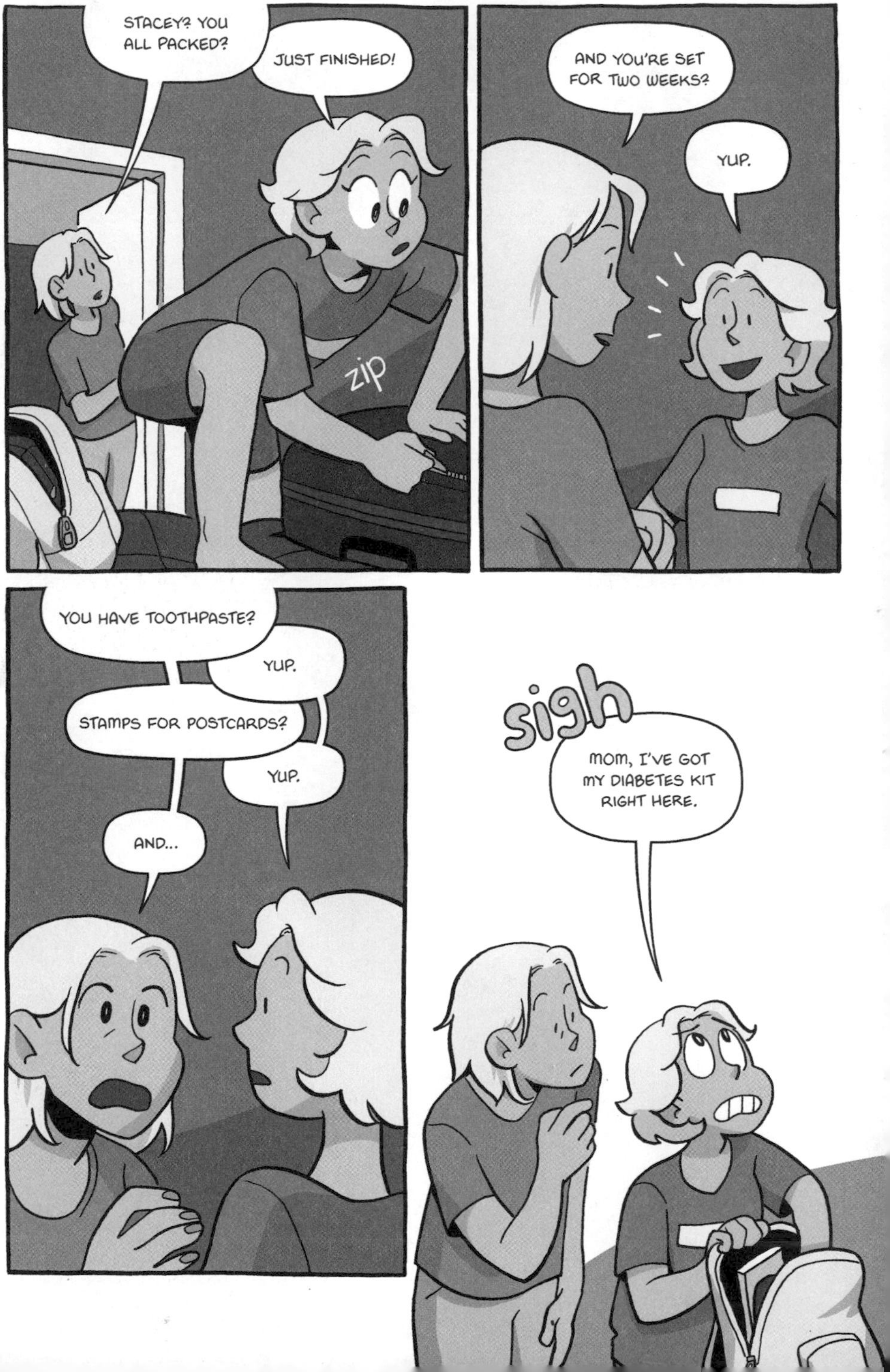
STACEY? YOU ALL PACKED?
JUST FINISHED!
zip
AND YOU'RE SET FOR TWO WEEKS?
YUP.
YOU HAVE TOOTHPASTE?
YUP.
STAMPS FOR POSTCARDS?
YUP.
AND...
sigh
MOM, I'VE GOT MY DIABETES KIT RIGHT HERE.

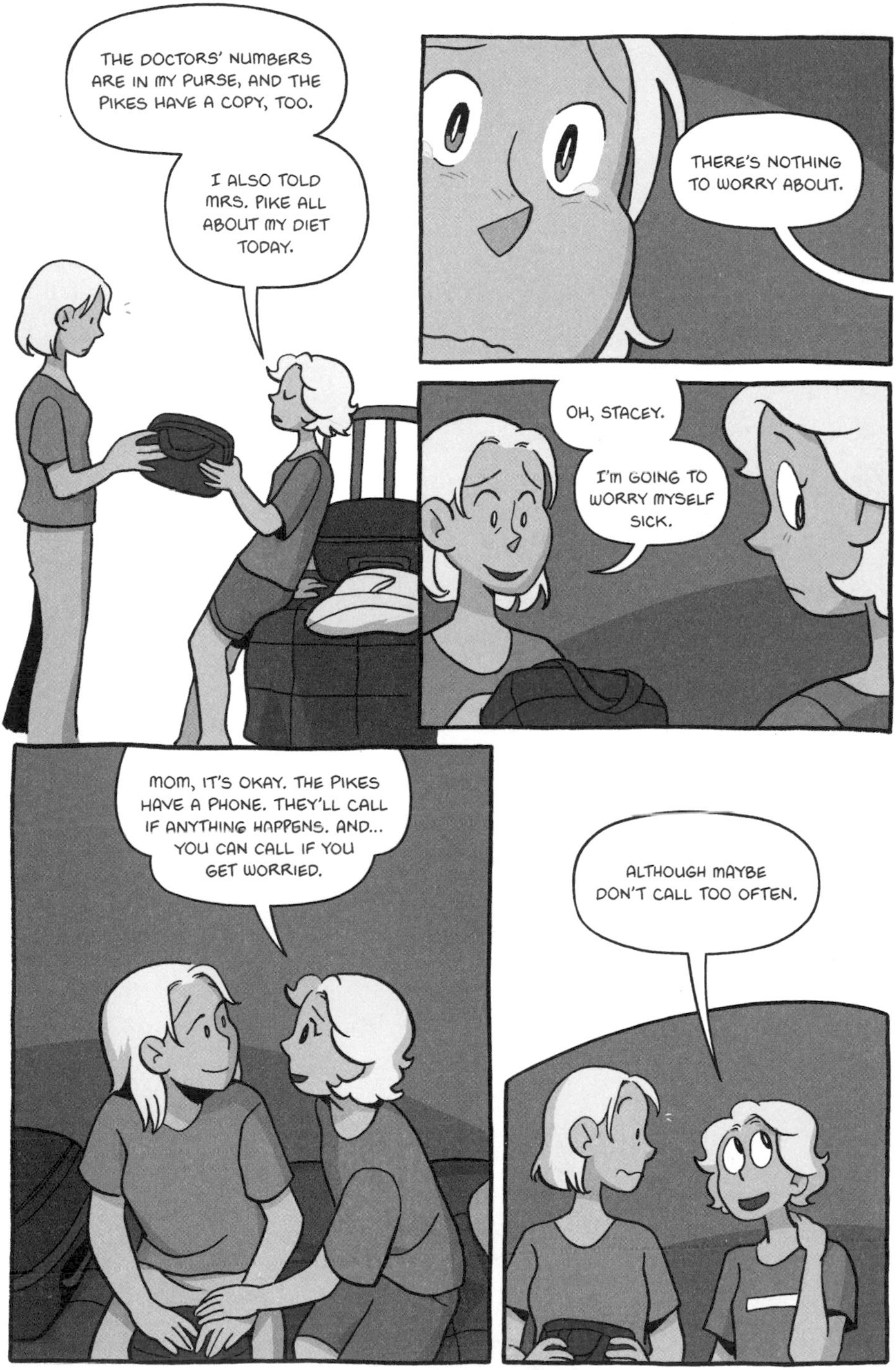
THE DOCTORS' NUMBERS ARE IN MY PURSE, AND THE PIKES HAVE A COPY, TOO.
I ALSO TOLD MRS. PIKE ALL ABOUT MY DIET TODAY.
THERE'S NOTHING TO WORRY ABOUT.
OH, STACEY.
I'M GOING TO WORRY MYSELF SICK.
MOM, IT'S OKAY. THE PIKES HAVE A PHONE. THEY'LL CALL IF ANYTHING HAPPENS. AND... YOU CAN CALL IF YOU GET WORRIED.
ALTHOUGH MAYBE DON'T CALL TOO OFTEN.

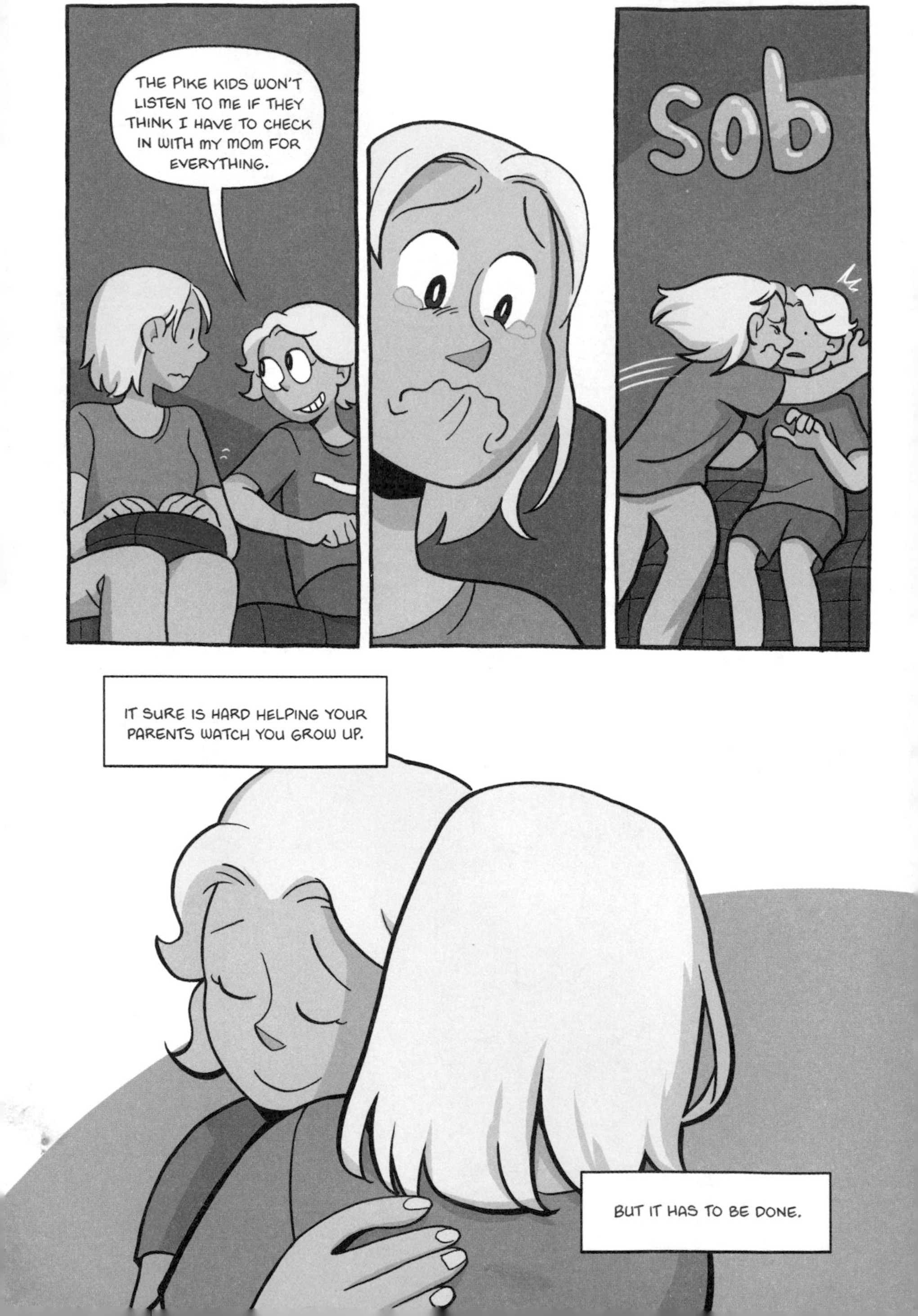
THE PIKE KIDS WON'T LISTEN TO ME IF THEY THINK I HAVE TO CHECK IN WITH MY MOM FOR EVERYTHING.
SOB
IT SURE IS HARD HELPING YOUR PARENTS WATCH YOU GROW UP.
BUT IT HAS TO BE DONE.

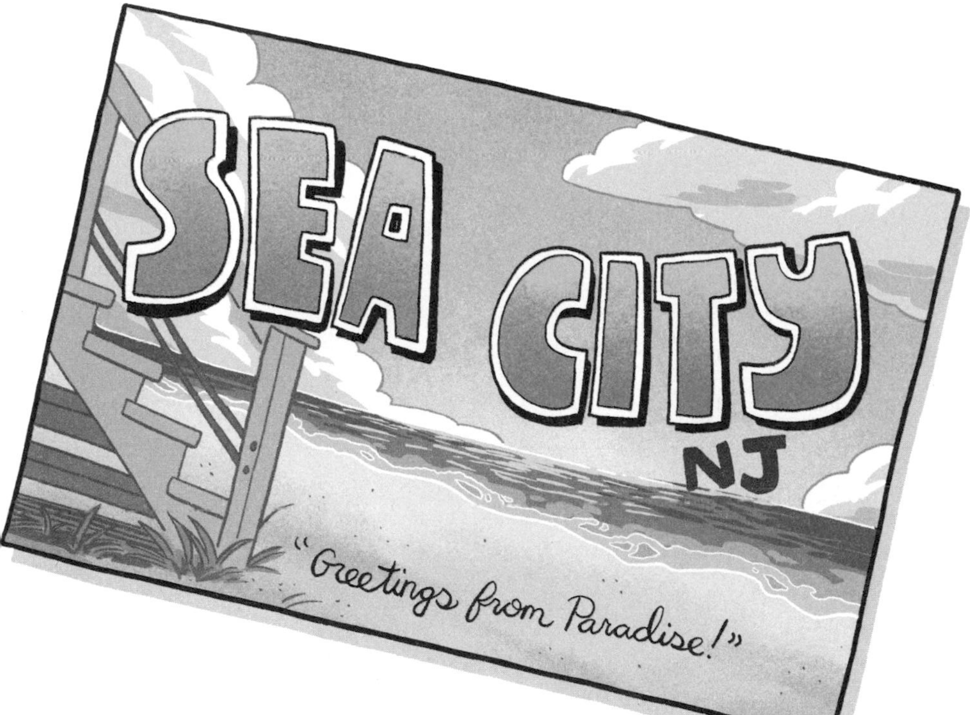
SEA CITY
NJ
"Greetings from Paradise!"

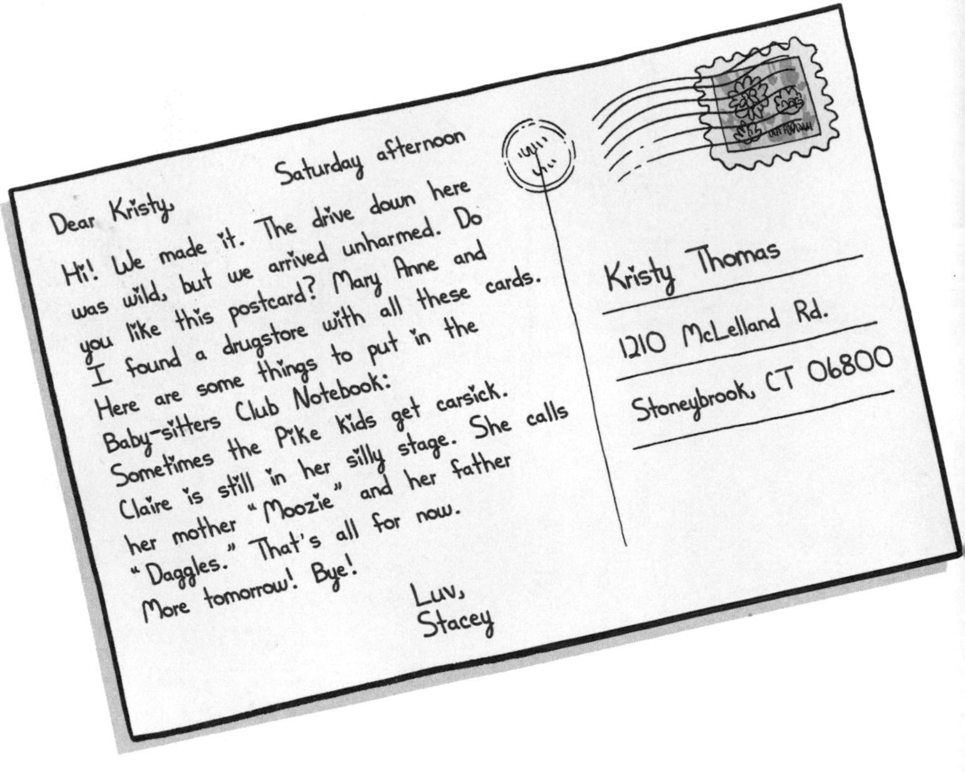
Saturday afternoon

Dear Kristy,

Hi! We made it. The drive down here was wild, but we arrived unharmed. Do you like this postcard? Mary Anne and I found a drugstore with all these cards. Here are some things to put in the Baby-sitters Club Notebook: Sometimes the Pike kids get carsick. Claire is still in her silly stage. She calls her mother "Moozie" and her father "Daggles." That's all for now. More tomorrow! Bye!

Luv,
Stacey

Kristy Thomas
1210 McLelland Rd.
Stoneybrook, CT 06800

CHAPTER 3

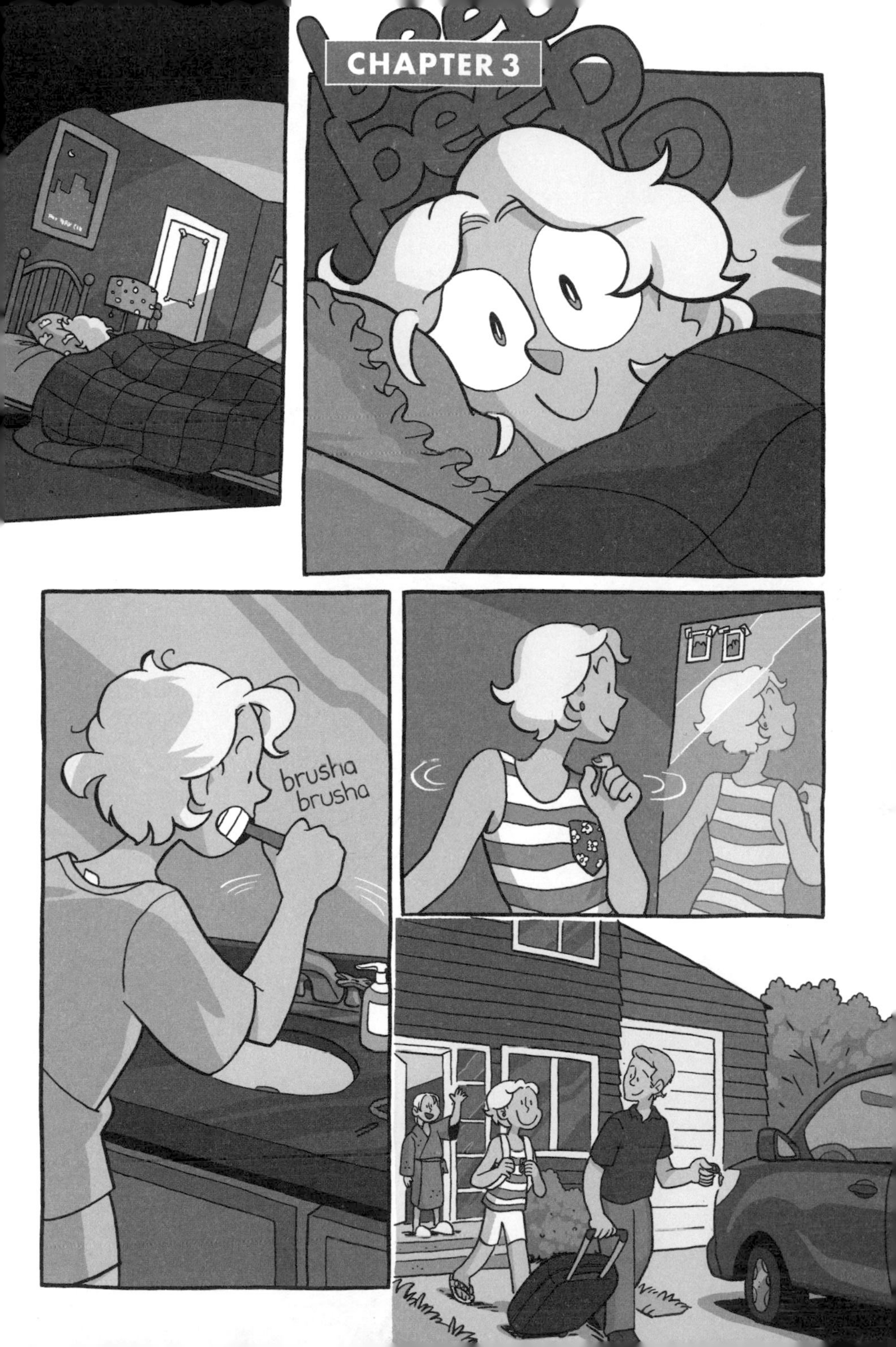
brusha
brusha

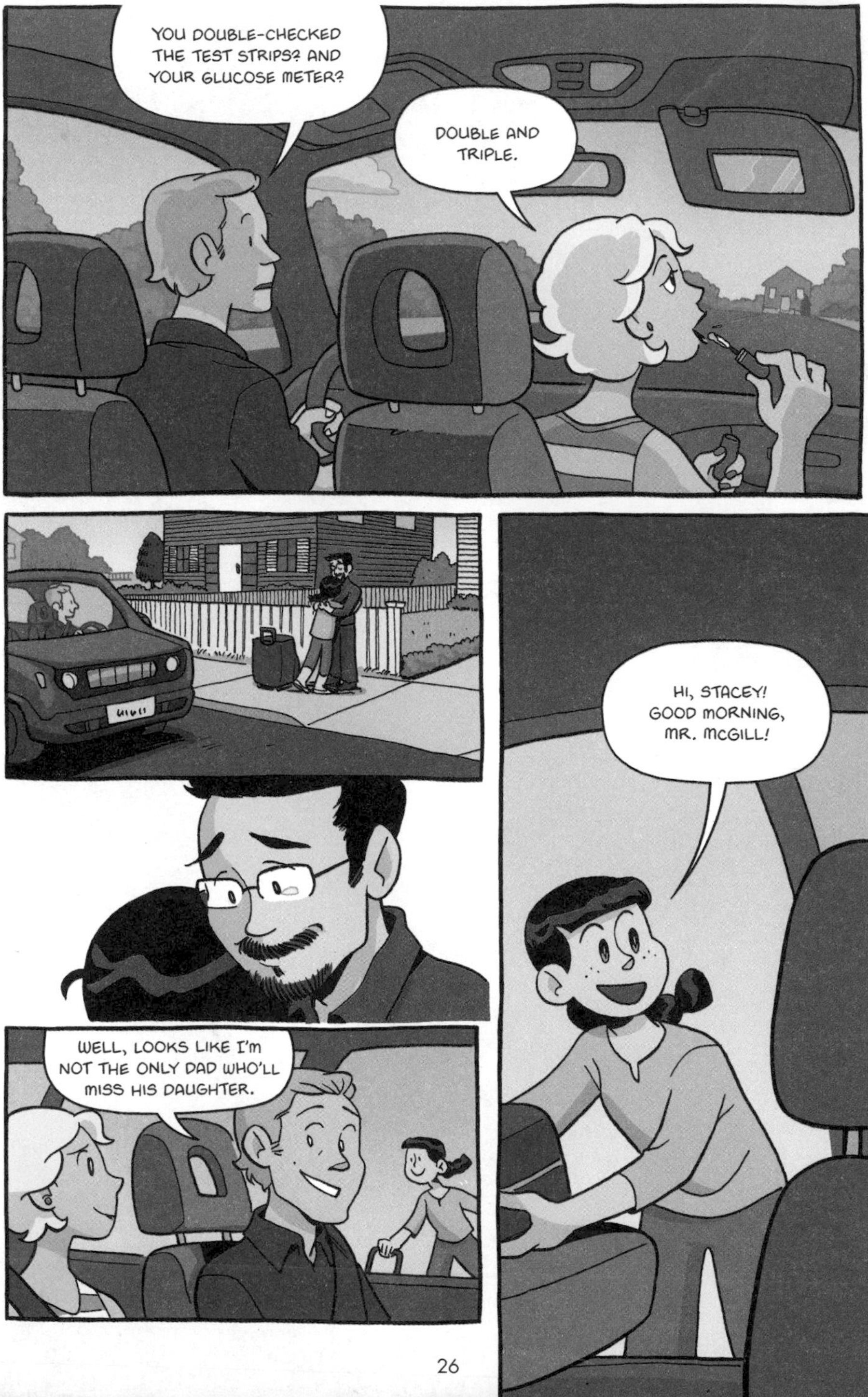
YOU DOUBLE-CHECKED THE TEST STRIPS? AND YOUR GLUCOSE METER?
DOUBLE AND TRIPLE.
WELL, LOOKS LIKE I'M NOT THE ONLY DAD WHO'LL MISS HIS DAUGHTER.
HI, STACEY! GOOD MORNING, MR. MCGILL!

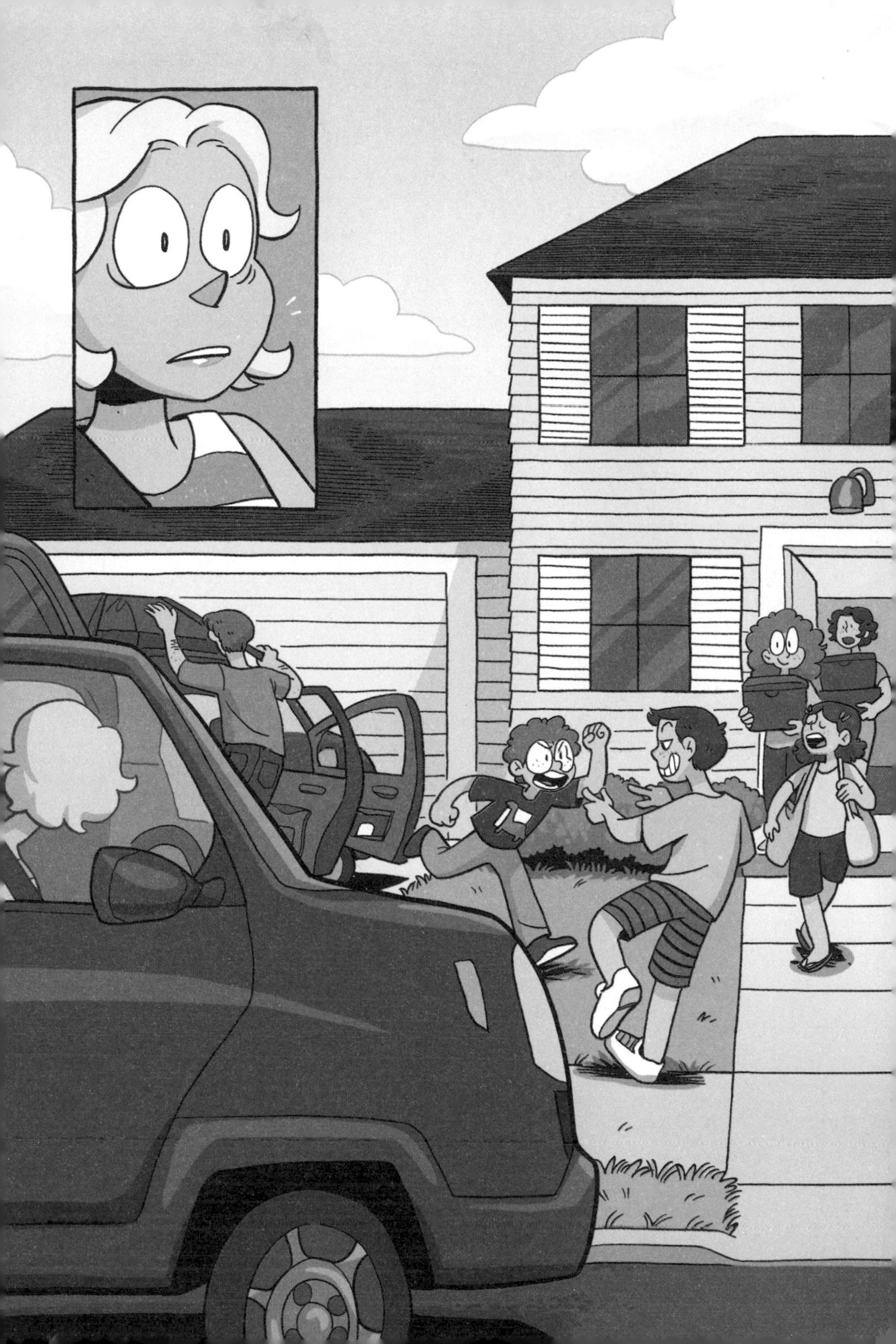

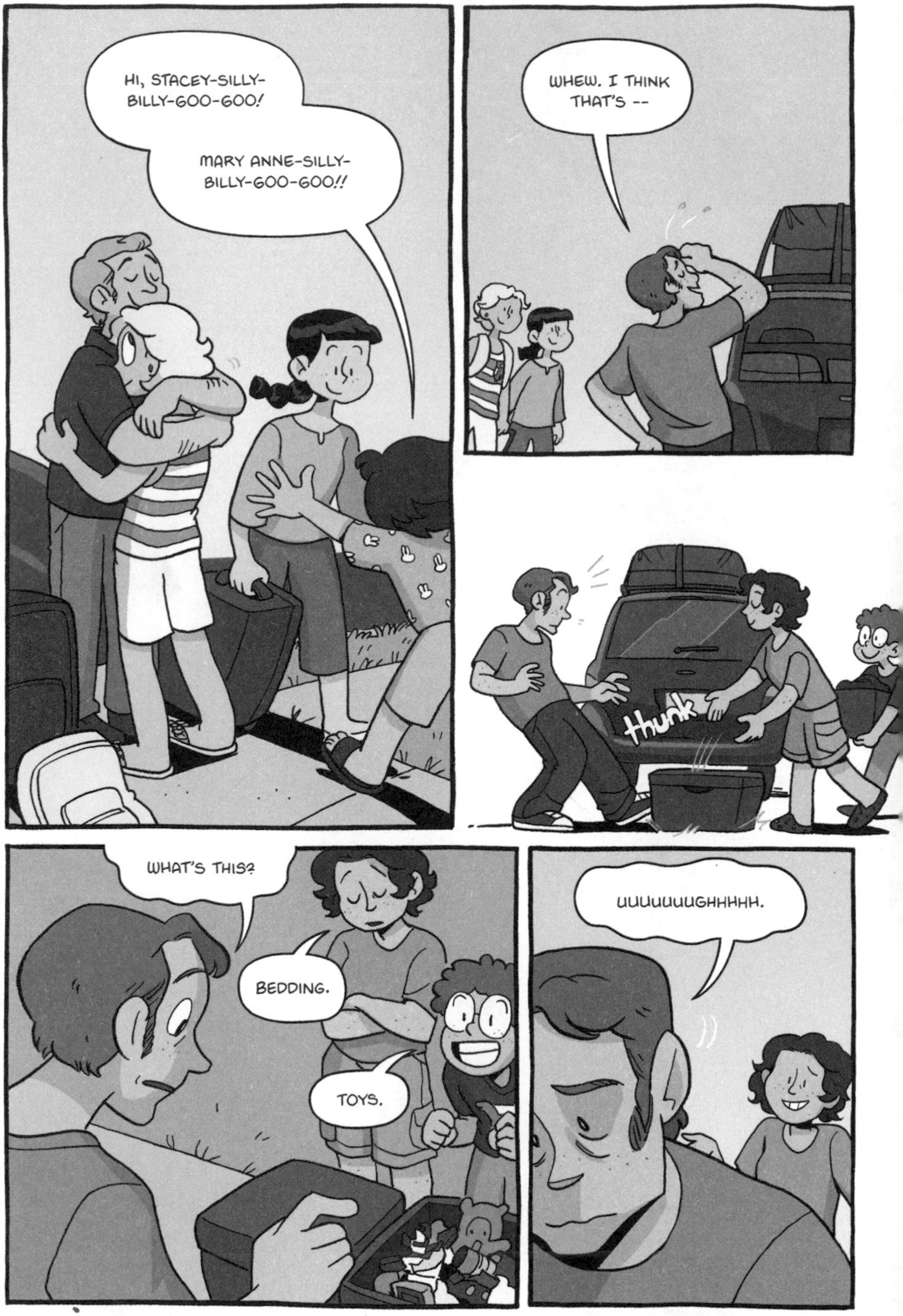
HI, STACEY-SILLY-BILLY-GOO-GOO!
MARY ANNE-SILLY-BILLY-GOO-GOO!!
WHEW. I THINK THAT'S --
thunk
WHAT'S THIS?
BEDDING.
TOYS.
UUUUUUUGHHHHH.

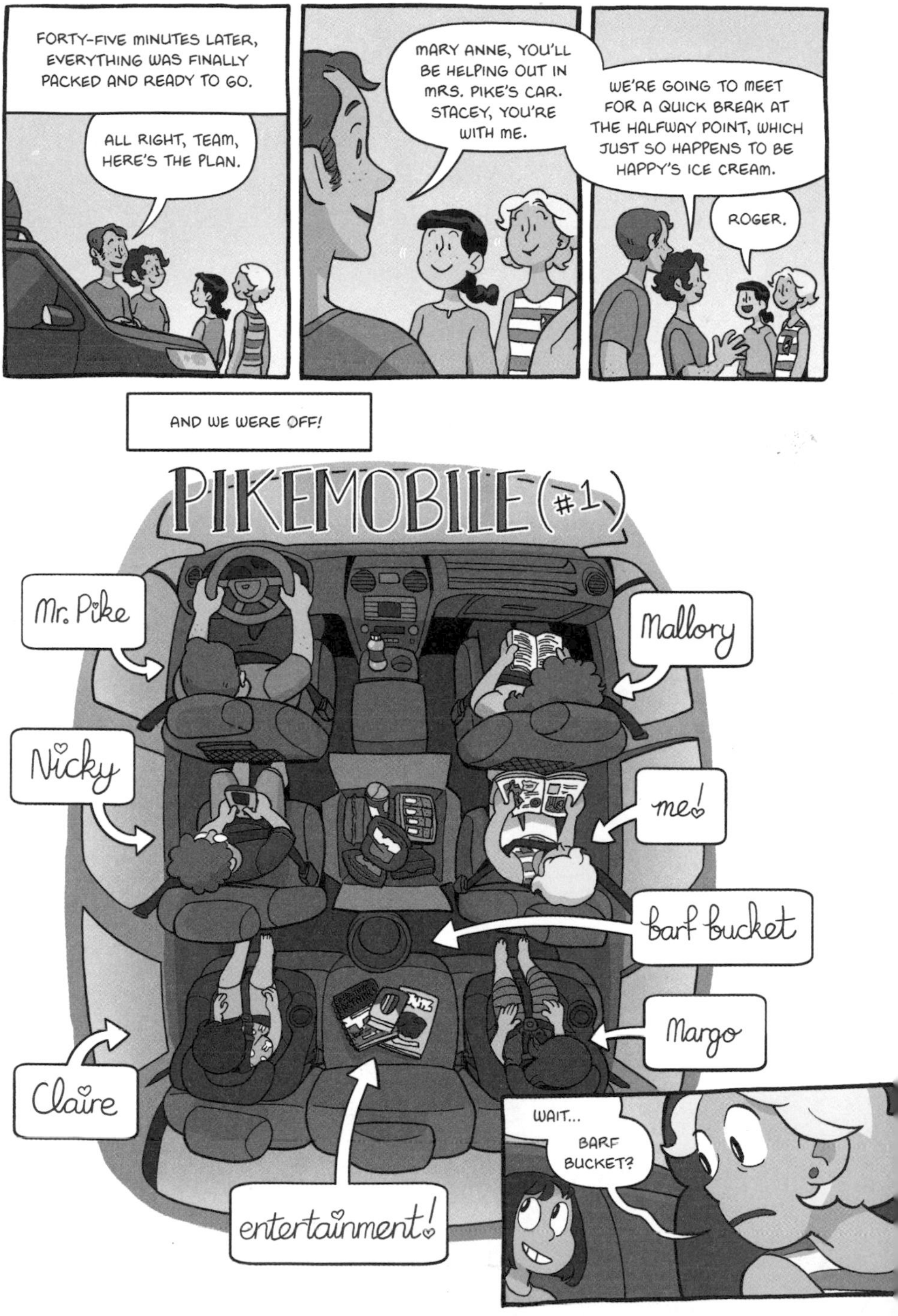
FORTY-FIVE MINUTES LATER, EVERYTHING WAS FINALLY PACKED AND READY TO GO.
ALL RIGHT, TEAM, HERE'S THE PLAN.
MARY ANNE, YOU'LL BE HELPING OUT IN MRS. PIKE'S CAR. STACEY, YOU'RE WITH ME.
WE'RE GOING TO MEET FOR A QUICK BREAK AT THE HALFWAY POINT, WHICH JUST SO HAPPENS TO BE HAPPY'S ICE CREAM.
ROGER.
AND WE WERE OFF!
PIKEMOBILE (#1)
Mr. Pike
Mallory
Nicky
me!
barf bucket
Margo
Claire
entertainment!
WAIT...
BARF BUCKET?

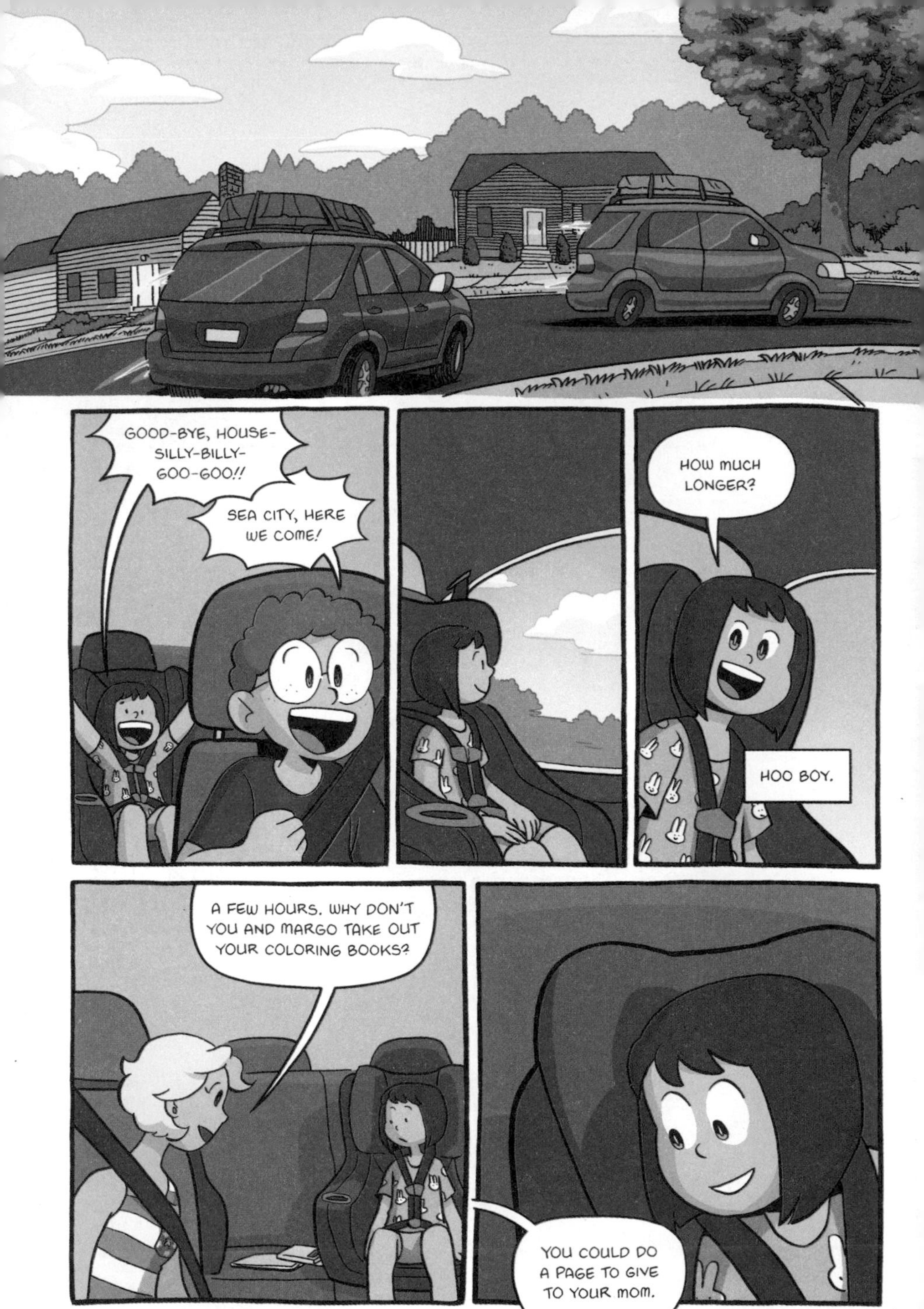
GOOD-BYE, HOUSE-SILLY-BILLY-GOO-GOO!!
SEA CITY, HERE WE COME!
HOW MUCH LONGER?
HOO BOY.
A FEW HOURS. WHY DON'T YOU AND MARGO TAKE OUT YOUR COLORING BOOKS?
YOU COULD DO A PAGE TO GIVE TO YOUR MOM.

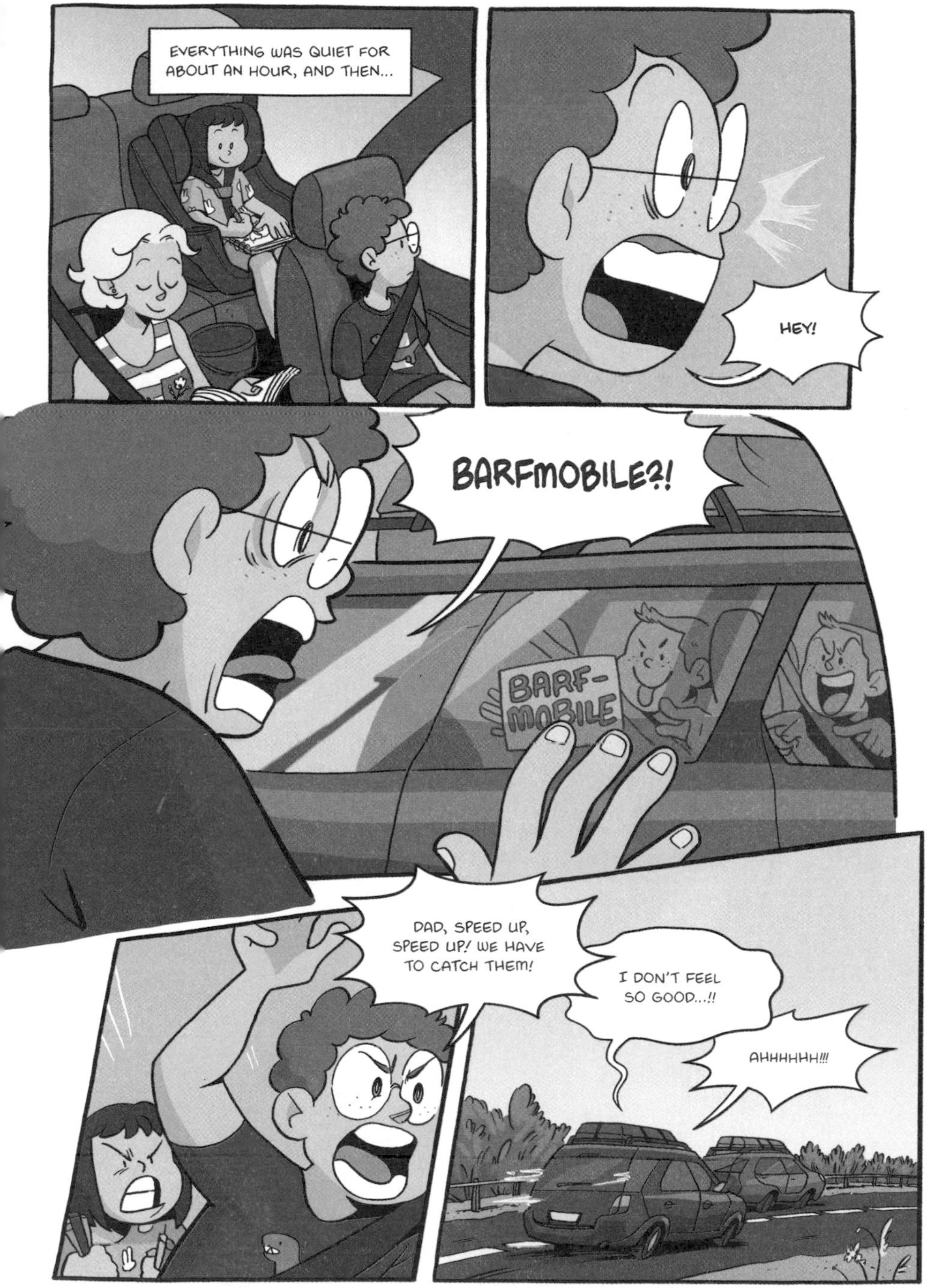
EVERYTHING WAS QUIET FOR ABOUT AN HOUR, AND THEN...
HEY!
BARFMOBILE?!
BARF-MOBILE
DAD, SPEED UP, SPEED UP! WE HAVE TO CATCH THEM!
I DON'T FEEL SO GOOD...!!
AHHHHHH!!!

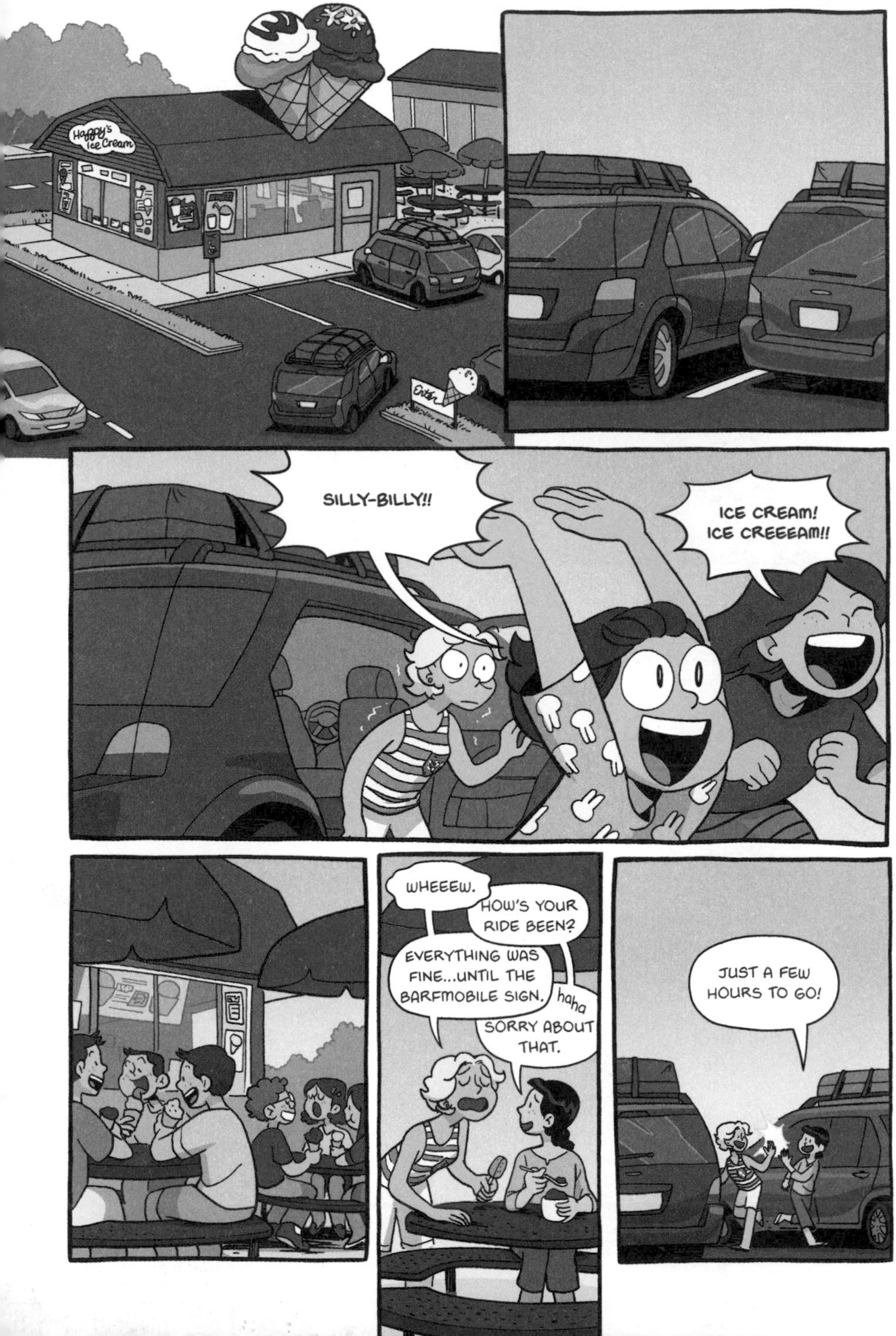
Happy's Ice Cream
Enter
SILLY-BILLY!!
ICE CREAM! ICE CREEEAM!!
WHEEEW.
HOW'S YOUR RIDE BEEN?
EVERYTHING WAS FINE...UNTIL THE BARFMOBILE SIGN.
haha
SORRY ABOUT THAT.
JUST A FEW HOURS TO GO!

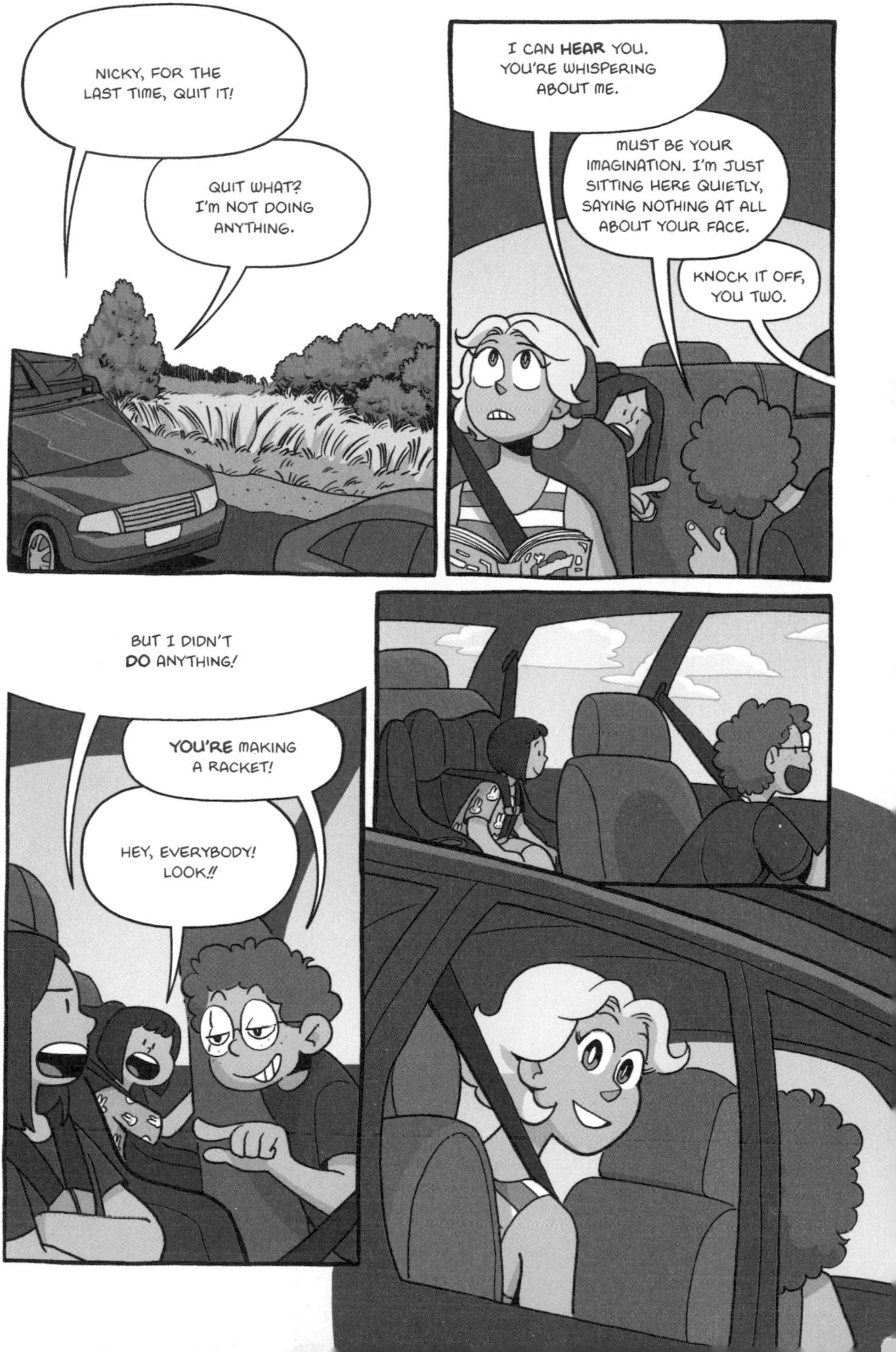
NICKY, FOR THE LAST TIME, QUIT IT!
QUIT WHAT? I'M NOT DOING ANYTHING.
I CAN **HEAR** YOU. YOU'RE WHISPERING ABOUT ME.
MUST BE YOUR IMAGINATION. I'M JUST SITTING HERE QUIETLY, SAYING NOTHING AT ALL ABOUT YOUR FACE.
KNOCK IT OFF, YOU TWO.
BUT I DIDN'T **DO** ANYTHING!
YOU'RE MAKING A RACKET!
HEY, EVERYBODY! LOOK!!

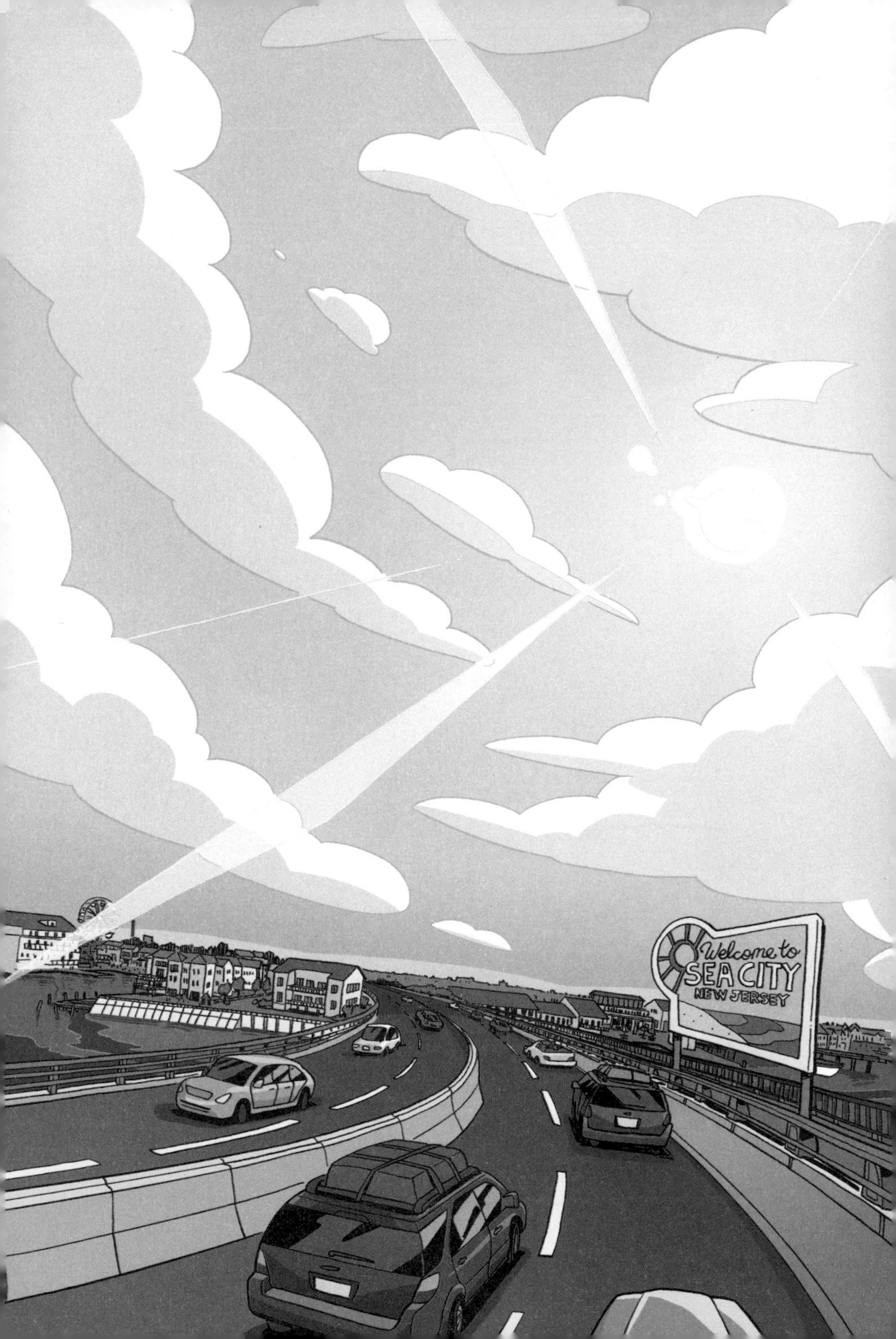
Welcome to
SEA CITY
NEW JERSEY

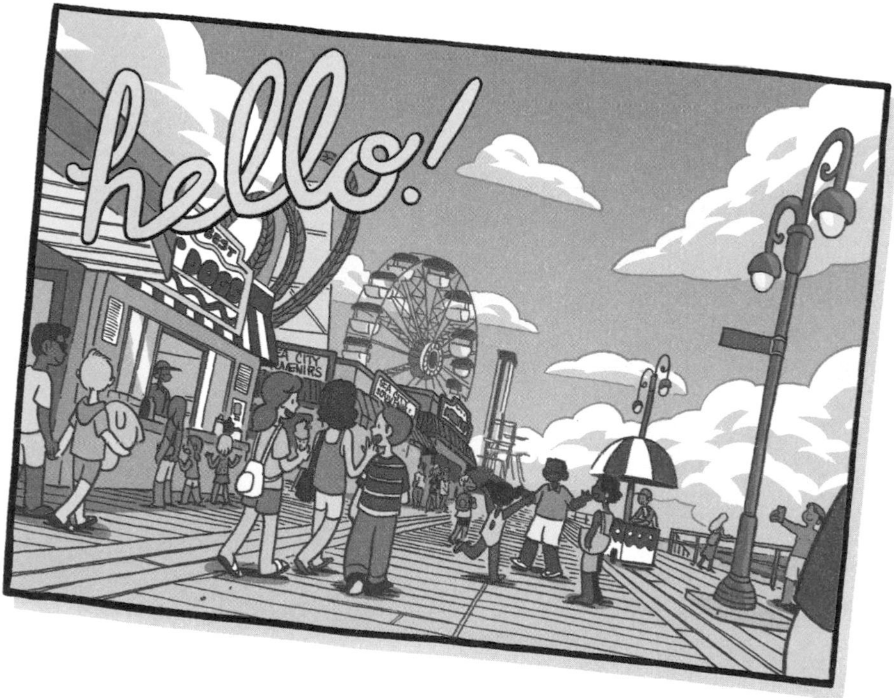
hello!
BEST
EA CITY
UVENIRS

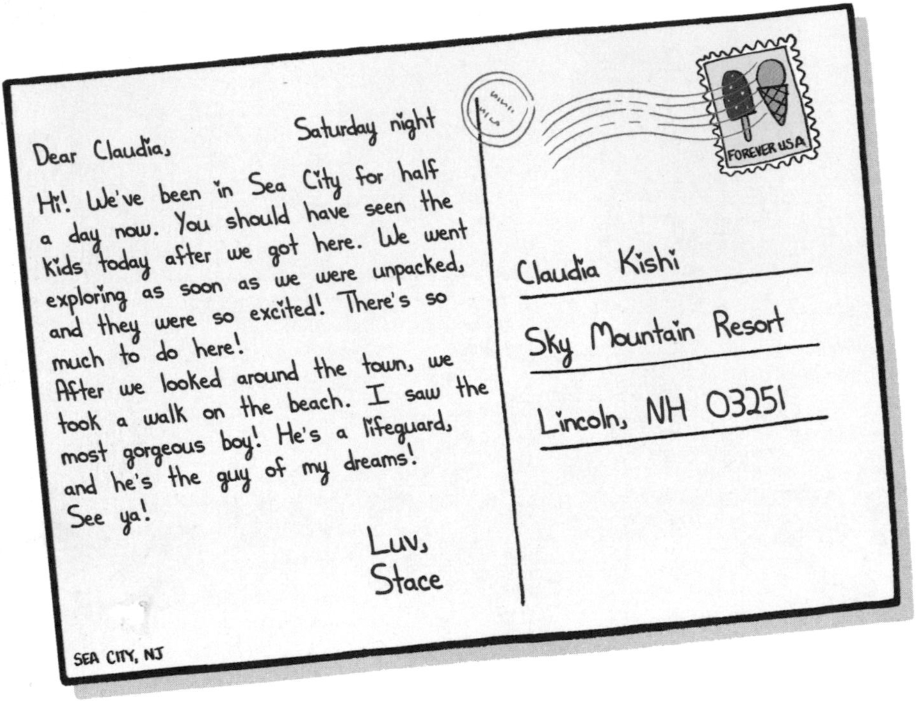

Saturday night

Dear Claudia,

Hi! We've been in Sea City for half a day now. You should have seen the kids today after we got here. We went exploring as soon as we were unpacked, and they were so excited! There's so much to do here!

After we looked around the town, we took a walk on the beach. I saw the most gorgeous boy! He's a lifeguard, and he's the guy of my dreams!

See ya!

Luv,
Stace

Claudia Kishi
Sky Mountain Resort
Lincoln, NH 03251

FOREVER USA

SEA CITY, NJ

CHAPTER 4

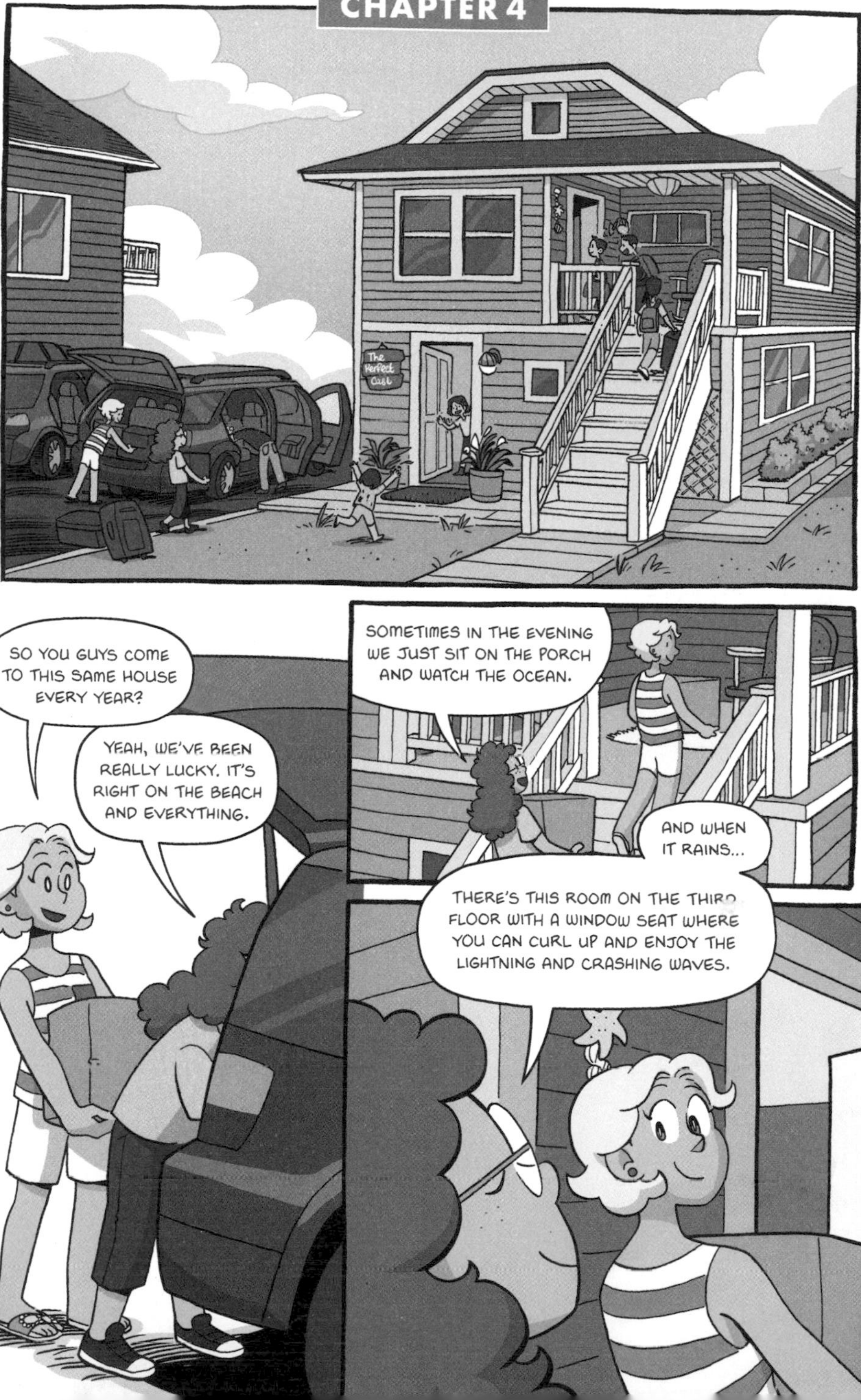
The Perfect Cast
SO YOU GUYS COME TO THIS SAME HOUSE EVERY YEAR?
YEAH, WE'VE BEEN REALLY LUCKY. IT'S RIGHT ON THE BEACH AND EVERYTHING.
SOMETIMES IN THE EVENING WE JUST SIT ON THE PORCH AND WATCH THE OCEAN.
AND WHEN IT RAINS...
THERE'S THIS ROOM ON THE THIRD FLOOR WITH A WINDOW SEAT WHERE YOU CAN CURL UP AND ENJOY THE LIGHTNING AND CRASHING WAVES.

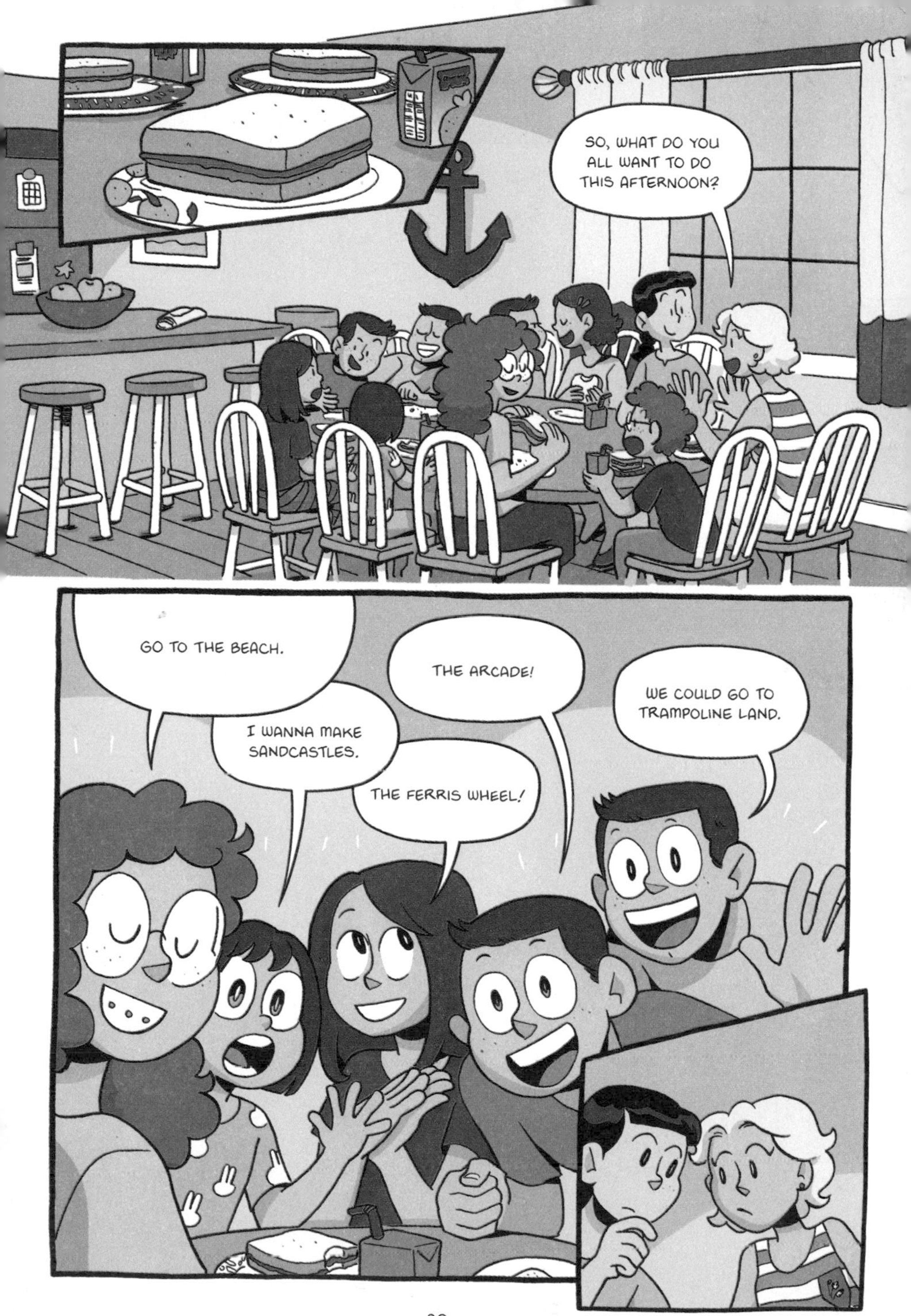
SO, WHAT DO YOU ALL WANT TO DO THIS AFTERNOON?
GO TO THE BEACH.
I WANNA MAKE SANDCASTLES.
THE ARCADE!
THE FERRIS WHEEL!
WE COULD GO TO TRAMPOLINE LAND.

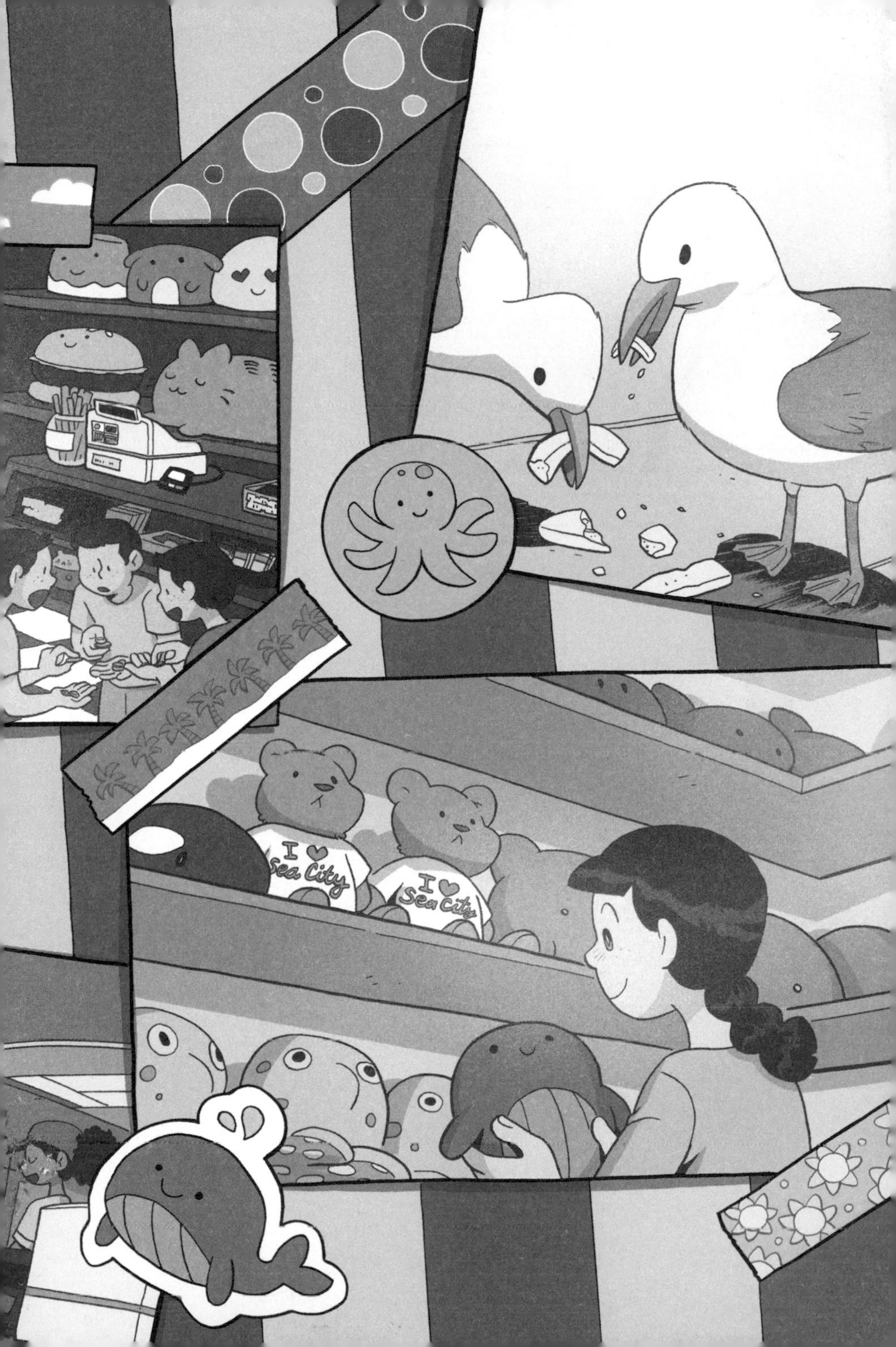
I ♥ Sea City
I ♥ Sea City

42

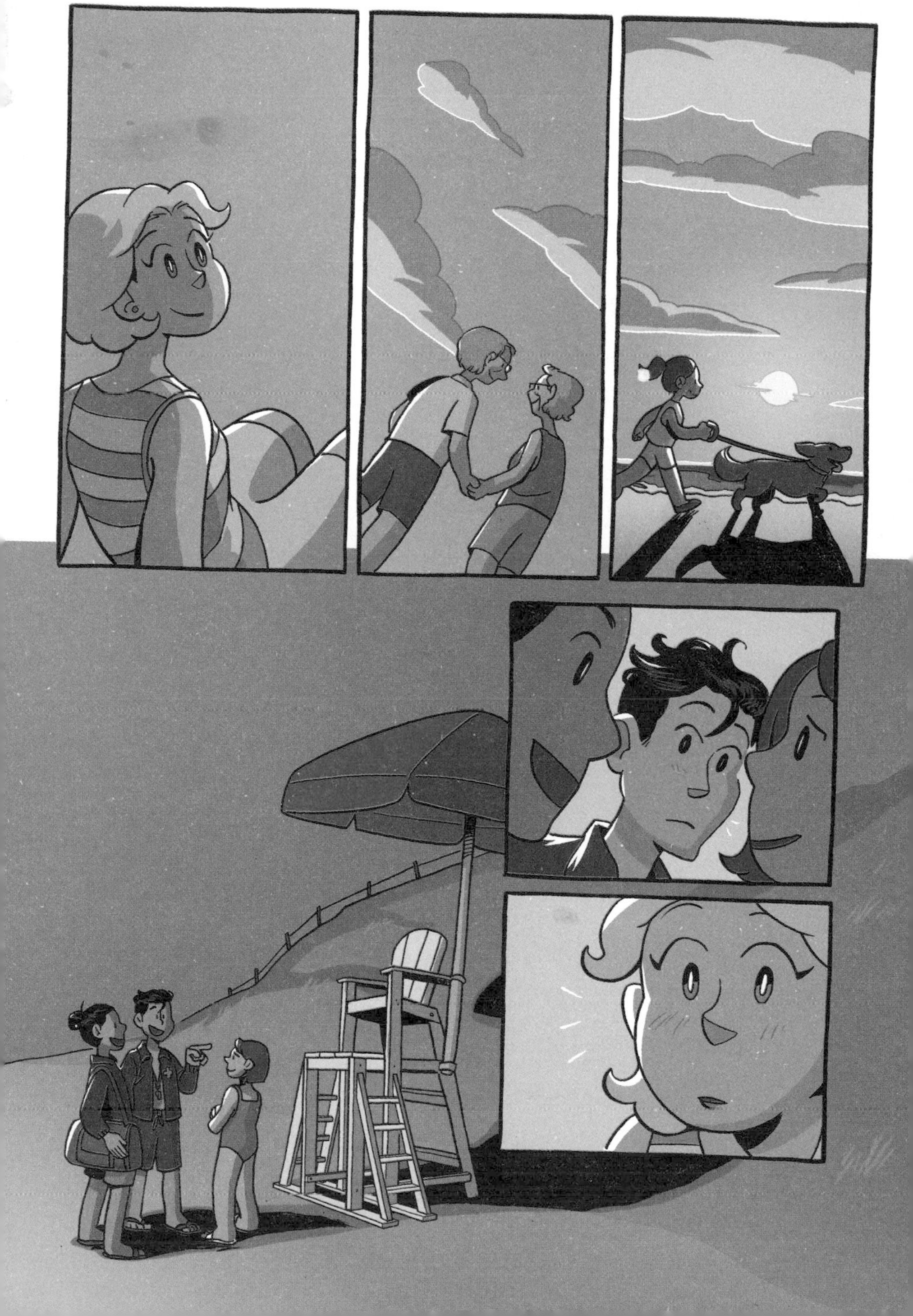

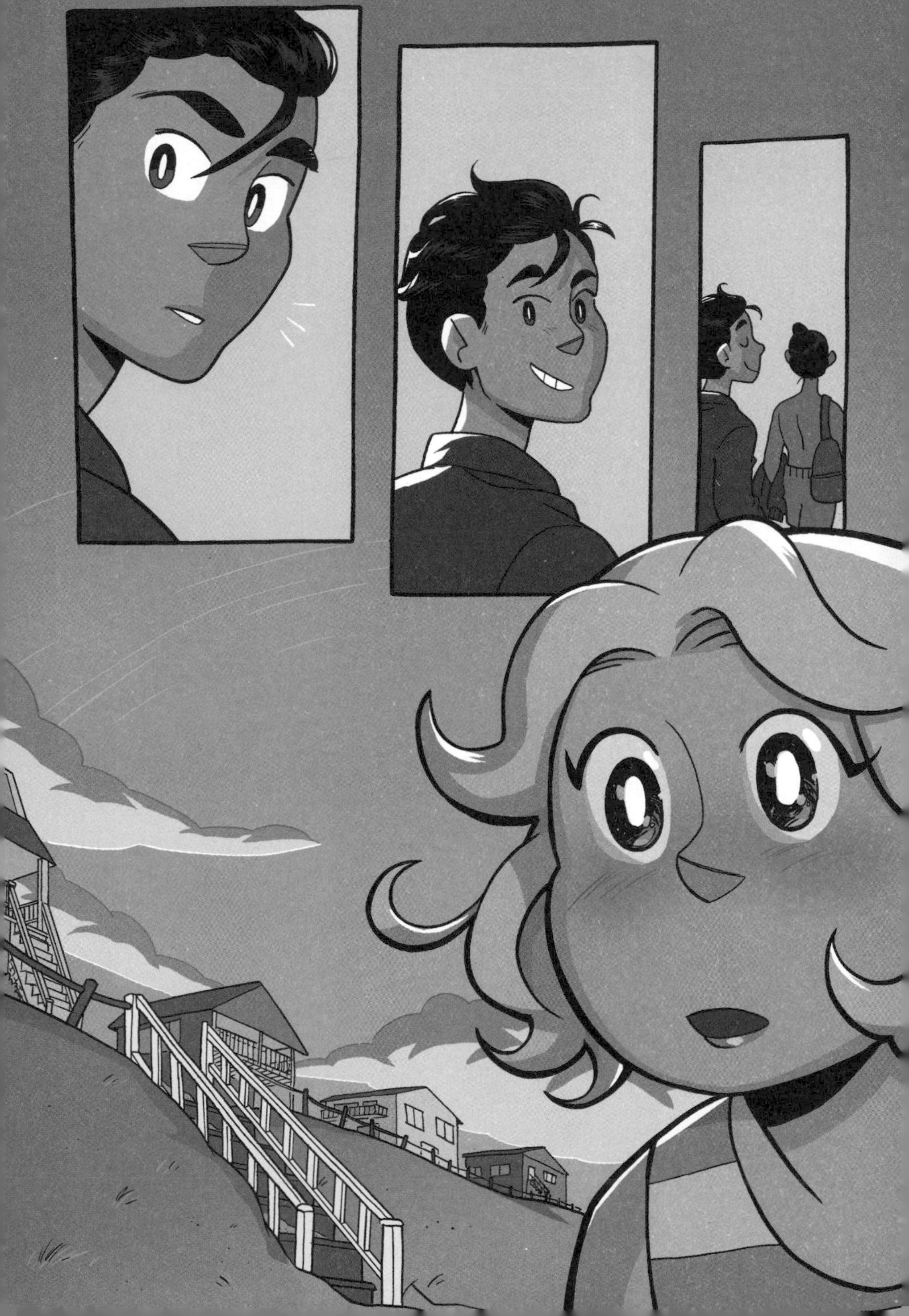

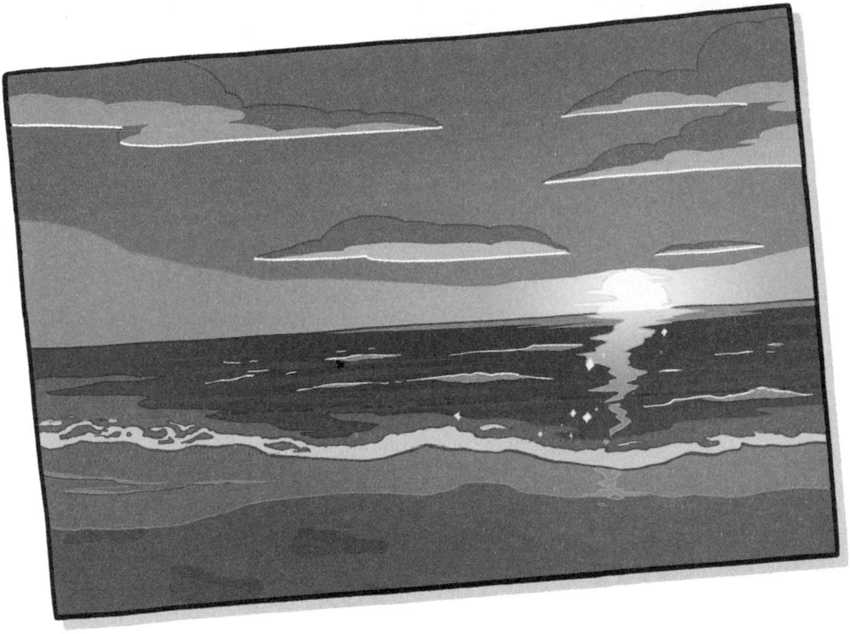

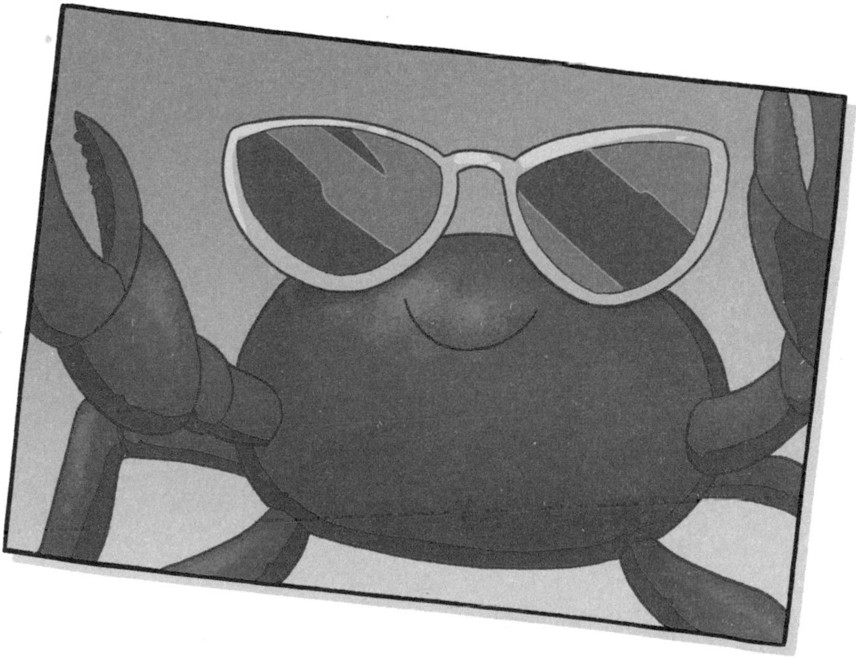

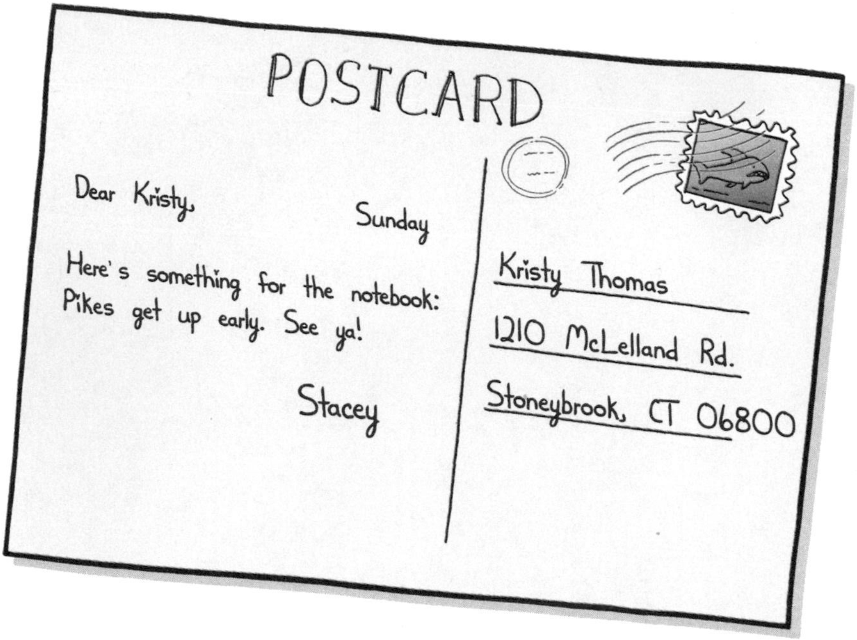

POSTCARD

Dear Kristy,

Sunday

Here's something for the notebook: Pikes get up early. See ya!

Stacey

Kristy Thomas
1210 McLelland Rd.
Stoneybrook, CT 06800

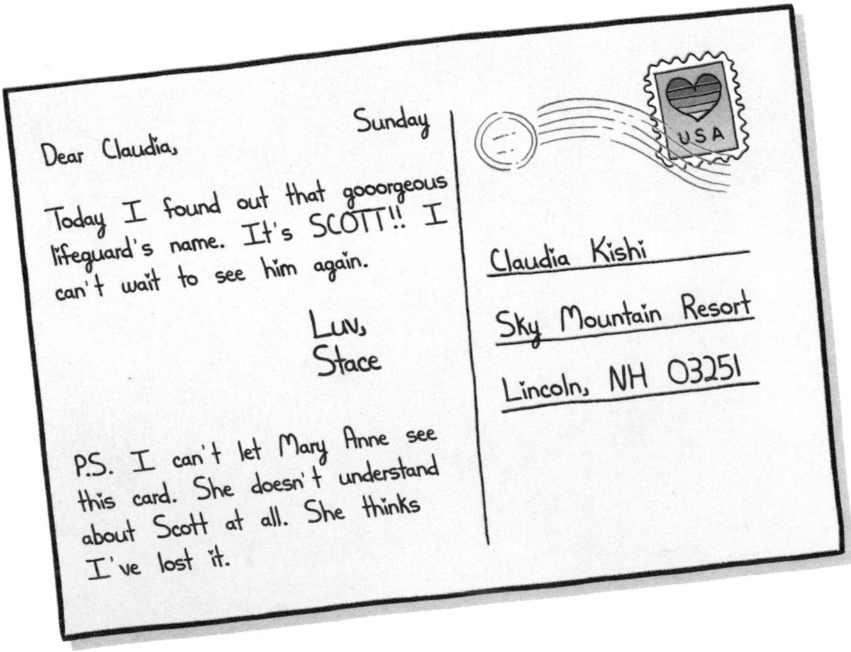

Sunday

Dear Claudia,

Today I found out that gooorgeous lifeguard's name. It's SCOTT!! I can't wait to see him again.

Luv,
Stace

P.S. I can't let Mary Anne see this card. She doesn't understand about Scott at all. She thinks I've lost it.

Claudia Kishi
Sky Mountain Resort
Lincoln, NH 03251

CHAPTER 5

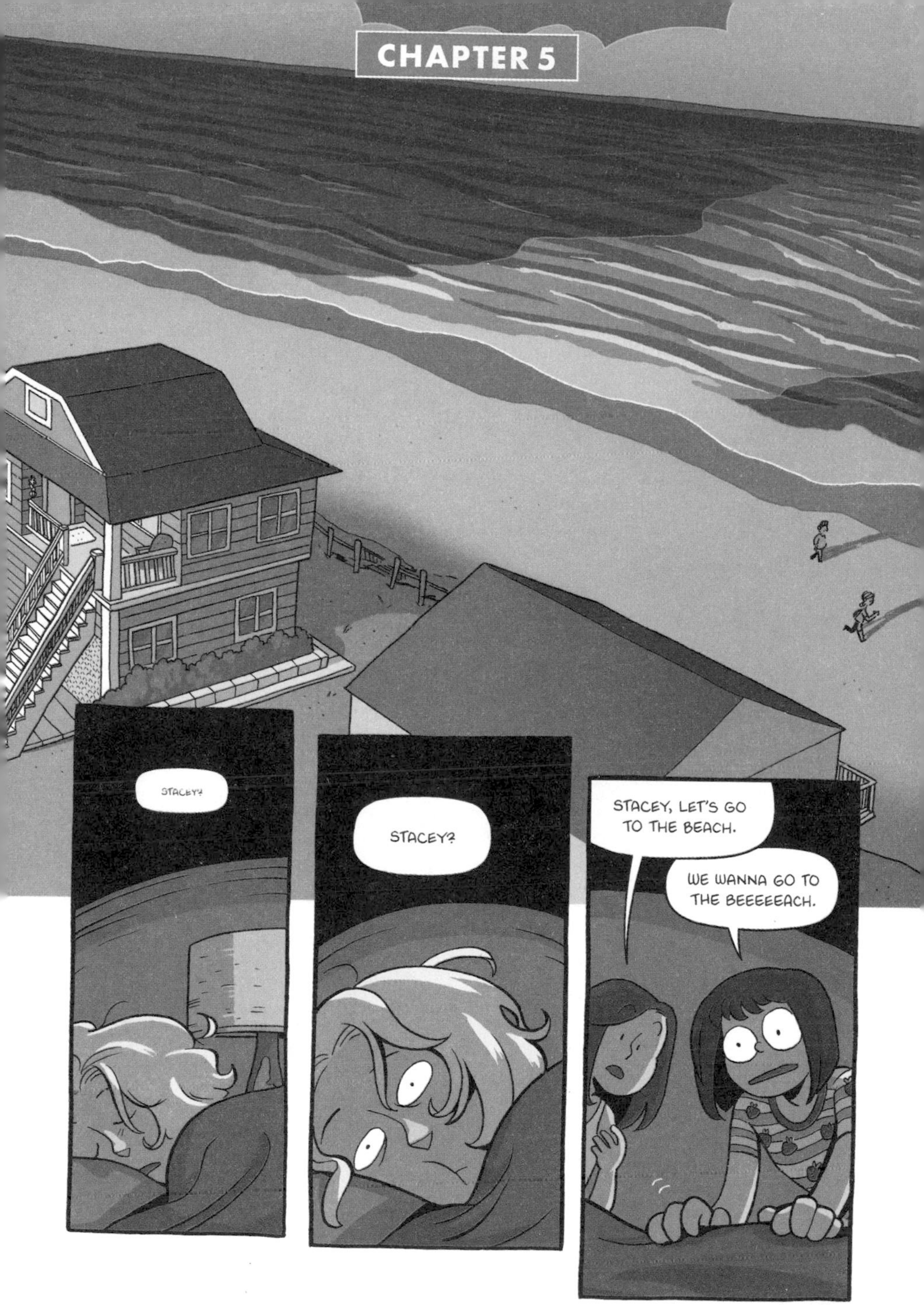

STACEY?
STACEY?
STACEY, LET'S GO TO THE BEACH.
WE WANNA GO TO THE BEEEEEACH.

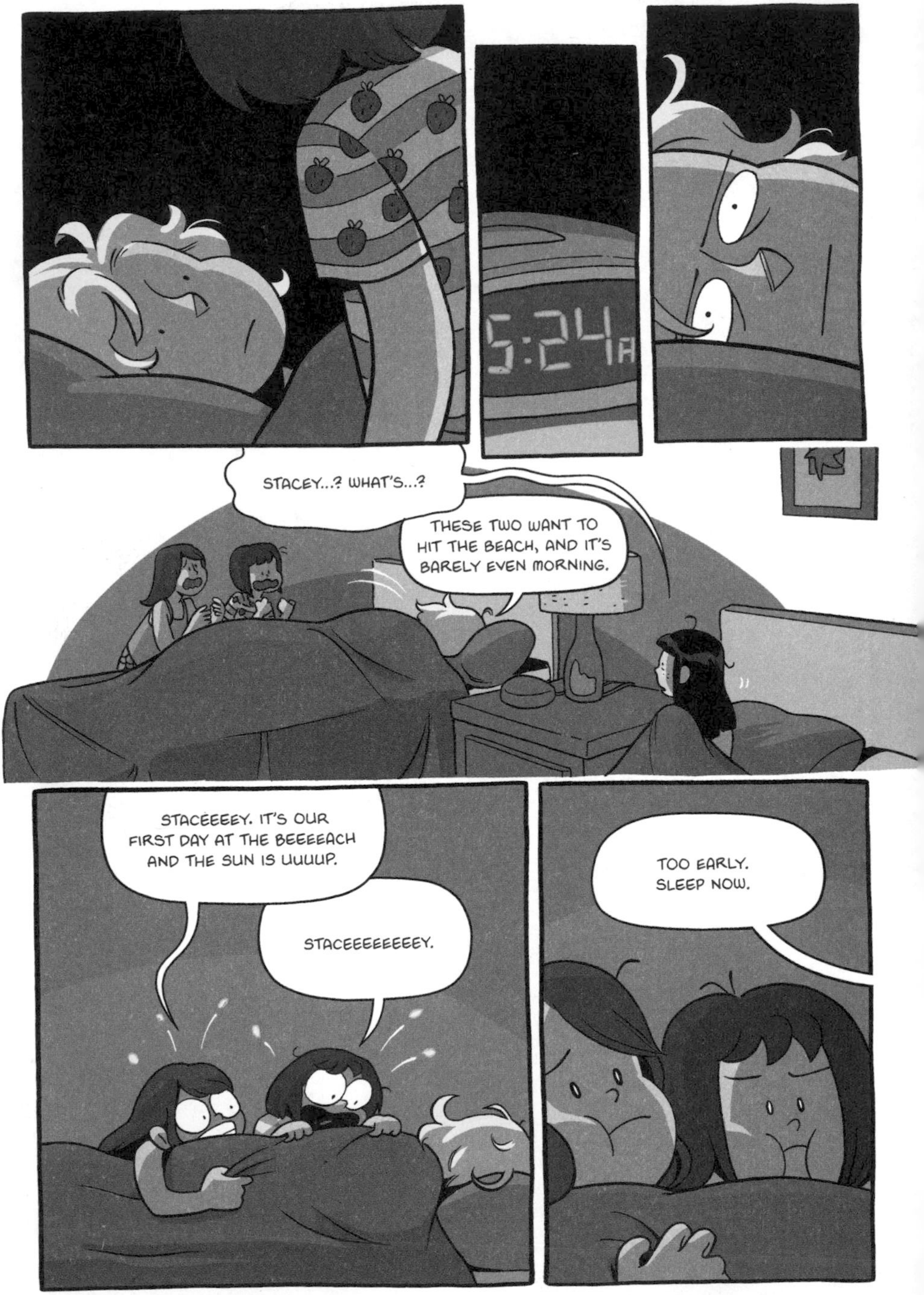
5:24 A
STACEY...? WHAT'S...?
THESE TWO WANT TO HIT THE BEACH, AND IT'S BARELY EVEN MORNING.
STACEEEEY. IT'S OUR FIRST DAY AT THE BEEEEACH AND THE SUN IS UUUUP.
STACEEEEEEEEY.
TOO EARLY. SLEEP NOW.

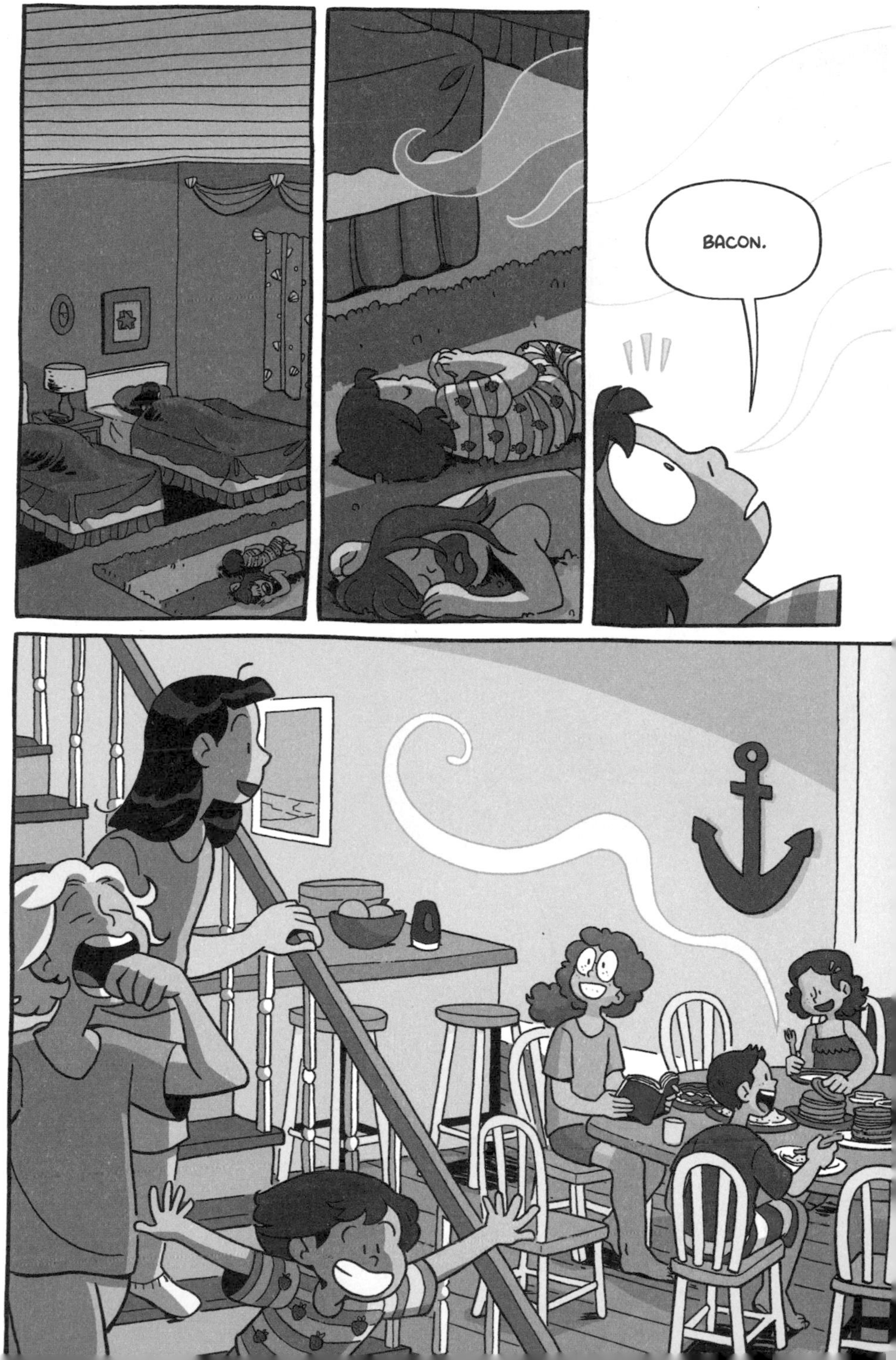
BACON.

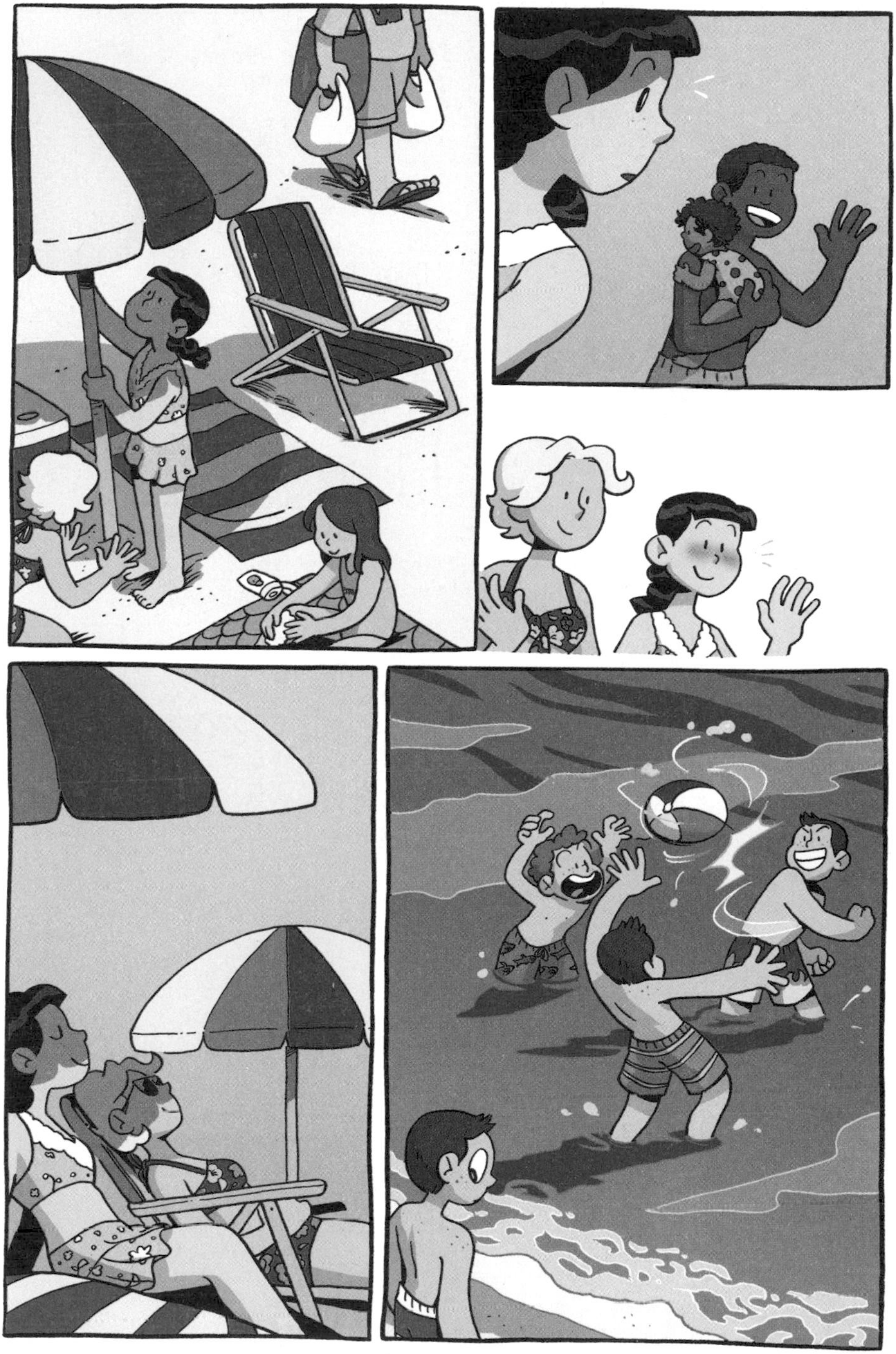

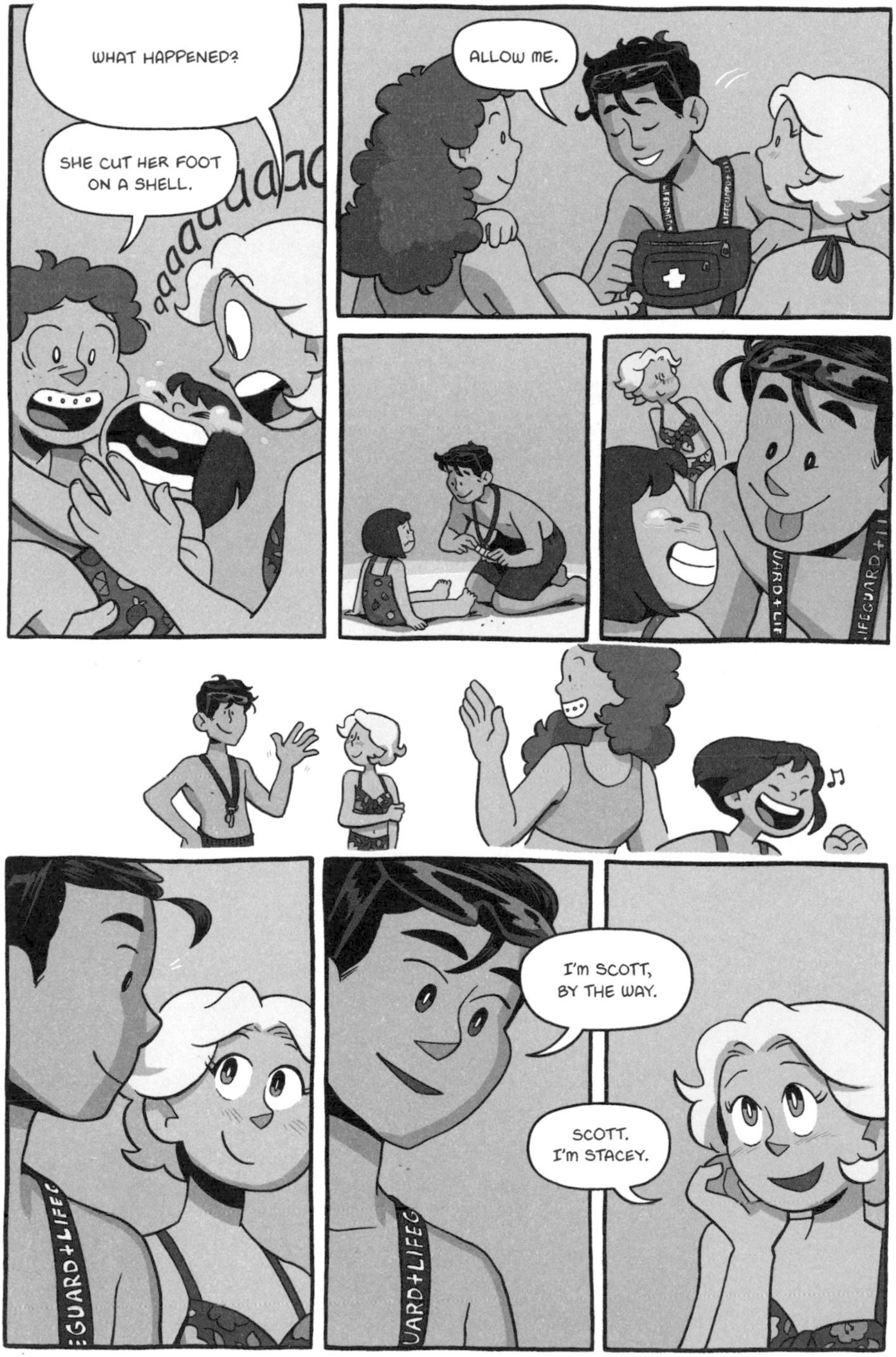
WHAT HAPPENED?
SHE CUT HER FOOT ON A SHELL.
ALLOW ME.
I'M SCOTT, BY THE WAY.
SCOTT. I'M STACEY.

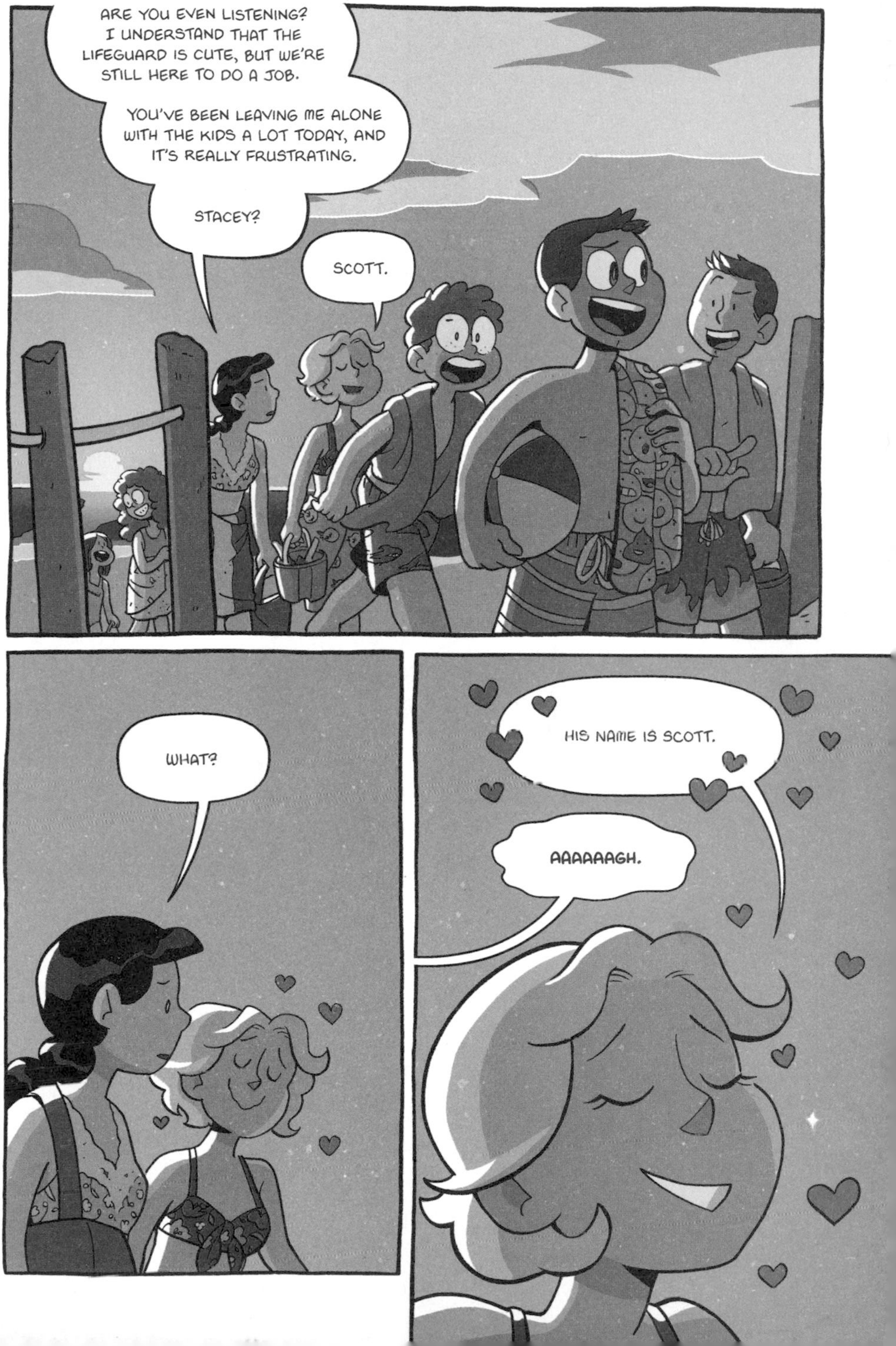
ARE YOU EVEN LISTENING? I UNDERSTAND THAT THE LIFEGUARD IS CUTE, BUT WE'RE STILL HERE TO DO A JOB.
YOU'VE BEEN LEAVING ME ALONE WITH THE KIDS A LOT TODAY, AND IT'S REALLY FRUSTRATING.
STACEY?
SCOTT.
WHAT?
HIS NAME IS SCOTT.
AAAAAAGH.

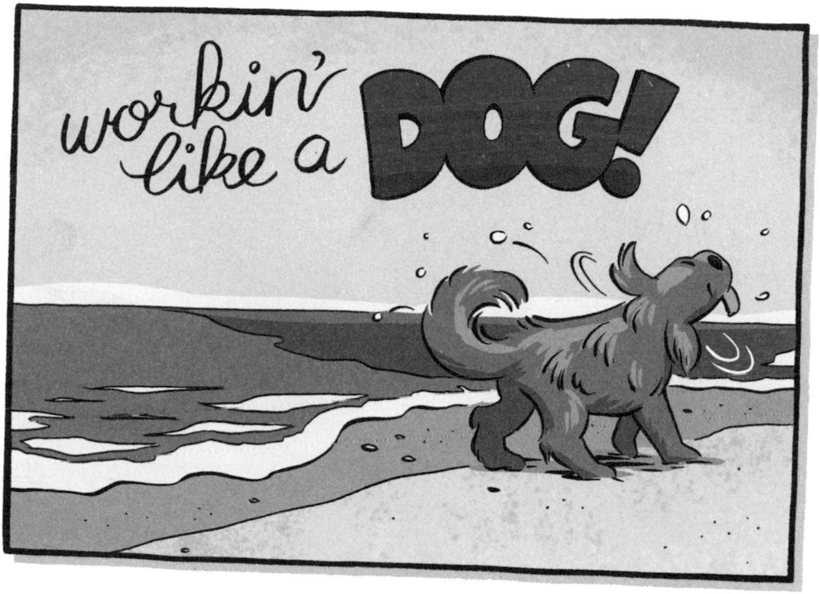
workin' like a DOG!

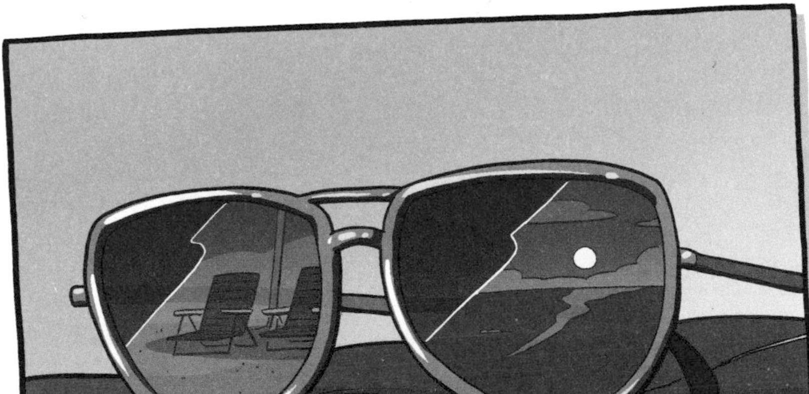

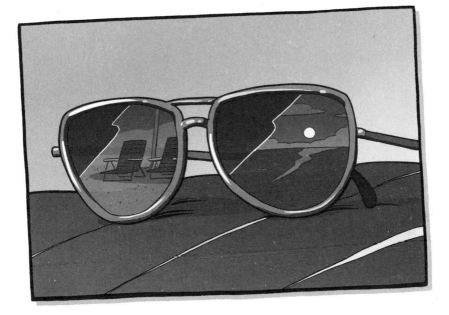

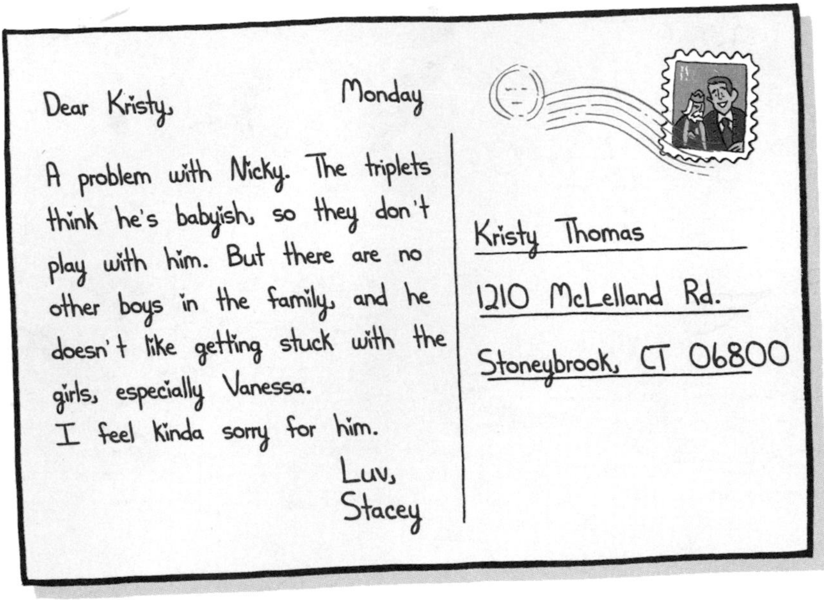
Dear Kristy,
Monday
A problem with Nicky. The triplets think he's babyish, so they don't play with him. But there are no other boys in the family, and he doesn't like getting stuck with the girls, especially Vanessa.
I feel kinda sorry for him.
Luv,
Stacey
Kristy Thomas
1210 McLelland Rd.
Stoneybrook, CT 06800

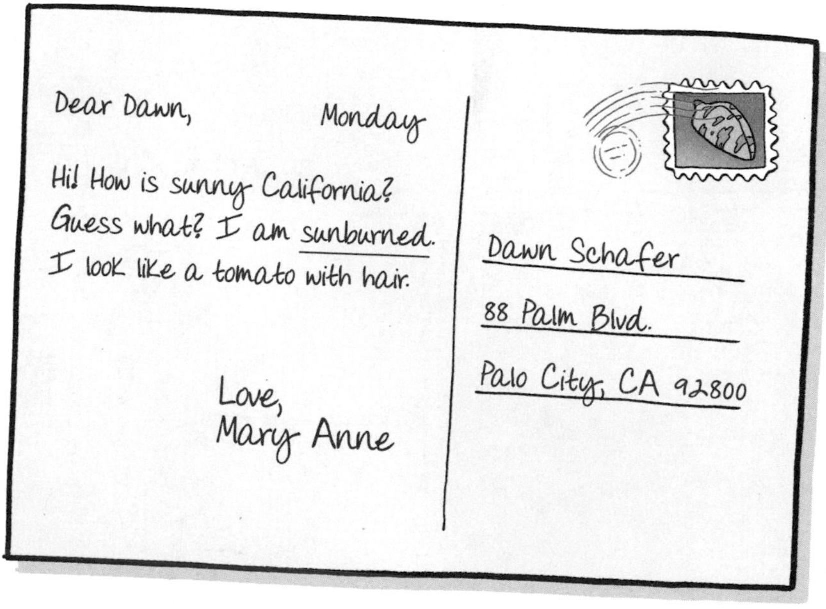
Dear Dawn,
Monday
Hi! How is sunny California?
Guess what? I am sunburned.
I look like a tomato with hair.
Love,
Mary Anne
Dawn Schafer
88 Palm Blvd.
Palo City, CA 92800

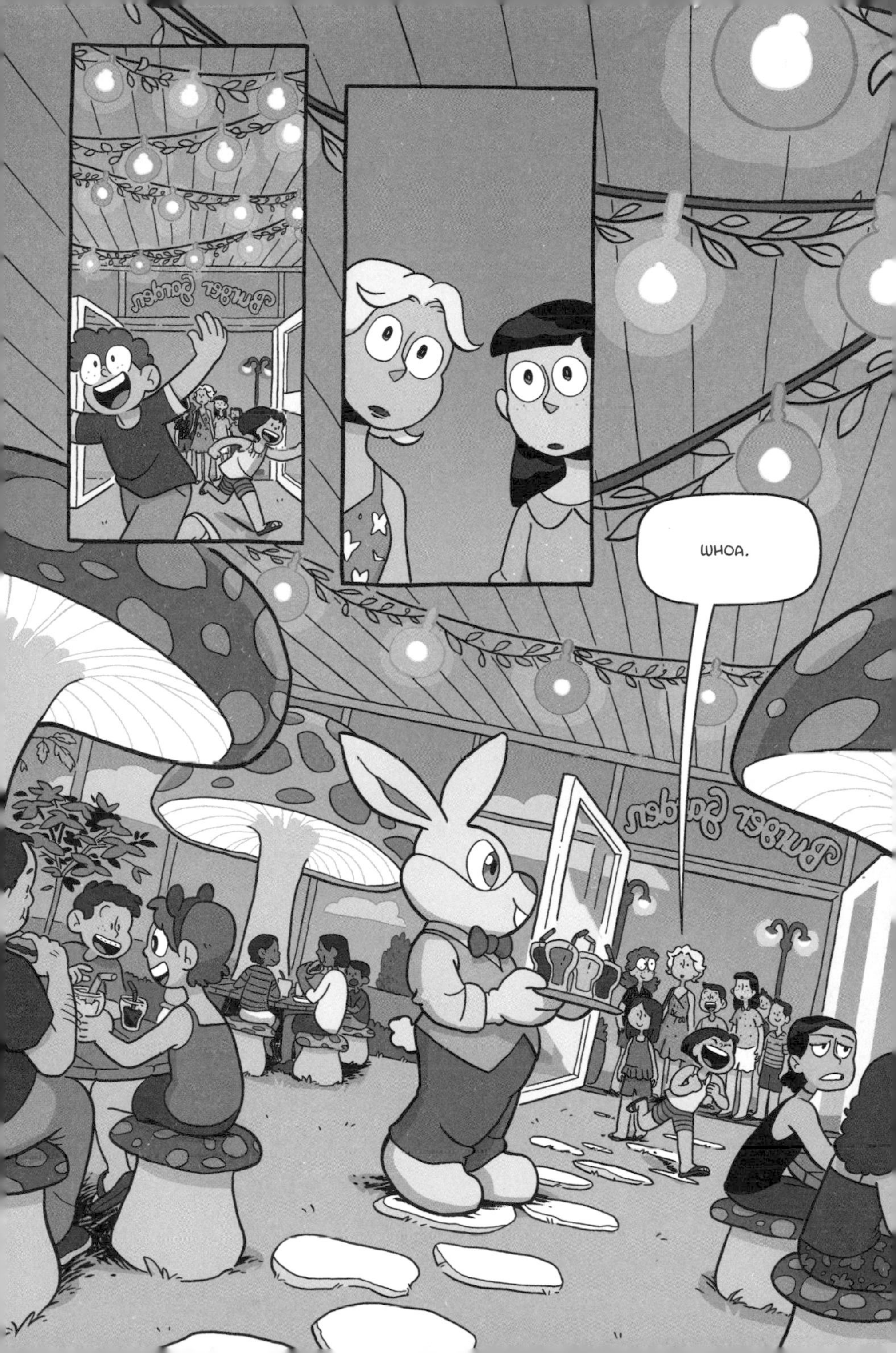
WHOA.

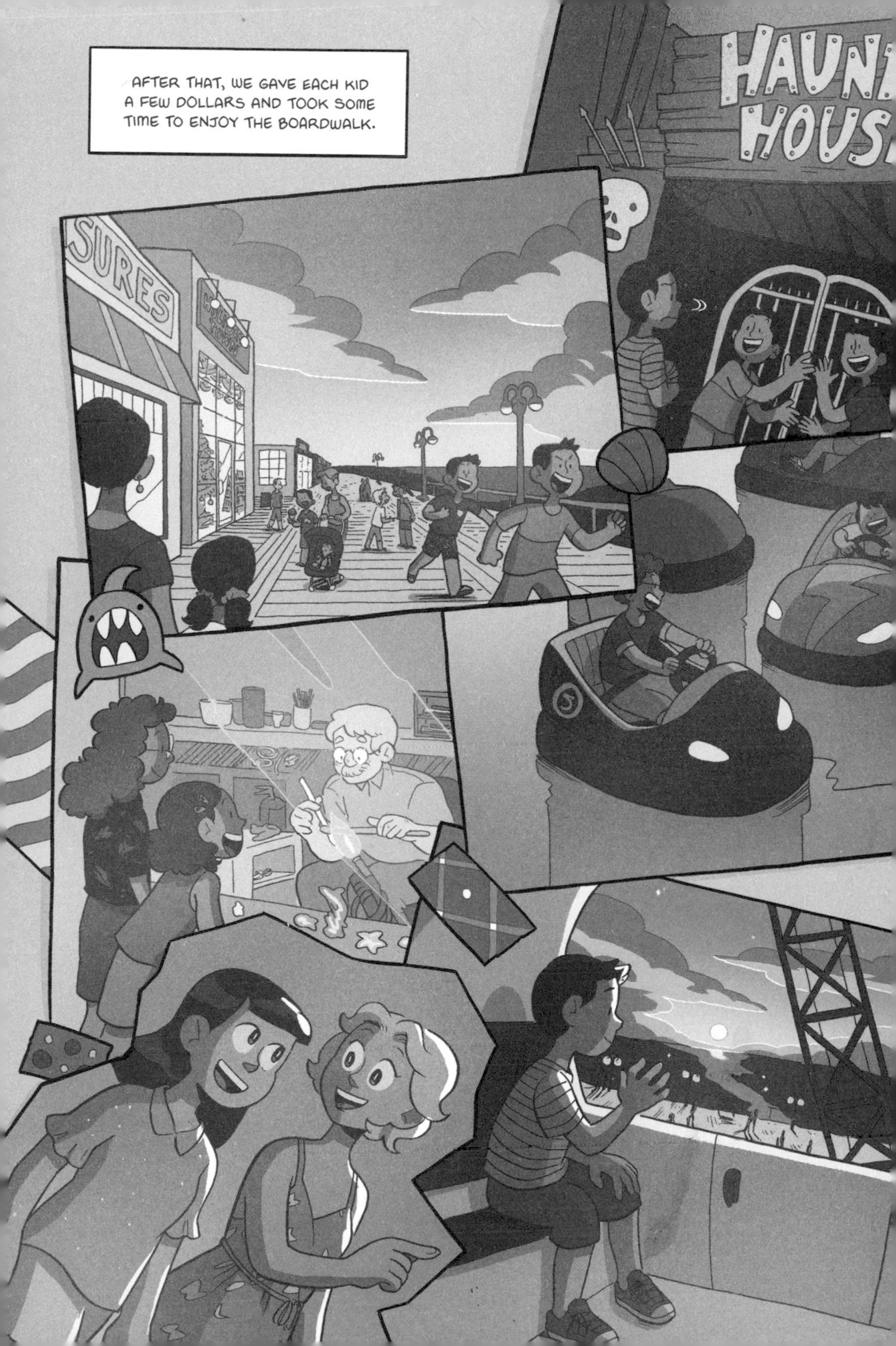
AFTER THAT, WE GAVE EACH KID A FEW DOLLARS AND TOOK SOME TIME TO ENJOY THE BOARDWALK.

71

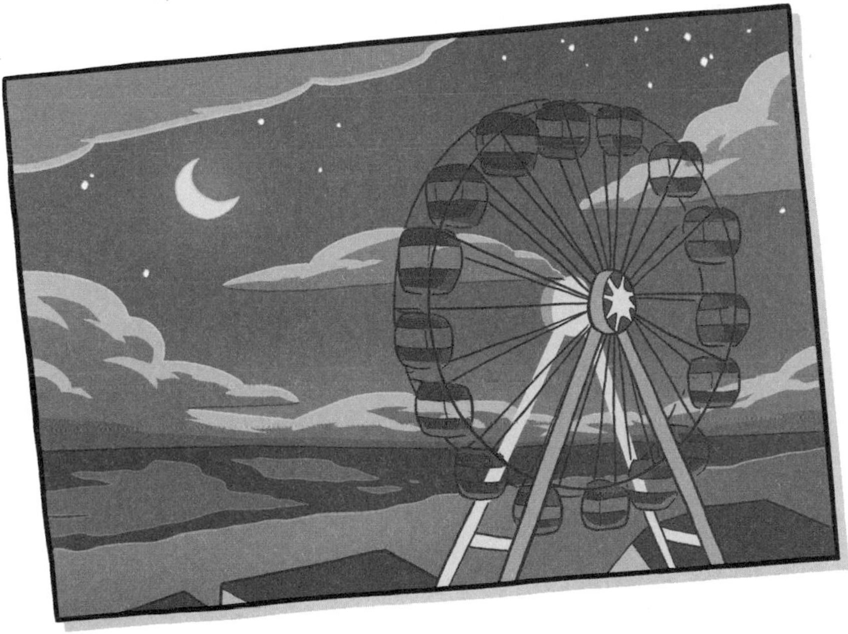

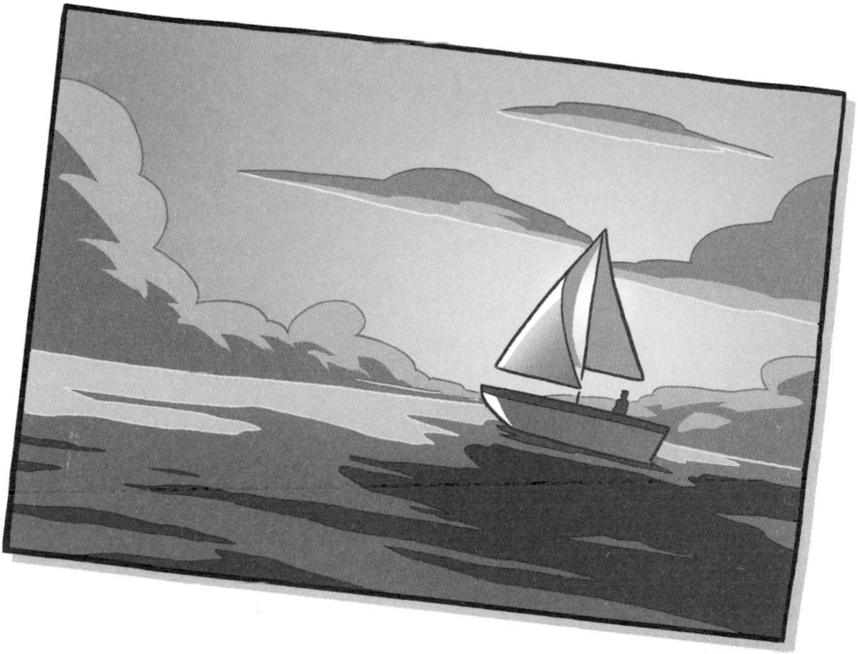

Dear Claudia,   Tuesday

I know I'm supposed to be baby-sitting, but Scott was on duty today and he's all I can think of. He said the sweetest thing when I went to say good-bye for the day . . . I can't wait to tell you all about it. Say hi to Mimi!

Luv,
Stace

P.S. Mary Anne thinks I'm overthinking it. She doesn't understand.

Claudia Kishi

Sky Mountain Resort

Lincoln, NH 03251

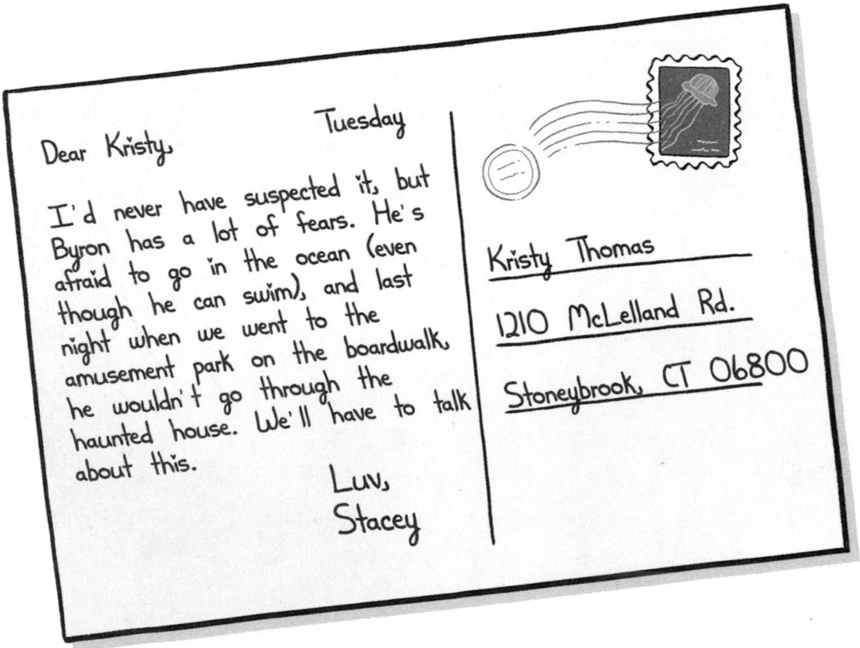

Dear Kristy,   Tuesday

I'd never have suspected it, but Byron has a lot of fears. He's afraid to go in the ocean (even though he can swim), and last night when we went to the amusement park on the boardwalk, he wouldn't go through the haunted house. We'll have to talk about this.

Luv,
Stacey

Kristy Thomas

1210 McLelland Rd.

Stoneybrook, CT 06800

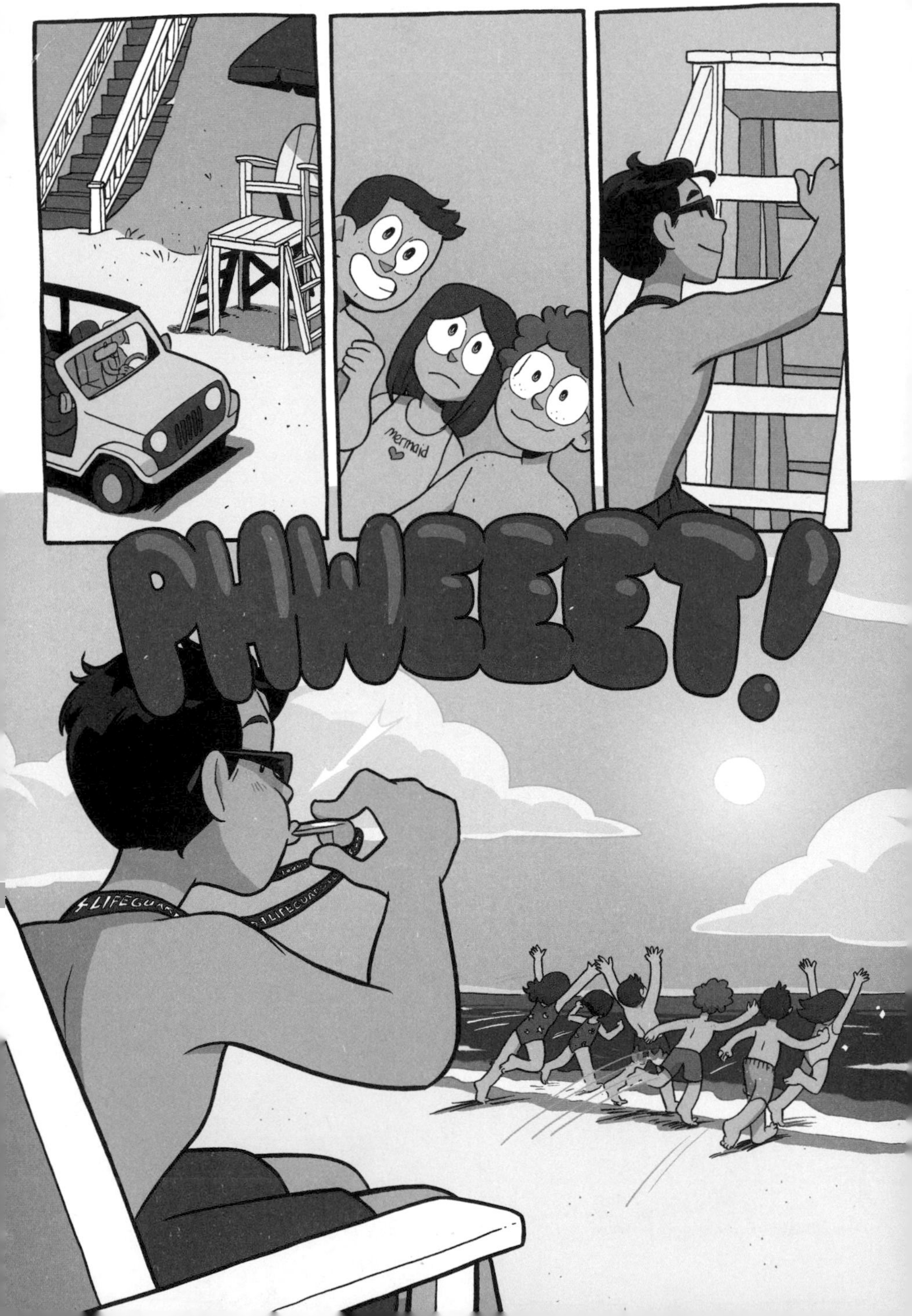
mermaid
PHWEEET!
LIFEGUARD

78

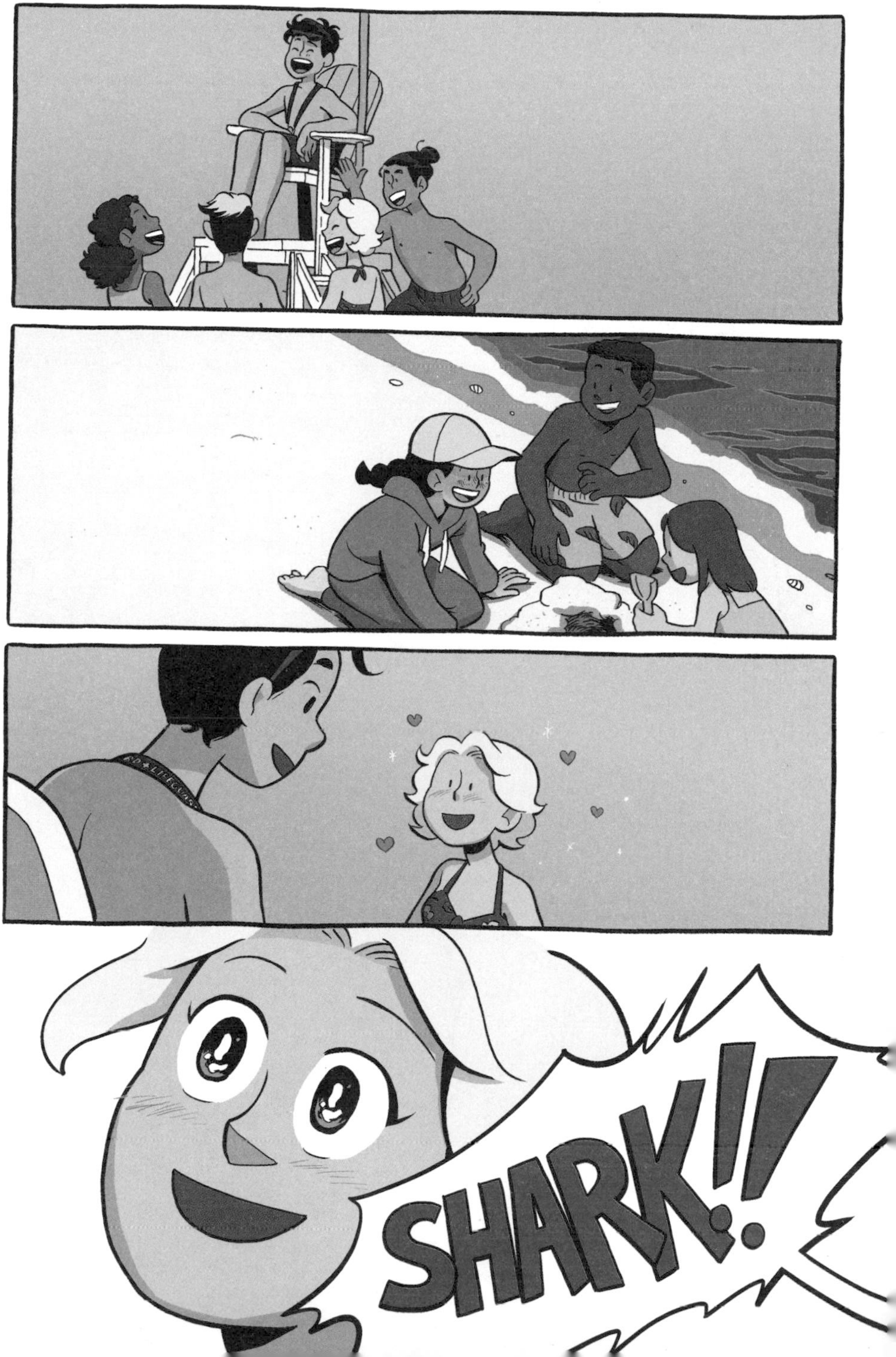
SHARK!!

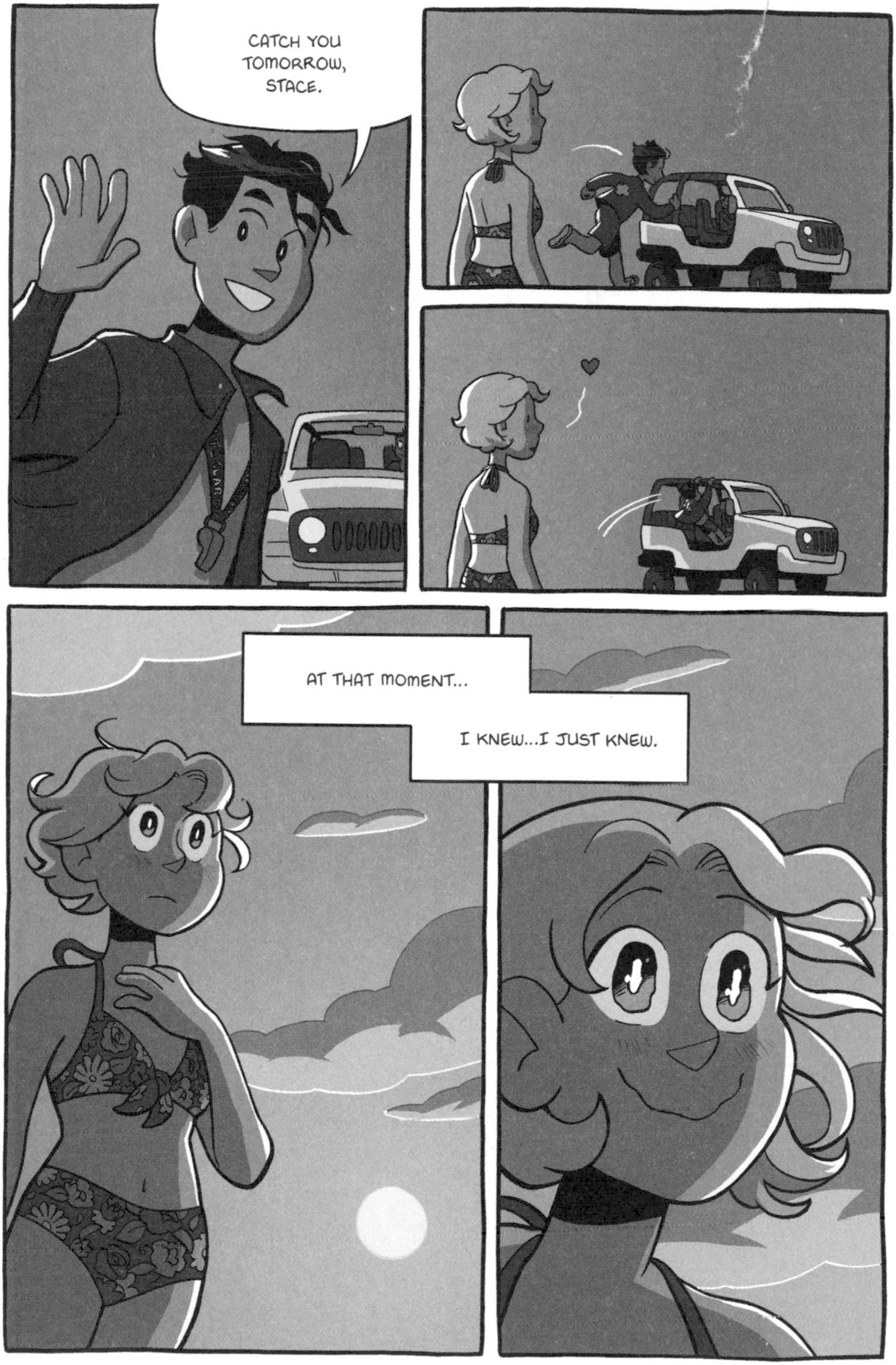
CATCH YOU TOMORROW, STACE.
AT THAT MOMENT...
I KNEW...I JUST KNEW.

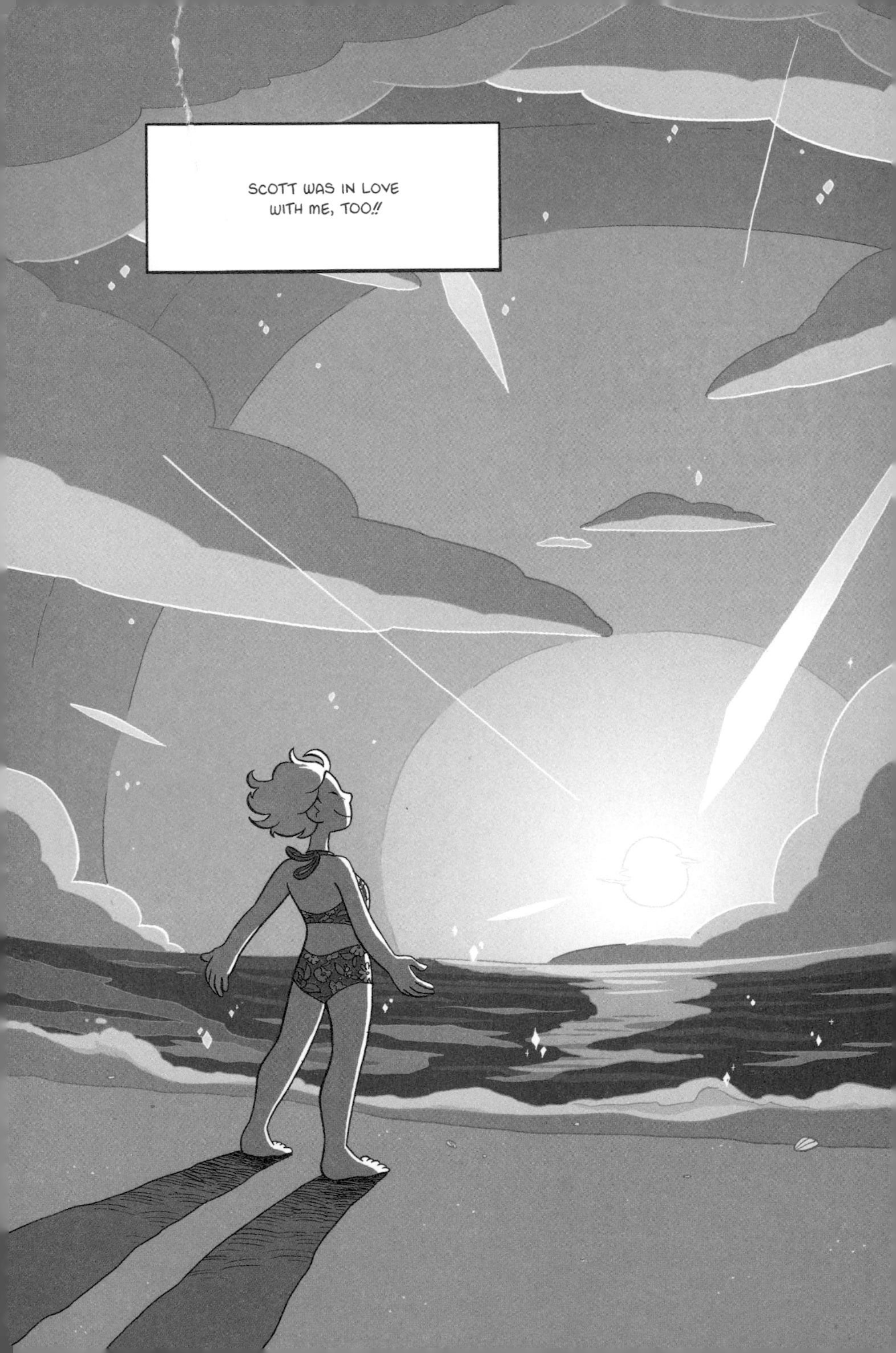
SCOTT WAS IN LOVE WITH ME, TOO!!

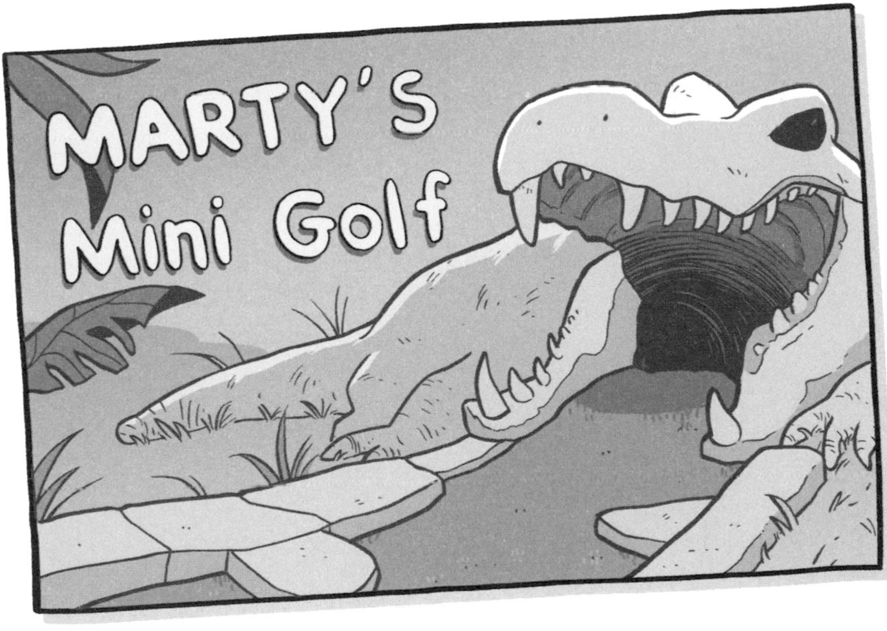
MARTY'S
Mini Golf

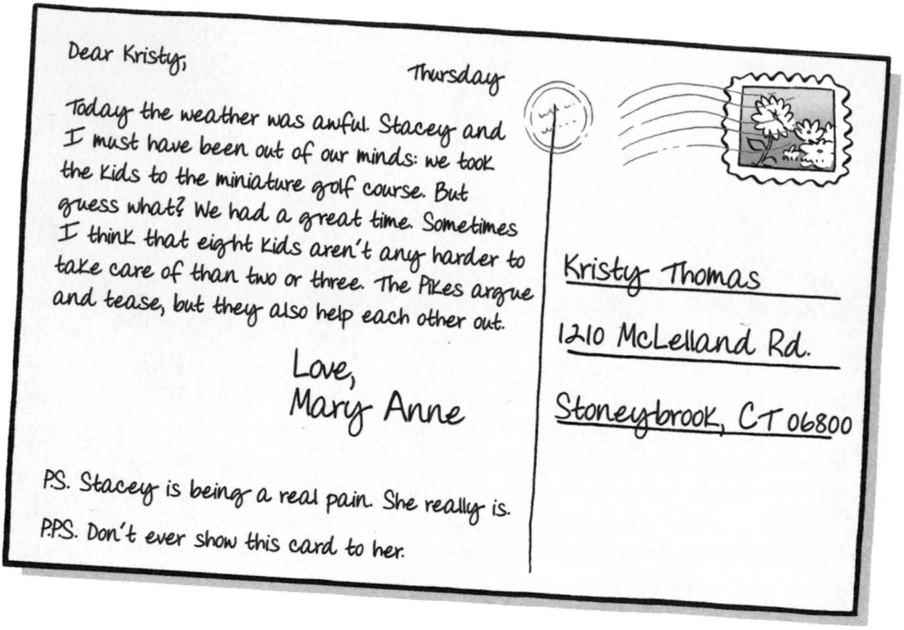
Dear Kristy,

Thursday

Today the weather was awful. Stacey and I must have been out of our minds: we took the kids to the miniature golf course. But guess what? We had a great time. Sometimes I think that eight kids aren't any harder to take care of than two or three. The Pikes argue and tease, but they also help each other out.

Love,
Mary Anne

P.S. Stacey is being a real pain. She really is.

P.P.S. Don't ever show this card to her.

Kristy Thomas
1210 McLelland Rd.
Stoneybrook, CT 06800

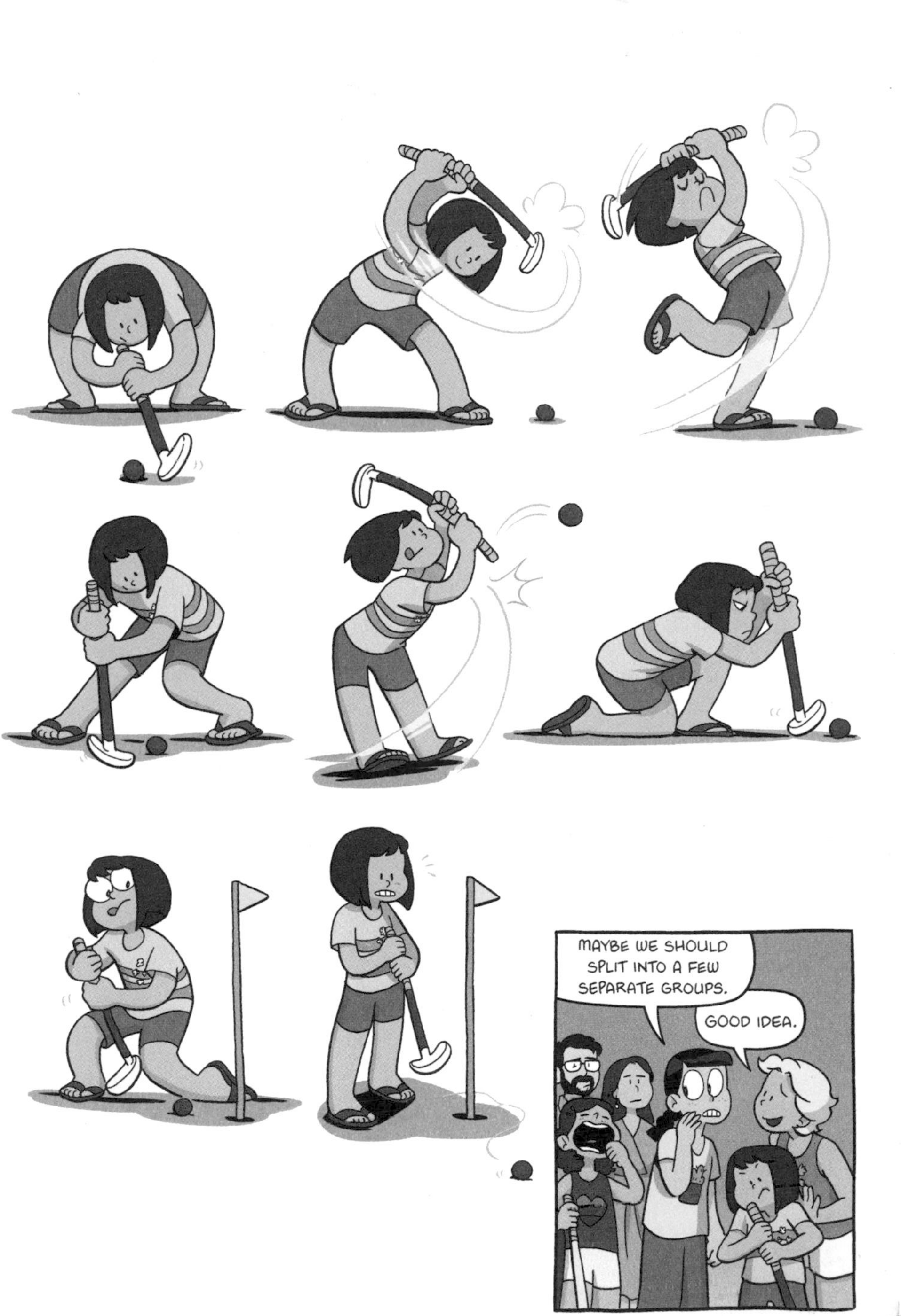
MAYBE WE SHOULD SPLIT INTO A FEW SEPARATE GROUPS.
GOOD IDEA.

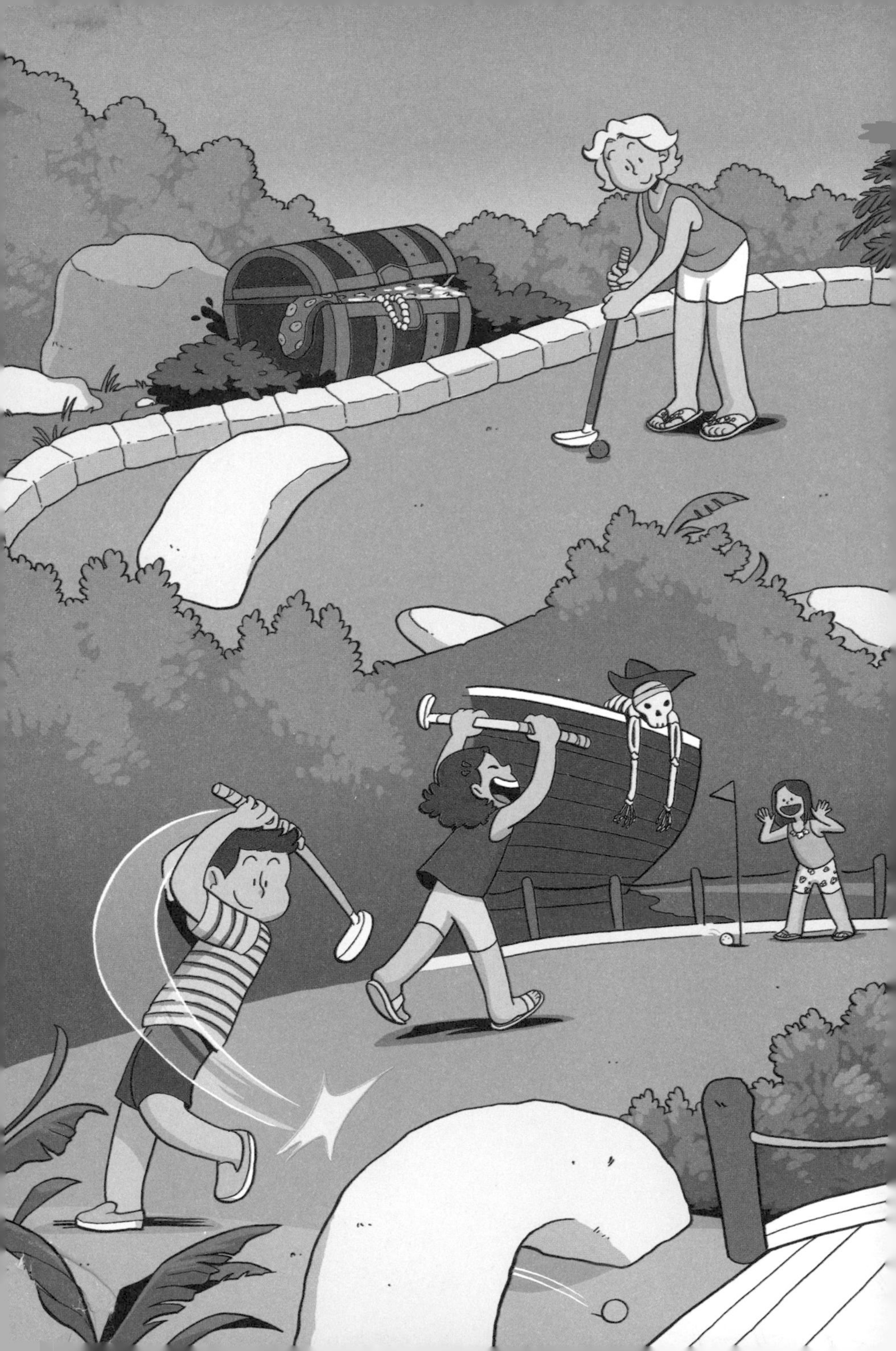

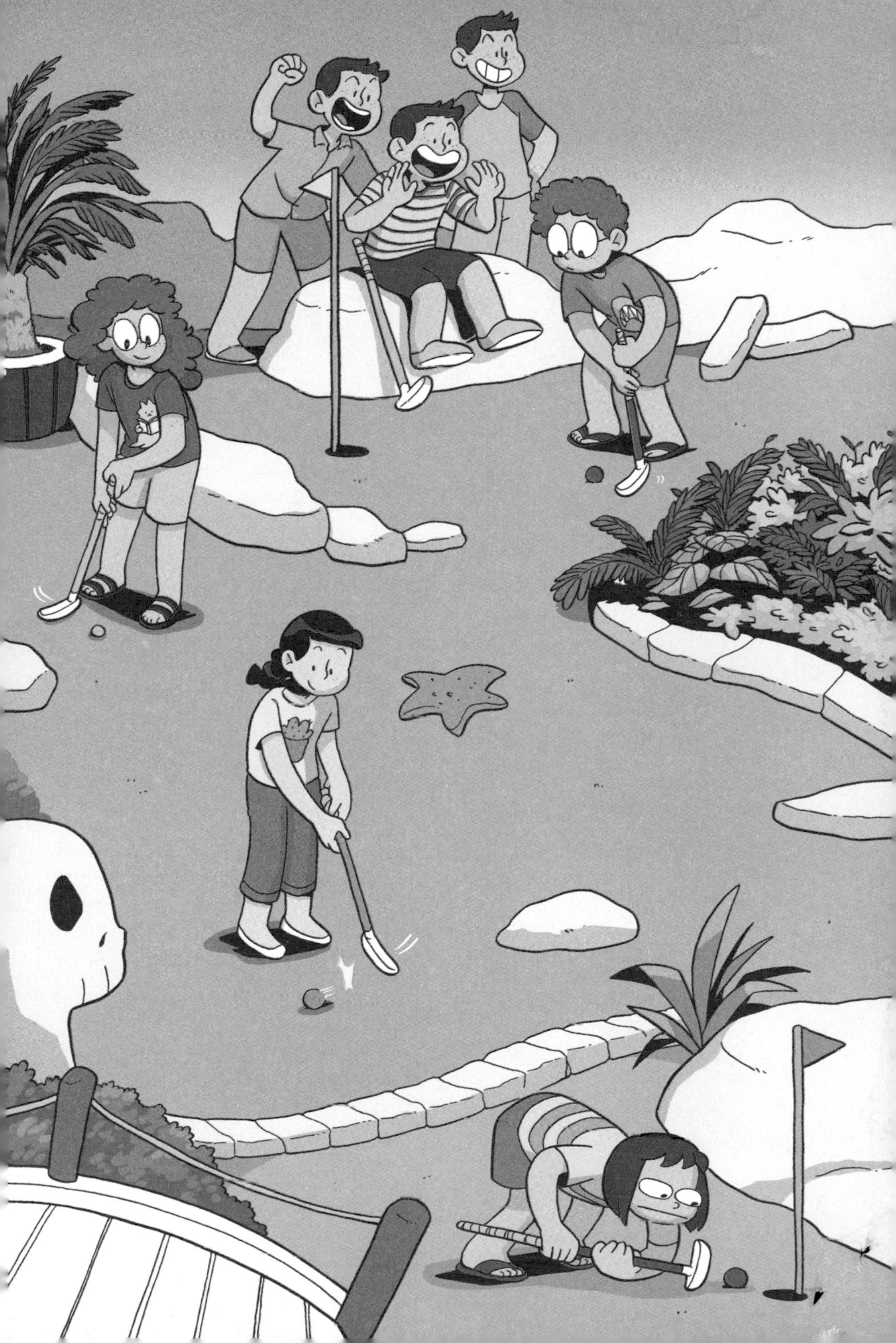

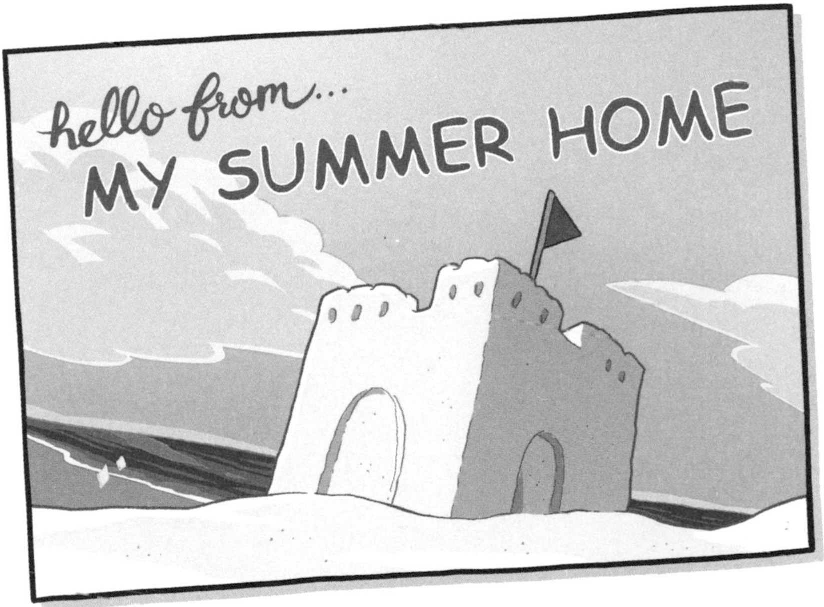
hello from...
MY SUMMER HOME

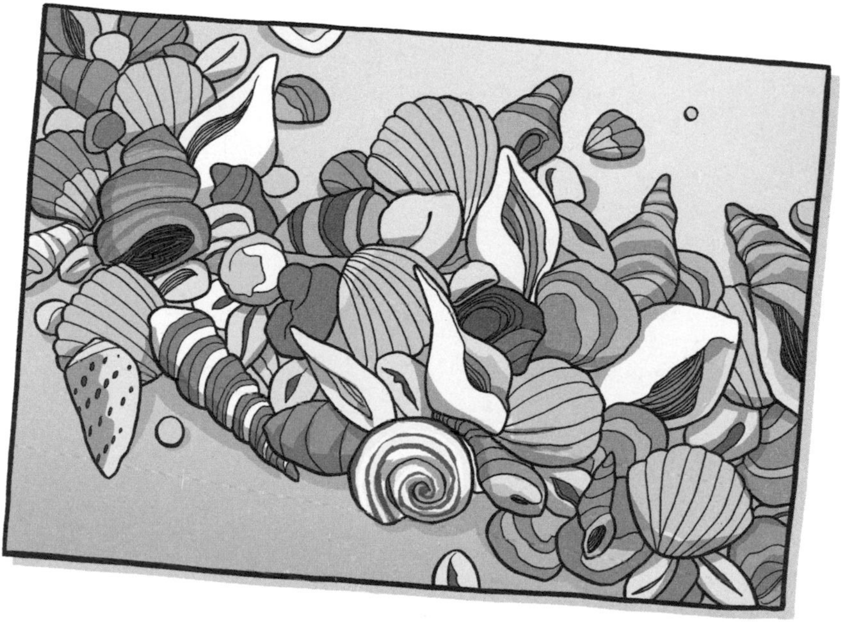

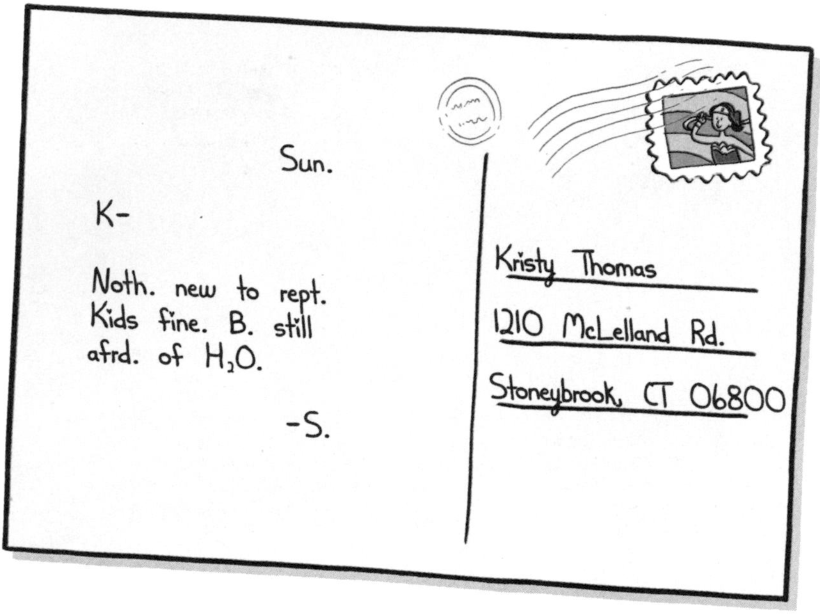
Sun.
K-
Noth. new to rept. Kids fine. B. still afrd. of H_2O.
-S.
Kristy Thomas
1210 McLelland Rd.
Stoneybrook, CT 06800

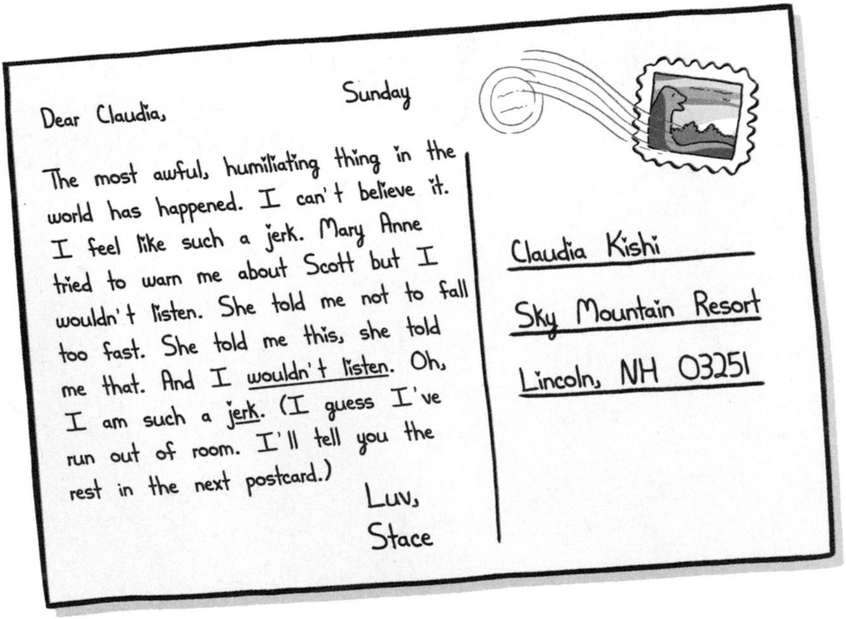
Sunday
Dear Claudia,
The most awful, humiliating thing in the world has happened. I can't believe it. I feel like such a jerk. Mary Anne tried to warn me about Scott but I wouldn't listen. She told me not to fall too fast. She told me this, she told me that. And I wouldn't listen. Oh, I am such a jerk. (I guess I've run out of room. I'll tell you the rest in the next postcard.)
Luv,
Stace
Claudia Kishi
Sky Mountain Resort
Lincoln, NH 03251

CHAPTER 9

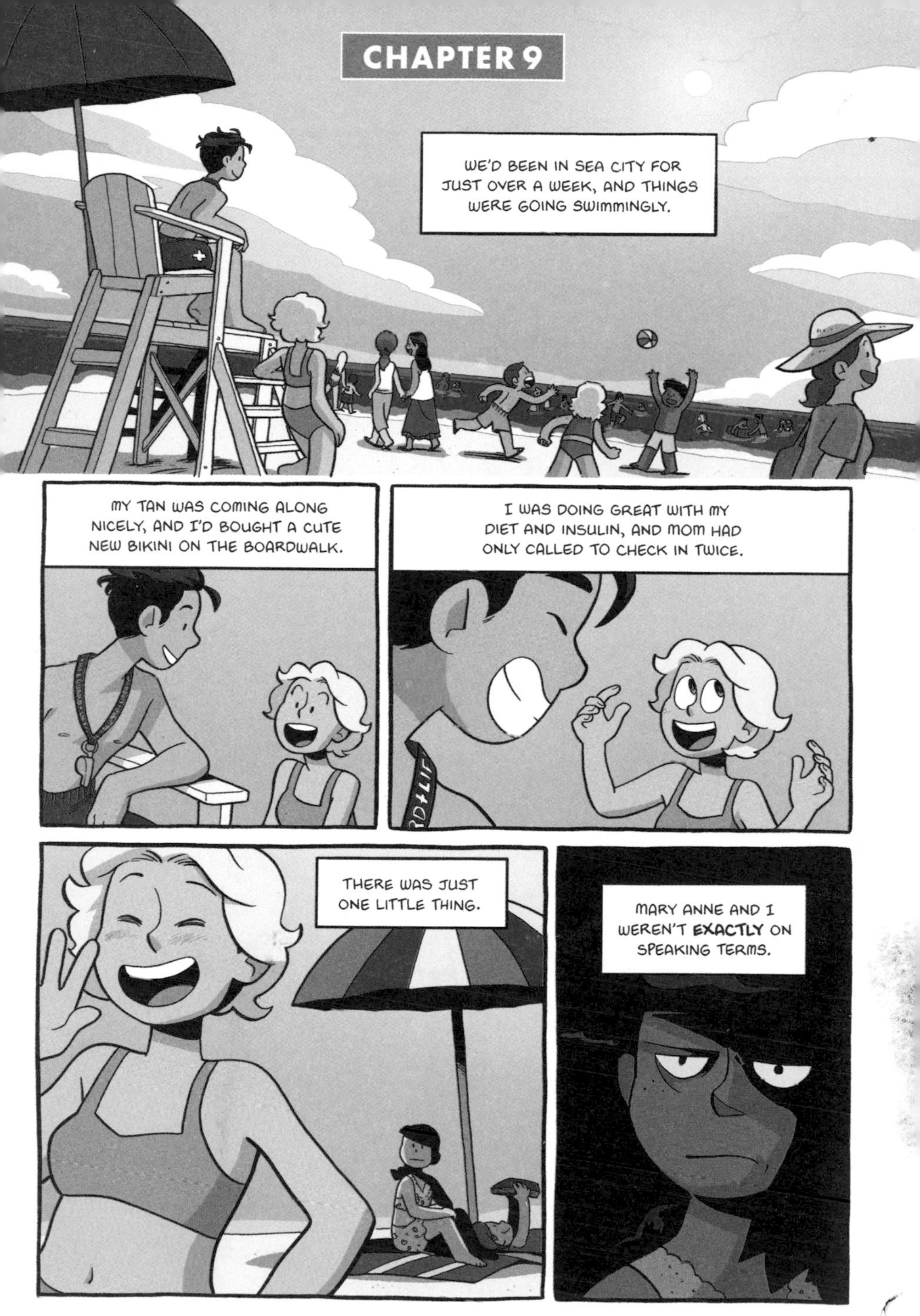
WE'D BEEN IN SEA CITY FOR JUST OVER A WEEK, AND THINGS WERE GOING SWIMMINGLY.
MY TAN WAS COMING ALONG NICELY, AND I'D BOUGHT A CUTE NEW BIKINI ON THE BOARDWALK.
I WAS DOING GREAT WITH MY DIET AND INSULIN, AND MOM HAD ONLY CALLED TO CHECK IN TWICE.
THERE WAS JUST ONE LITTLE THING.
MARY ANNE AND I WEREN'T **EXACTLY** ON SPEAKING TERMS.

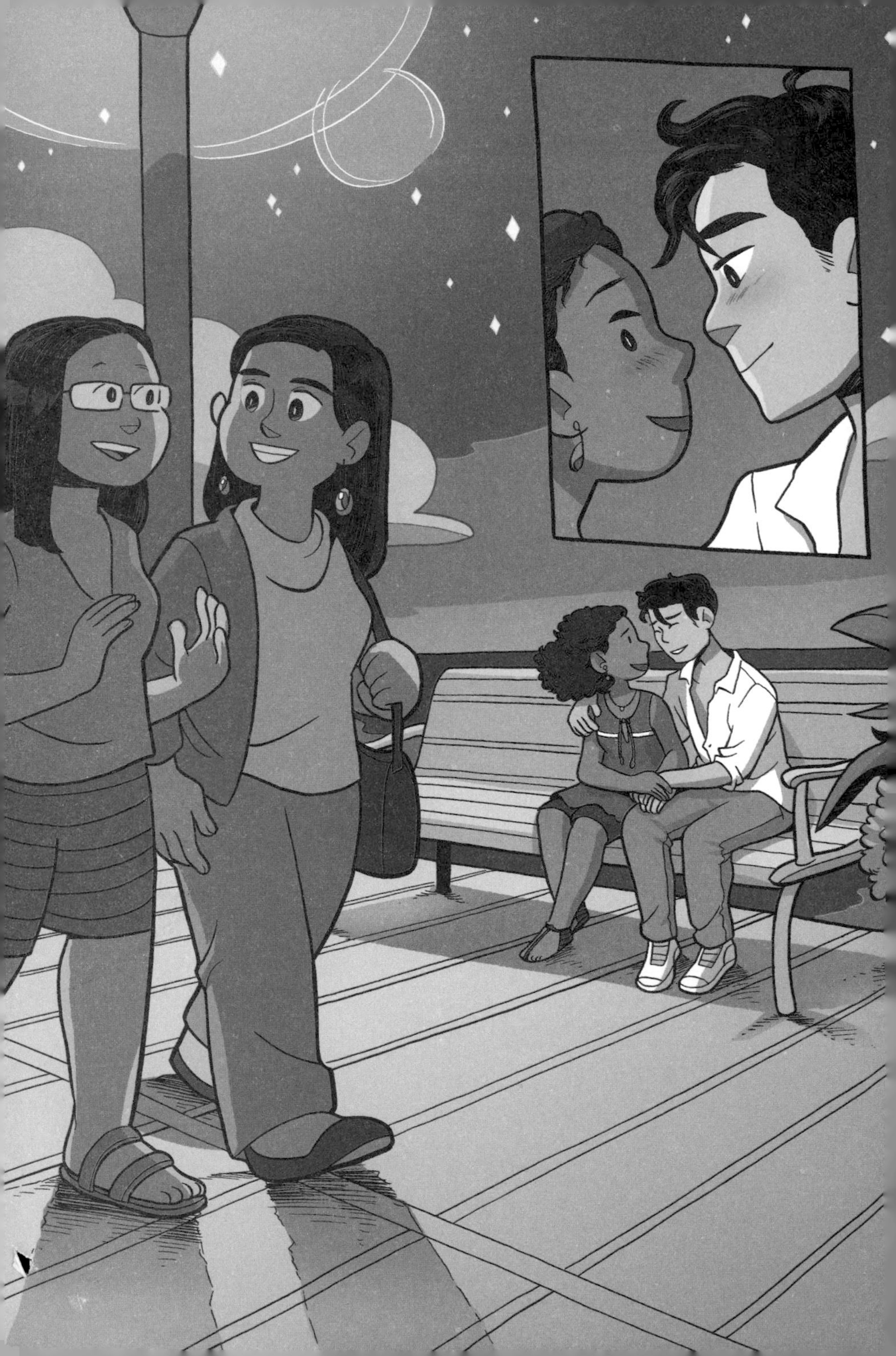

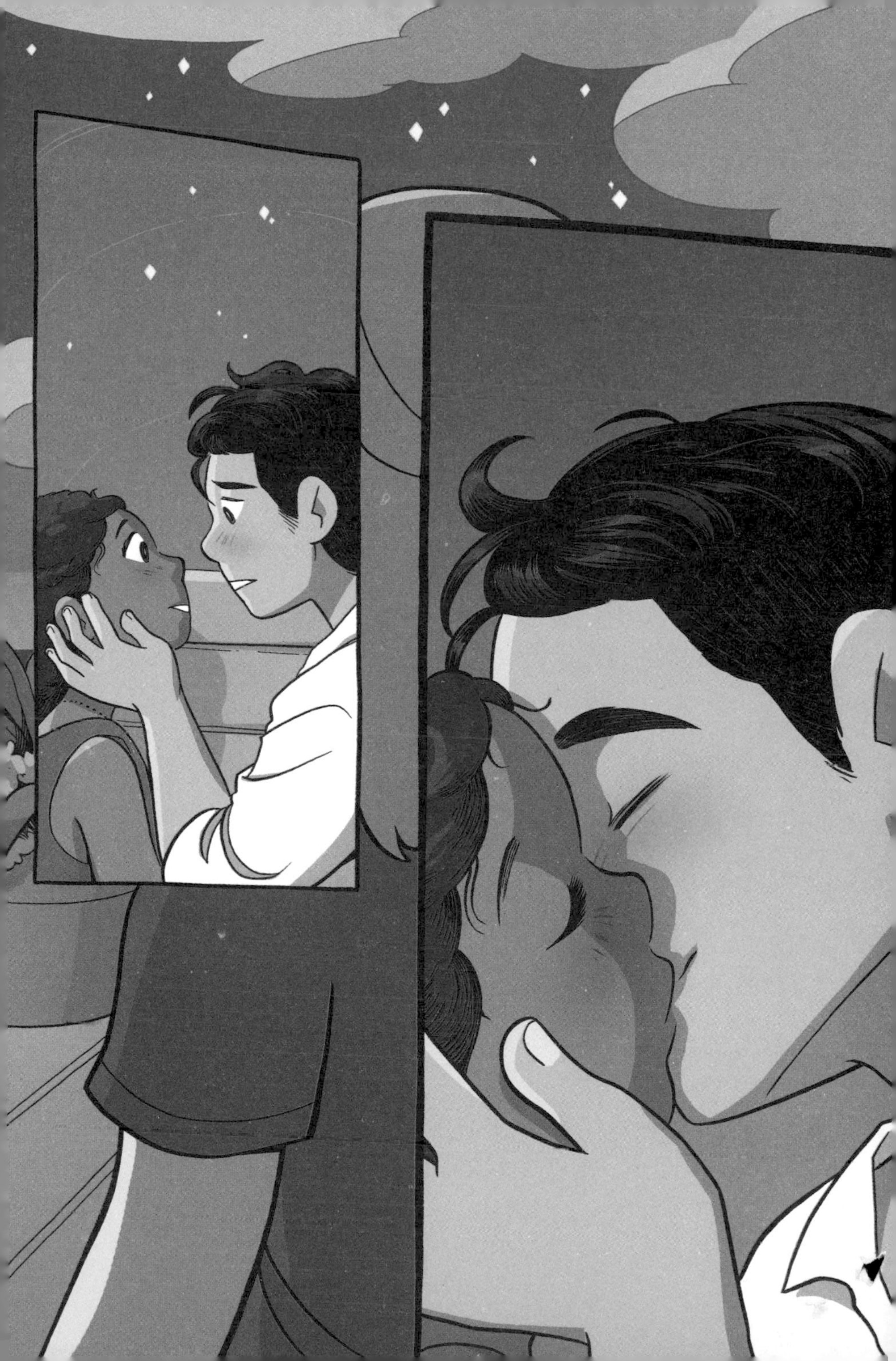

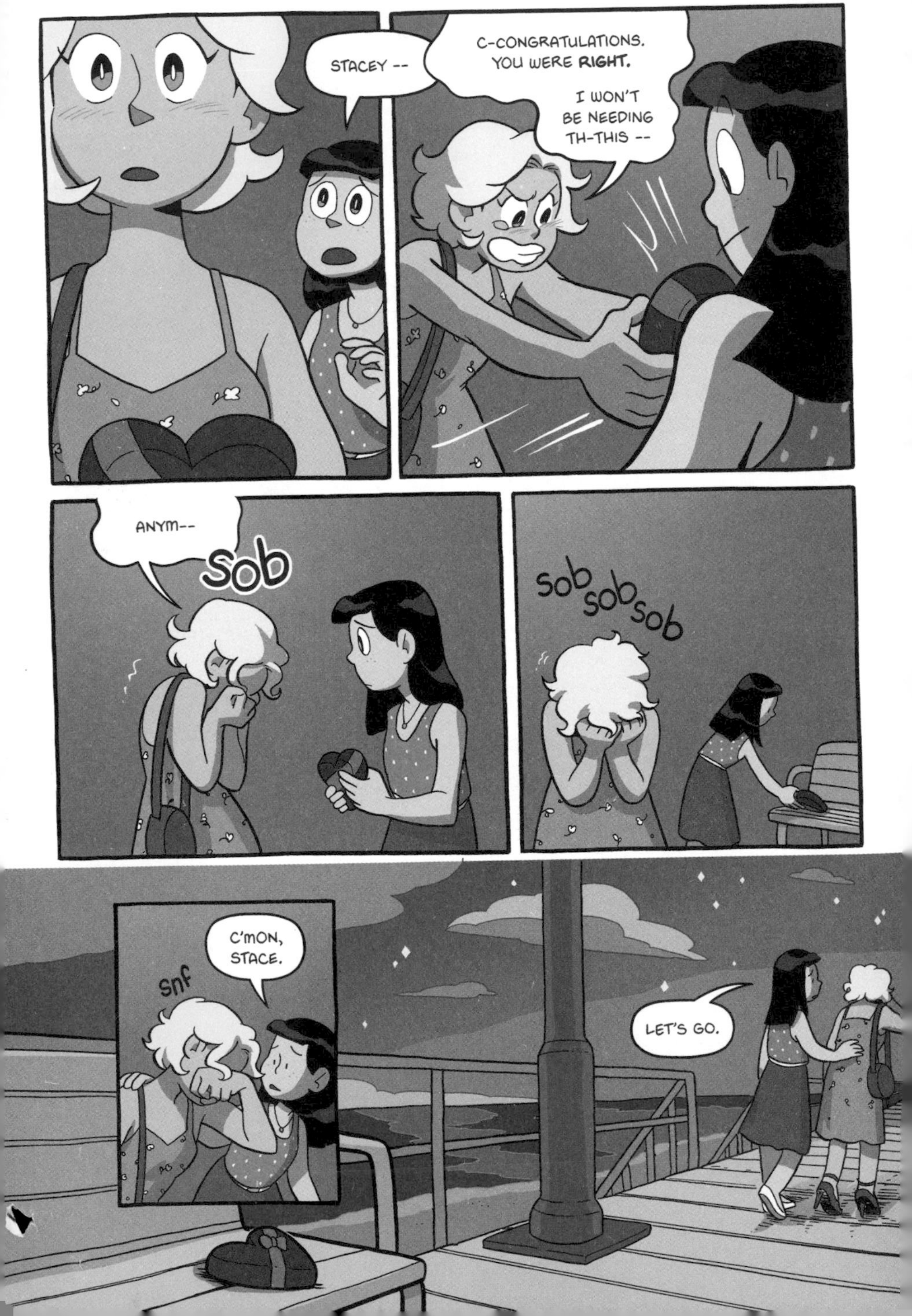
STACEY --
C-CONGRATULATIONS. YOU WERE **RIGHT.**
I WON'T BE NEEDING TH-THIS --
ANYM--
sob
sob sob sob
C'MON, STACE.
snf
LET'S GO.

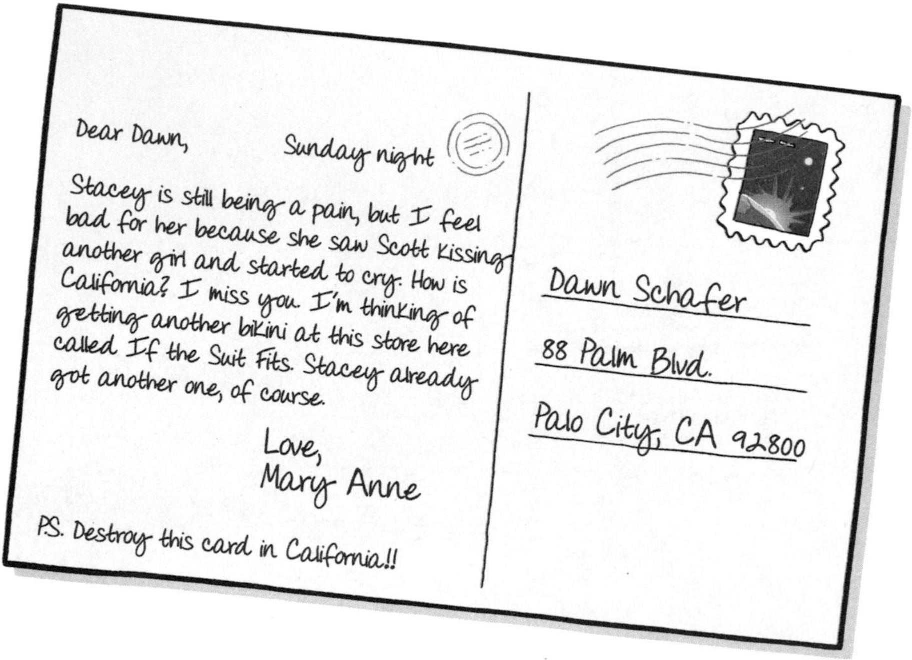
Dear Dawn,
Sunday night
Stacey is still being a pain, but I feel bad for her because she saw Scott kissing another girl and started to cry. How is California? I miss you. I'm thinking of getting another bikini at this store here called If the Suit Fits. Stacey already got another one, of course.
Love,
Mary Anne
P.S. Destroy this card in California!!
Dawn Schafer
88 Palm Blvd.
Palo City, CA 92800

CHAPTER 10

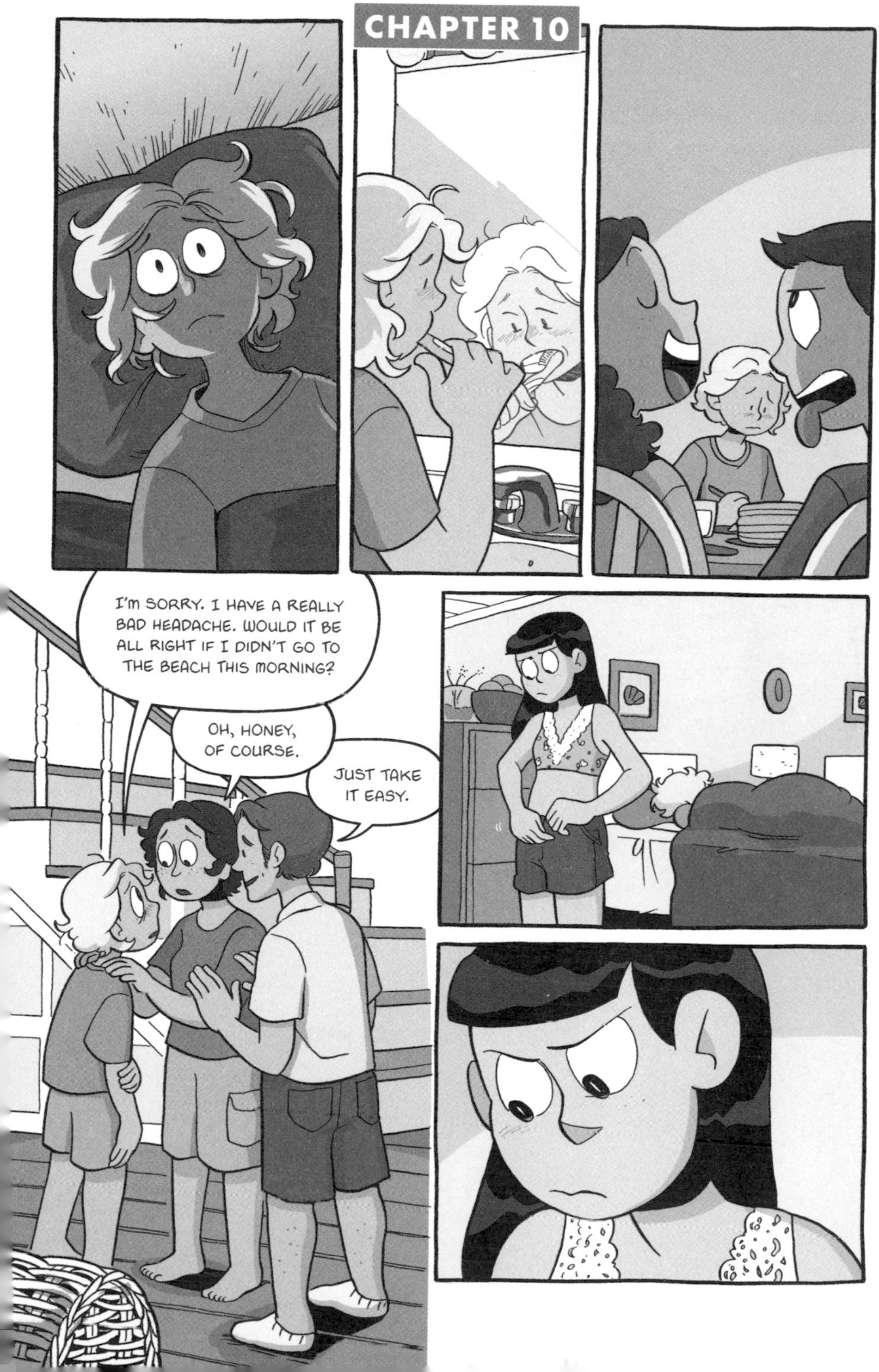
I'M SORRY. I HAVE A REALLY BAD HEADACHE. WOULD IT BE ALL RIGHT IF I DIDN'T GO TO THE BEACH THIS MORNING?
OH, HONEY, OF COURSE.
JUST TAKE IT EASY.

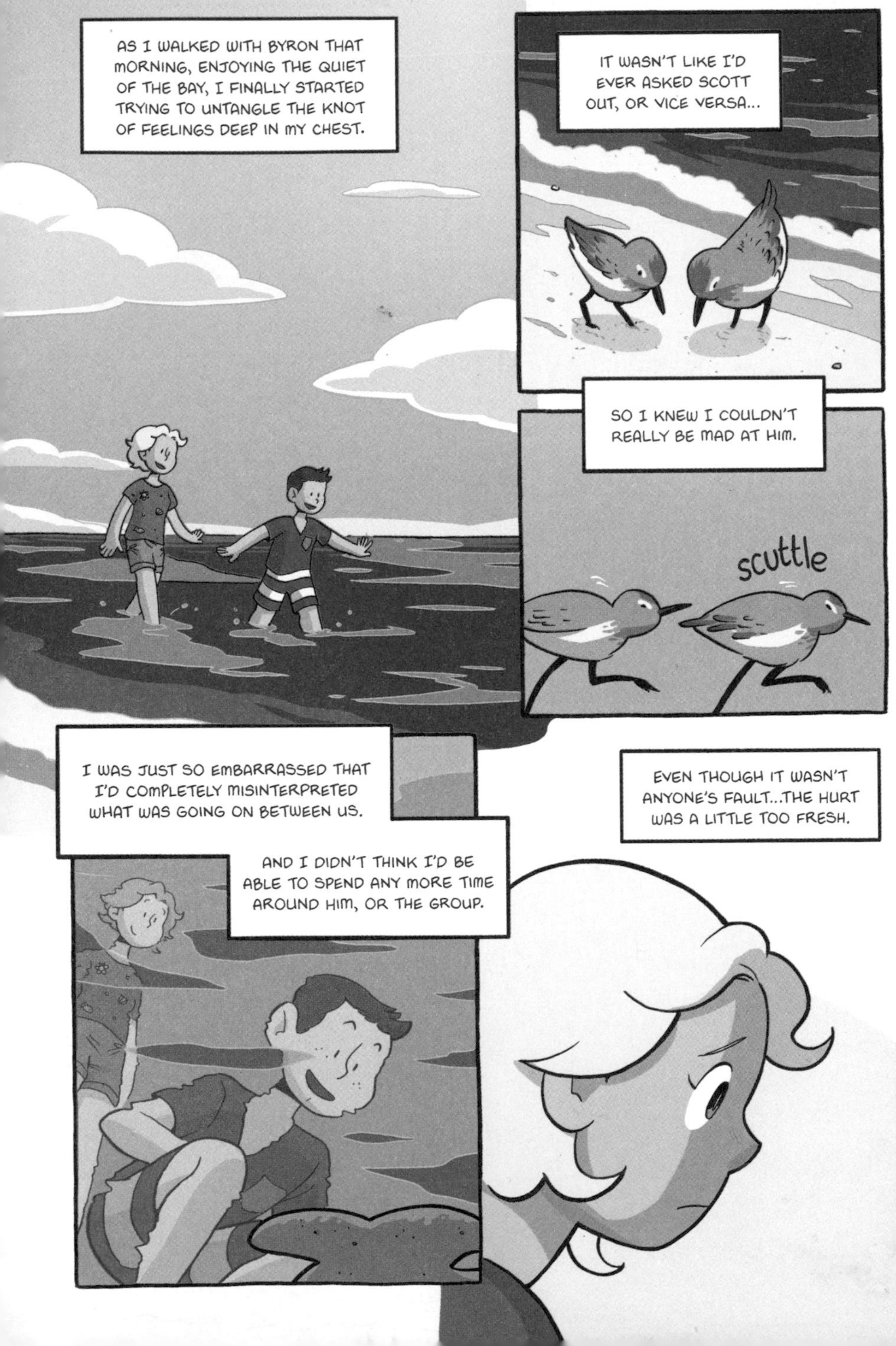
AS I WALKED WITH BYRON THAT MORNING, ENJOYING THE QUIET OF THE BAY, I FINALLY STARTED TRYING TO UNTANGLE THE KNOT OF FEELINGS DEEP IN MY CHEST.
IT WASN'T LIKE I'D EVER ASKED SCOTT OUT, OR VICE VERSA...
SO I KNEW I COULDN'T REALLY BE MAD AT HIM.
scuttle
I WAS JUST SO EMBARRASSED THAT I'D COMPLETELY MISINTERPRETED WHAT WAS GOING ON BETWEEN US.
AND I DIDN'T THINK I'D BE ABLE TO SPEND ANY MORE TIME AROUND HIM, OR THE GROUP.
EVEN THOUGH IT WASN'T ANYONE'S FAULT...THE HURT WAS A LITTLE TOO FRESH.

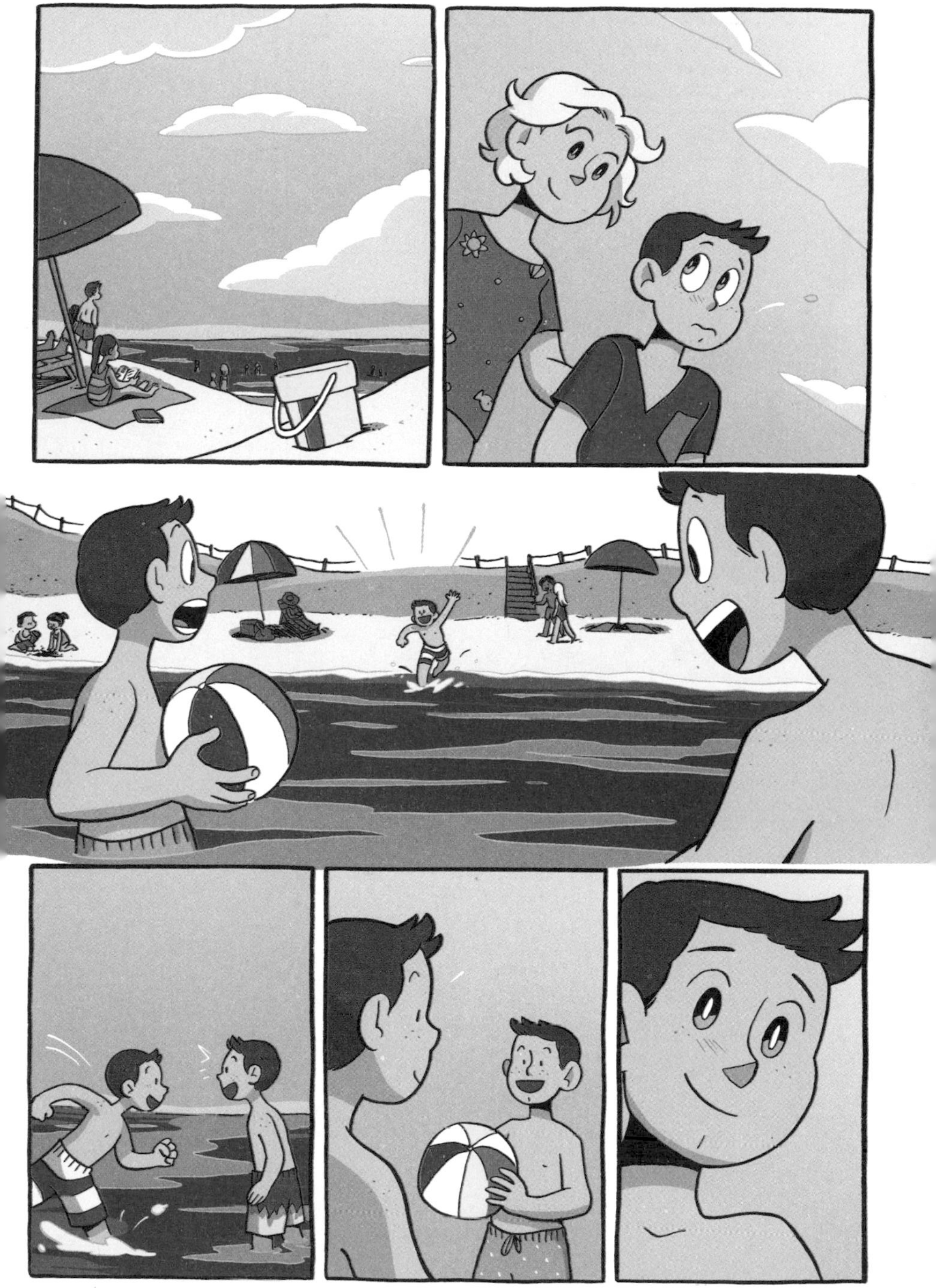

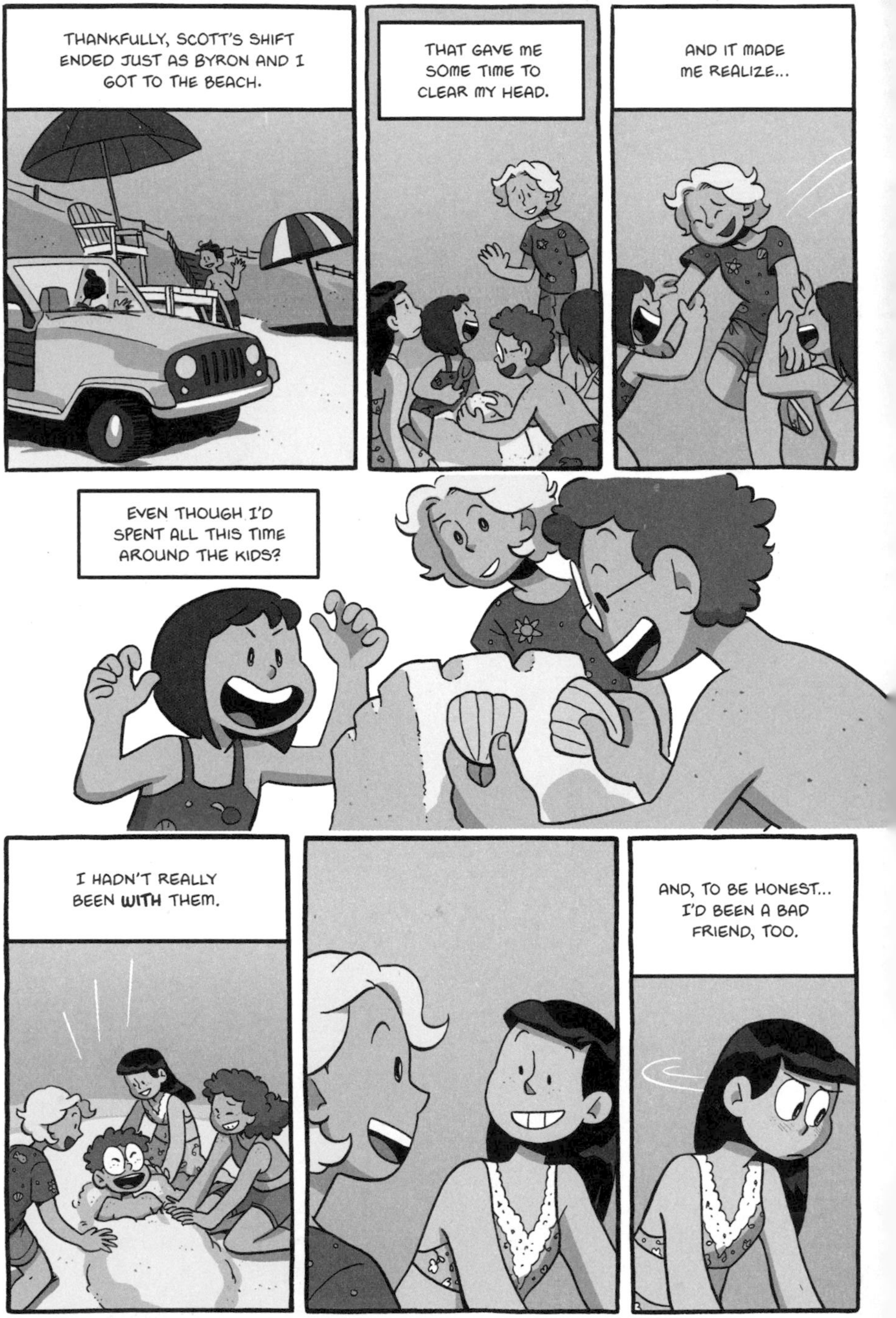

THANKFULLY, SCOTT'S SHIFT ENDED JUST AS BYRON AND I GOT TO THE BEACH.
THAT GAVE ME SOME TIME TO CLEAR MY HEAD.
AND IT MADE ME REALIZE...
EVEN THOUGH I'D SPENT ALL THIS TIME AROUND THE KIDS?
I HADN'T REALLY BEEN **WITH** THEM.
AND, TO BE HONEST... I'D BEEN A BAD FRIEND, TOO.

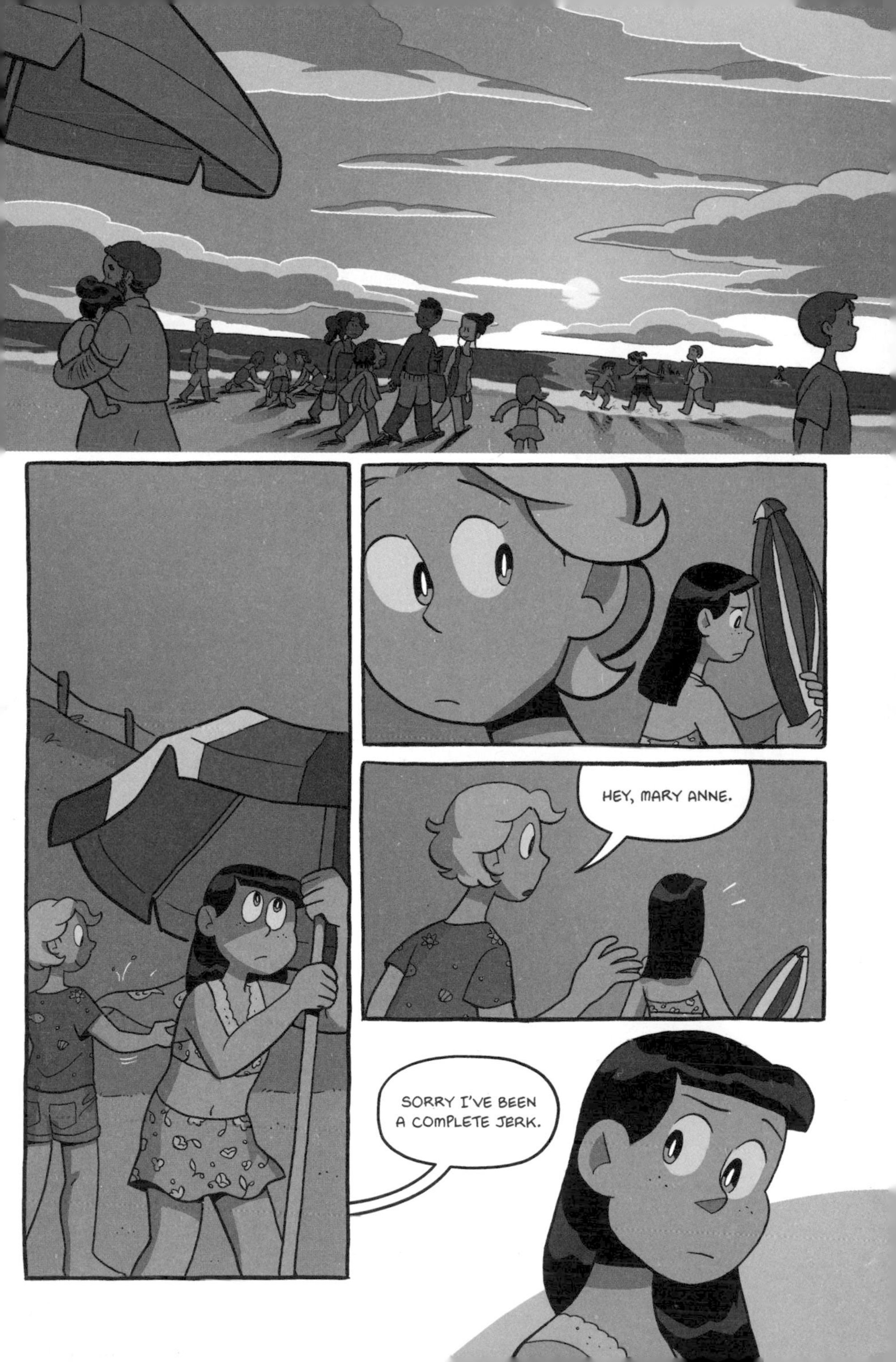
HEY, MARY ANNE.
SORRY I'VE BEEN A COMPLETE JERK.

Dear Kristy,

Wednesday

Byron went in the water! (Sort of.) I know what he's afraid of. We'll talk about it at the next BSC meeting. I heard a really funny joke today. I'll tell that at the next meeting, too.

Luv,
Stacey

Kristy Thomas

1210 McLelland Rd.

Stoneybrook, CT 06800

Dear Claudia,

Wednesday

Sadness over! I met a cute guy named Toby. I mean, _really_ cute. He has brown hair, brown eyes, and a few freckles. His clothes are _extremely_ cool.

Luv ya,
Stace

Claudia Kishi

Sky Mountain Resort

Lincoln, NH 03251

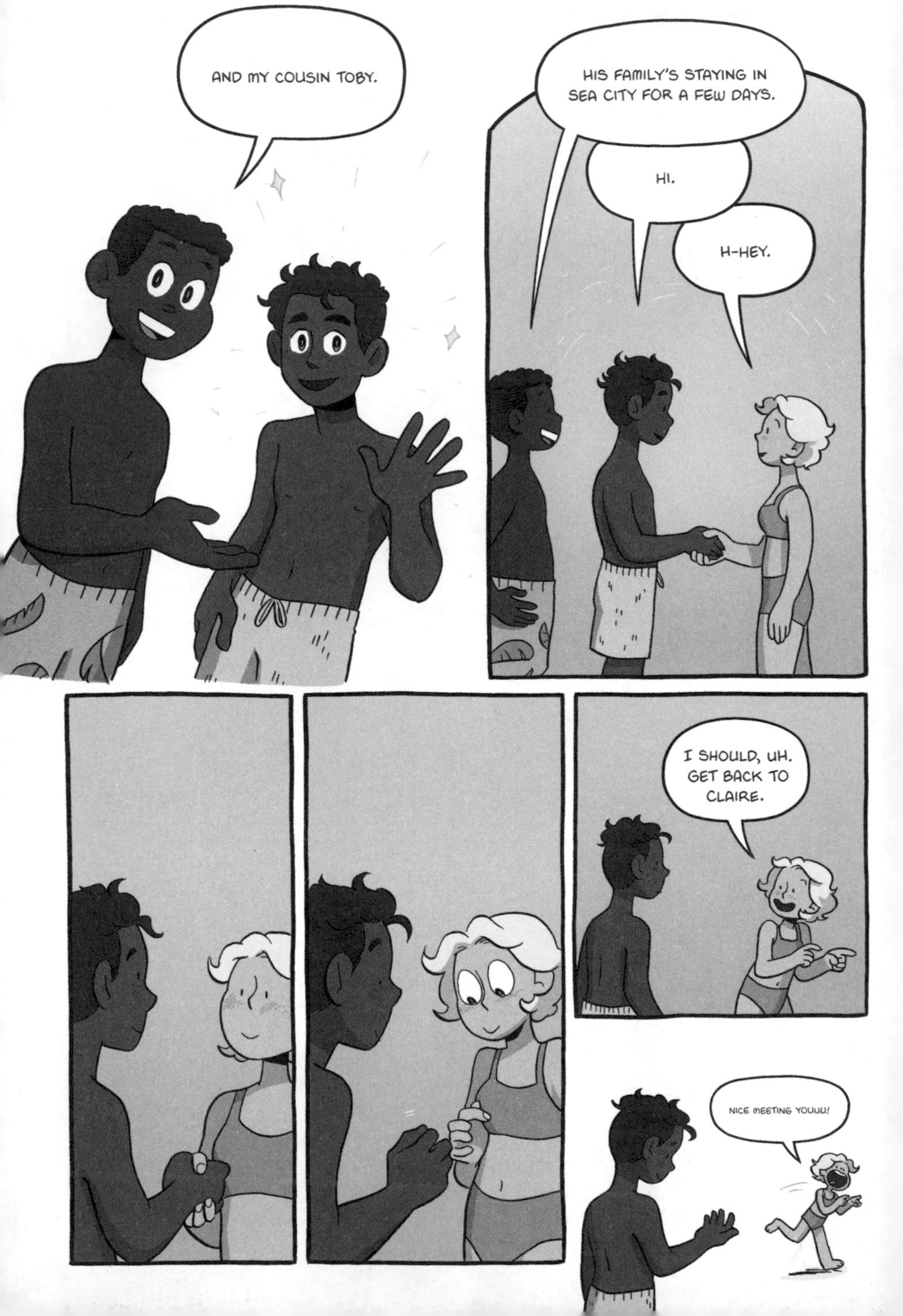
AND MY COUSIN TOBY.
HIS FAMILY'S STAYING IN SEA CITY FOR A FEW DAYS.
HI.
H-HEY.
I SHOULD, UH. GET BACK TO CLAIRE.
NICE MEETING YOUUU!

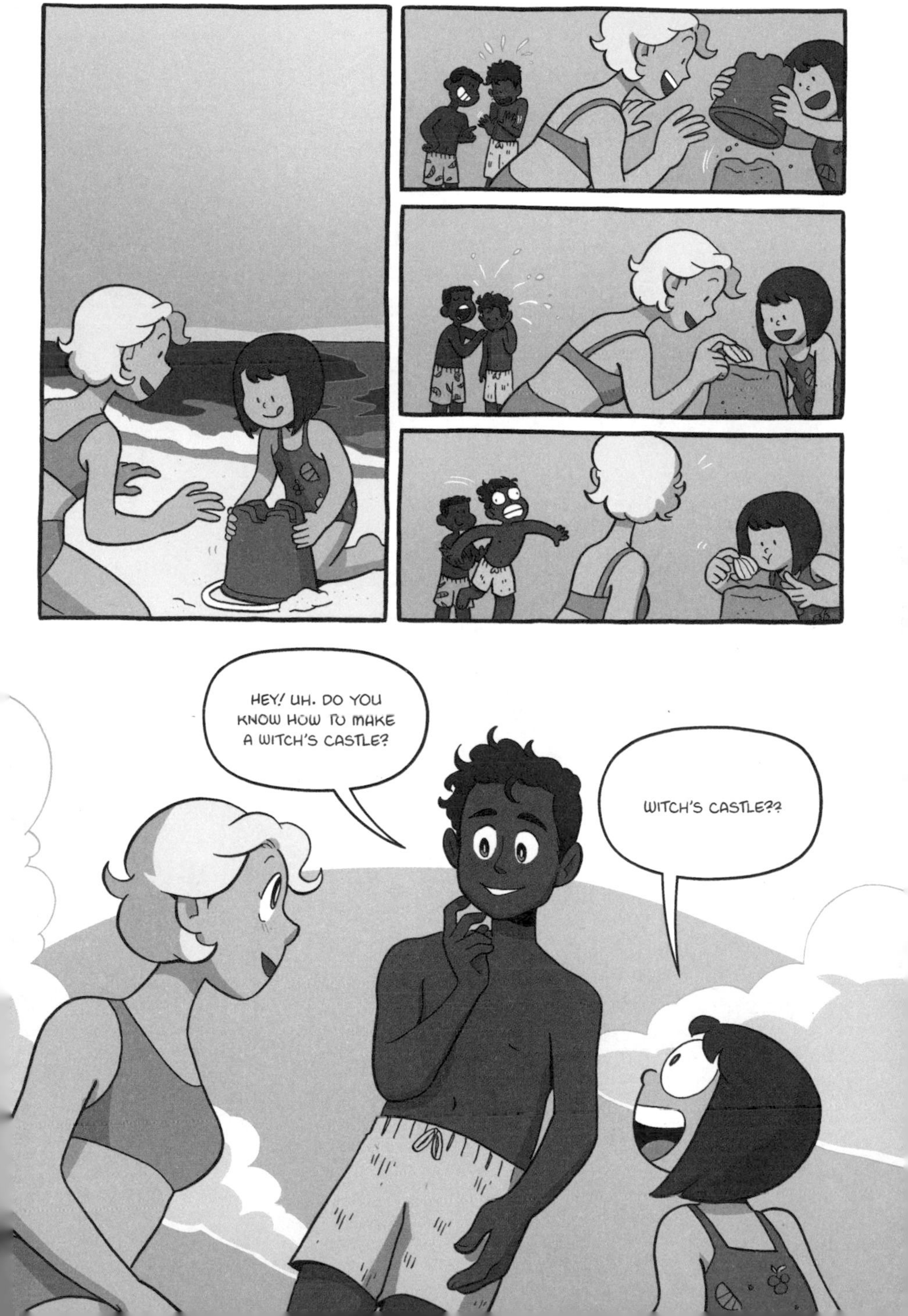
HEY! UH. DO YOU KNOW HOW TO MAKE A WITCH'S CASTLE?
WITCH'S CASTLE??

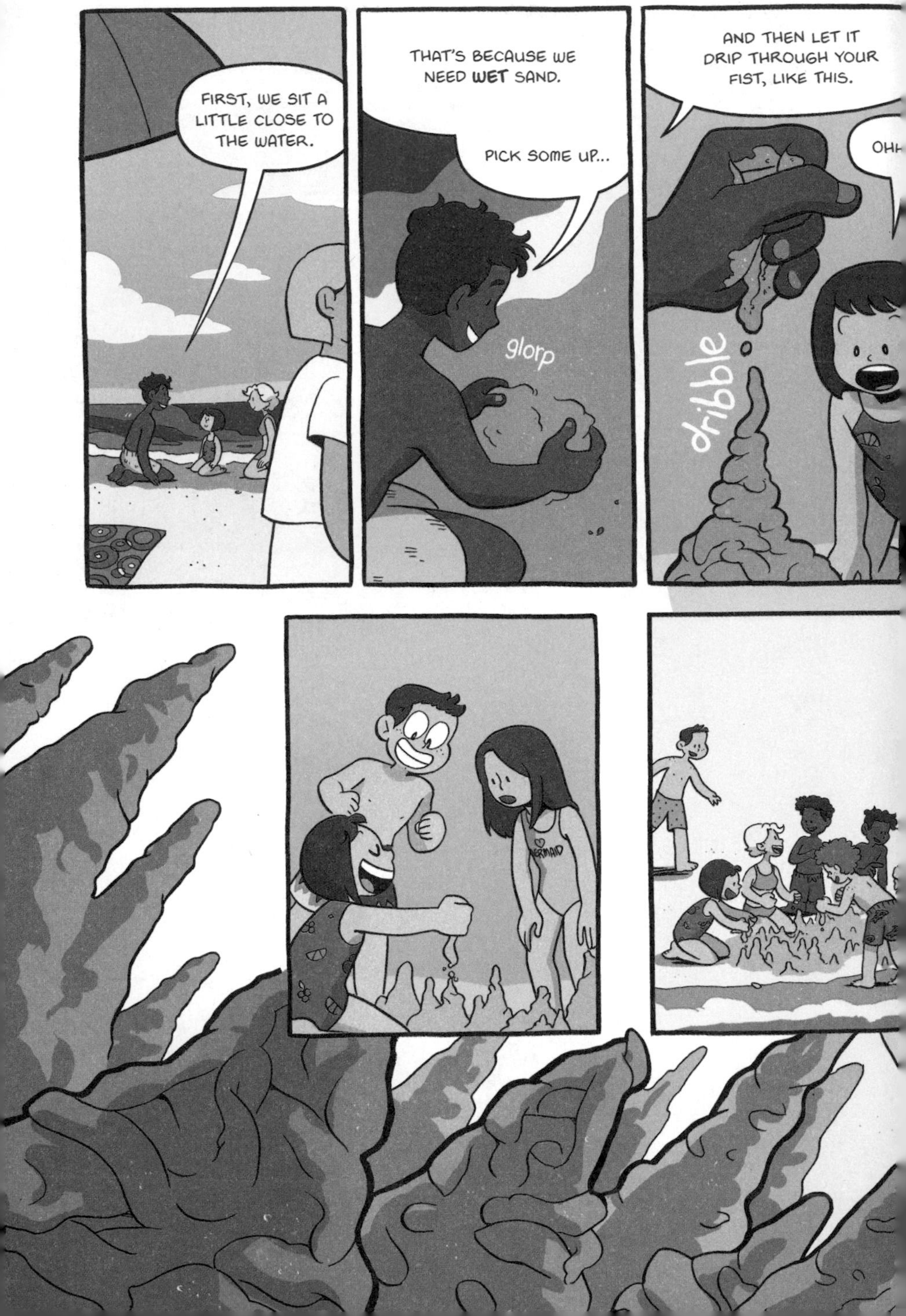
FIRST, WE SIT A LITTLE CLOSE TO THE WATER.
THAT'S BECAUSE WE NEED **WET** SAND.
PICK SOME UP...
glorp
AND THEN LET IT DRIP THROUGH YOUR FIST, LIKE THIS.
dribble
MERMAID

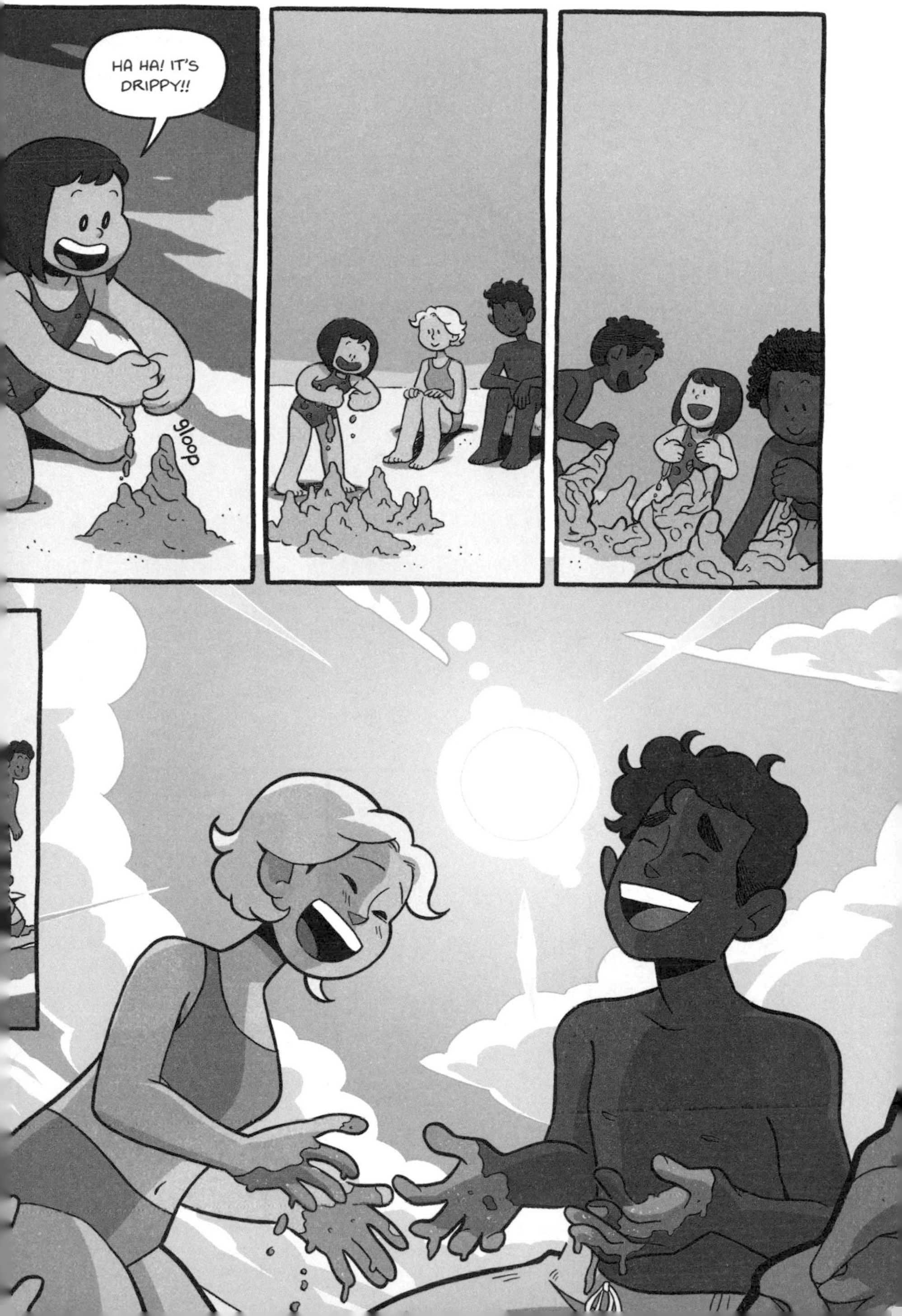
HA HA! IT'S DRIPPY!!
gloop

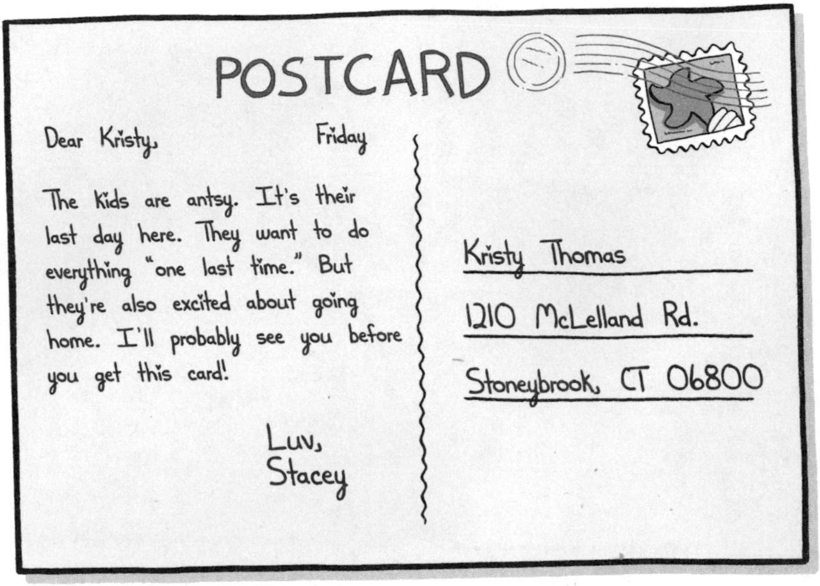
POSTCARD
Dear Kristy,
Friday
The kids are antsy. It's their last day here. They want to do everything "one last time." But they're also excited about going home. I'll probably see you before you get this card!
Luv,
Stacey
Kristy Thomas
1210 McLelland Rd.
Stoneybrook, CT 06800

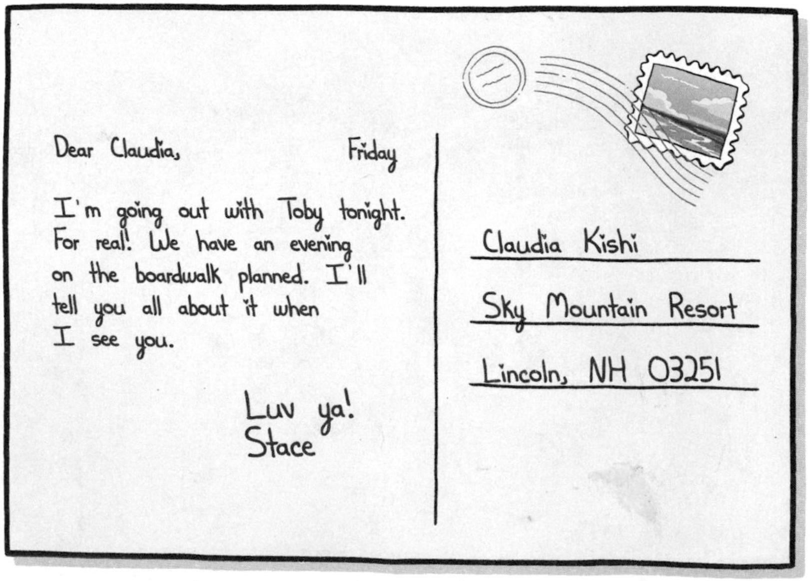
Dear Claudia,
Friday
I'm going out with Toby tonight. For real! We have an evening on the boardwalk planned. I'll tell you all about it when I see you.
Luv ya!
Stace
Claudia Kishi
Sky Mountain Resort
Lincoln, NH 03251

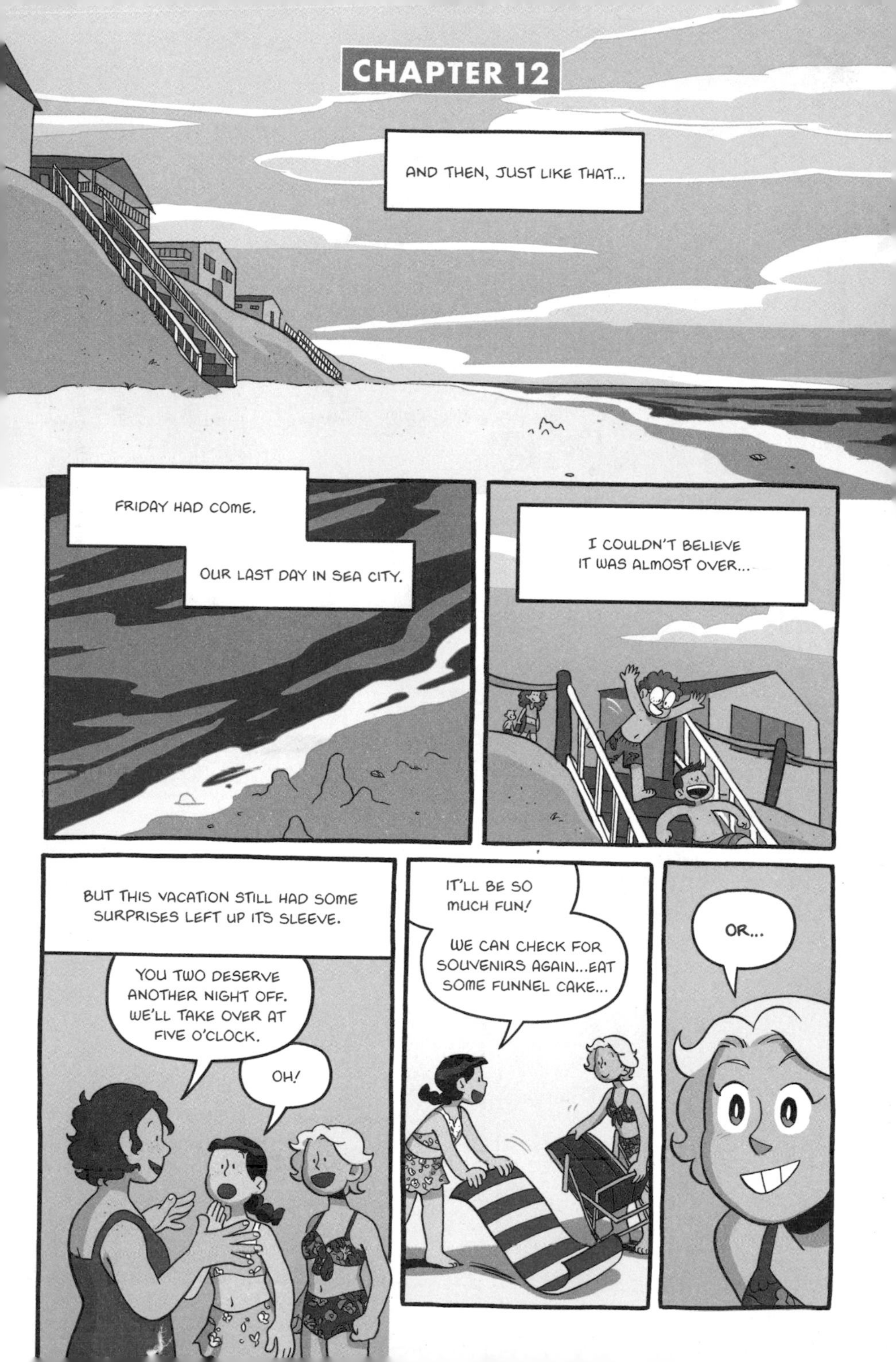
CHAPTER 12
AND THEN, JUST LIKE THAT...
FRIDAY HAD COME.
OUR LAST DAY IN SEA CITY.
I COULDN'T BELIEVE IT WAS ALMOST OVER...
BUT THIS VACATION STILL HAD SOME SURPRISES LEFT UP ITS SLEEVE.
YOU TWO DESERVE ANOTHER NIGHT OFF. WE'LL TAKE OVER AT FIVE O'CLOCK.
OH!
IT'LL BE SO MUCH FUN!
WE CAN CHECK FOR SOUVENIRS AGAIN...EAT SOME FUNNEL CAKE...
OR...

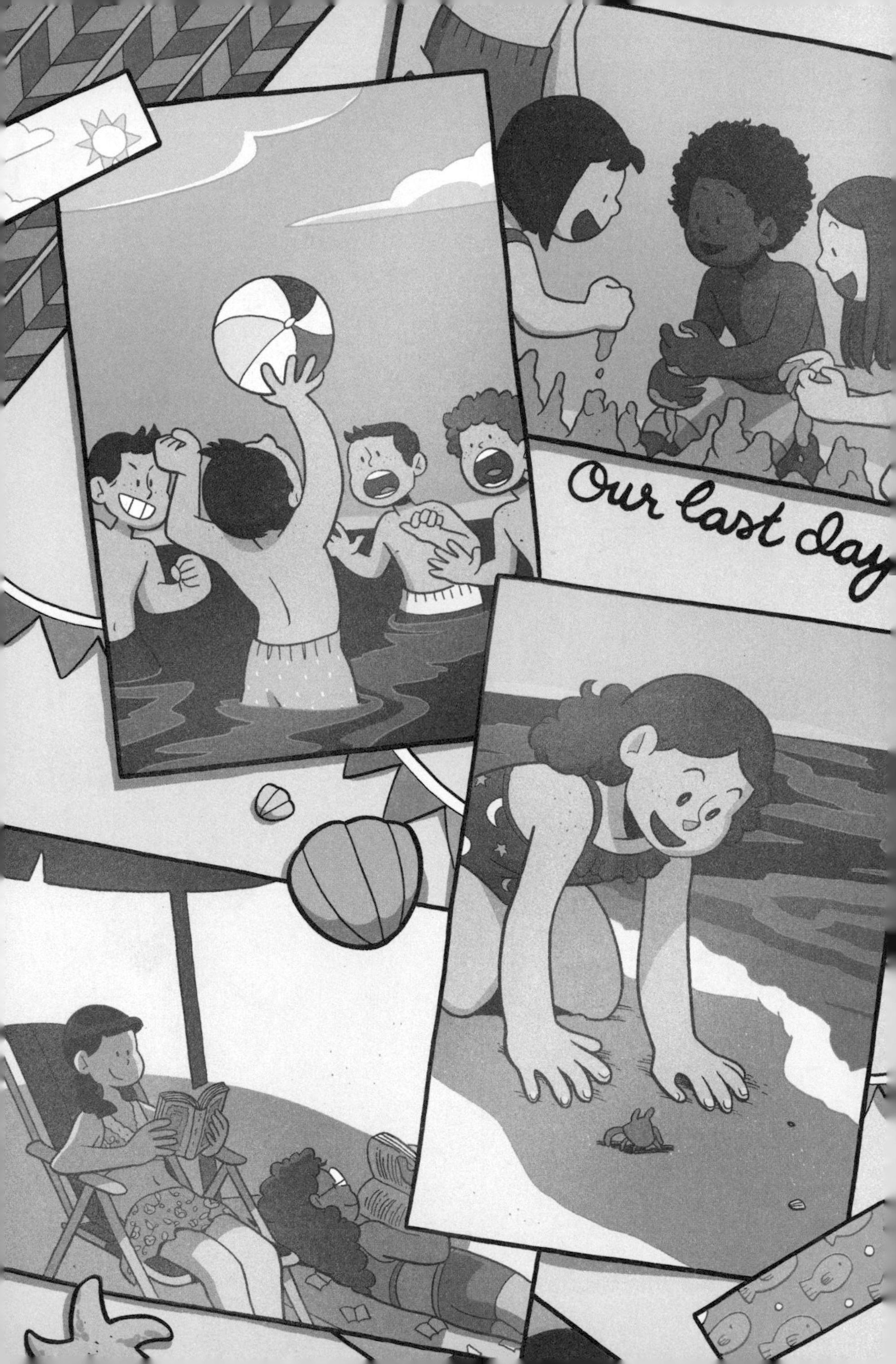
Our last day

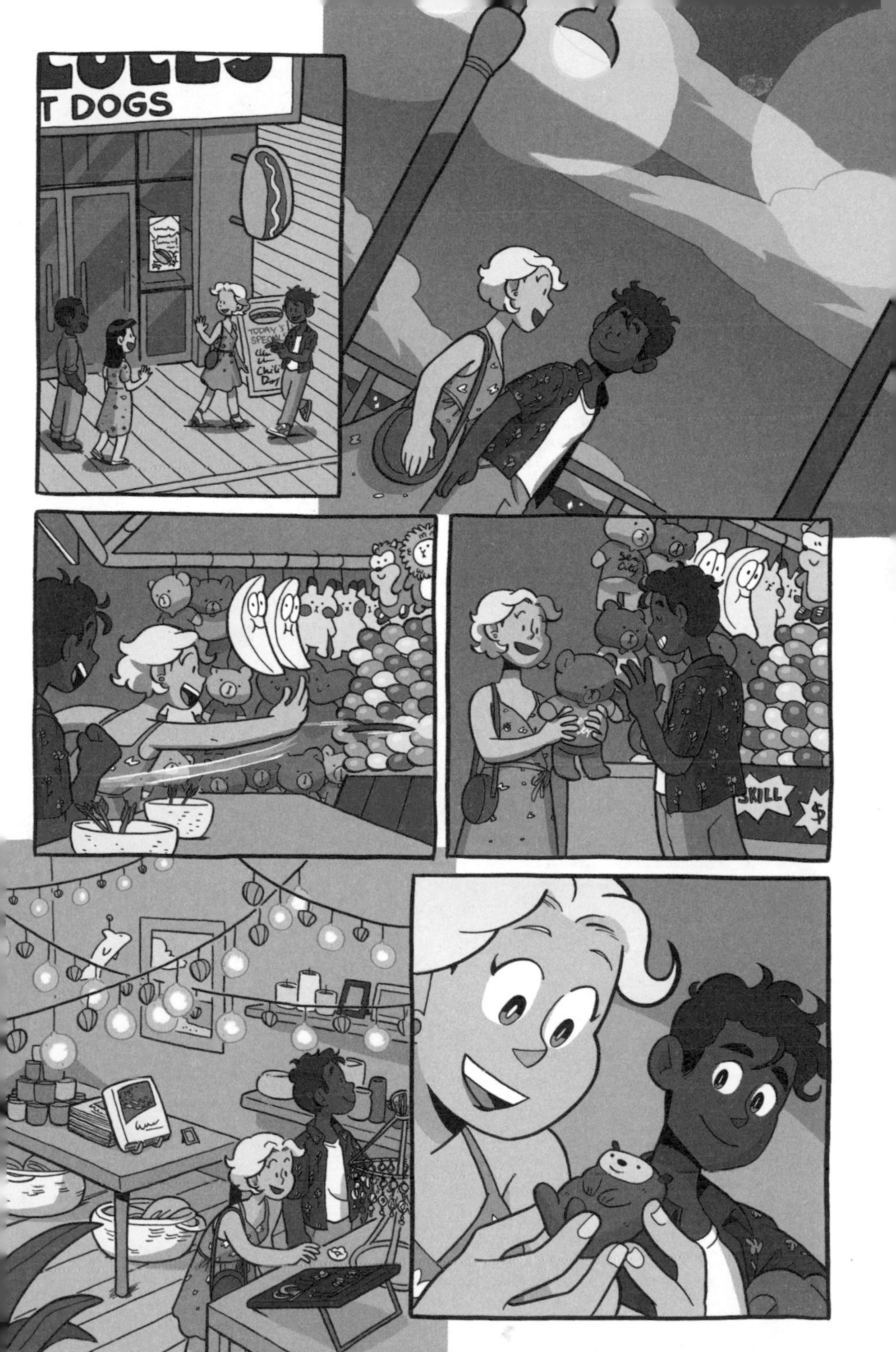

T DOGS
TODAY'S SPECIALS
Chili Dog
SKILL
$

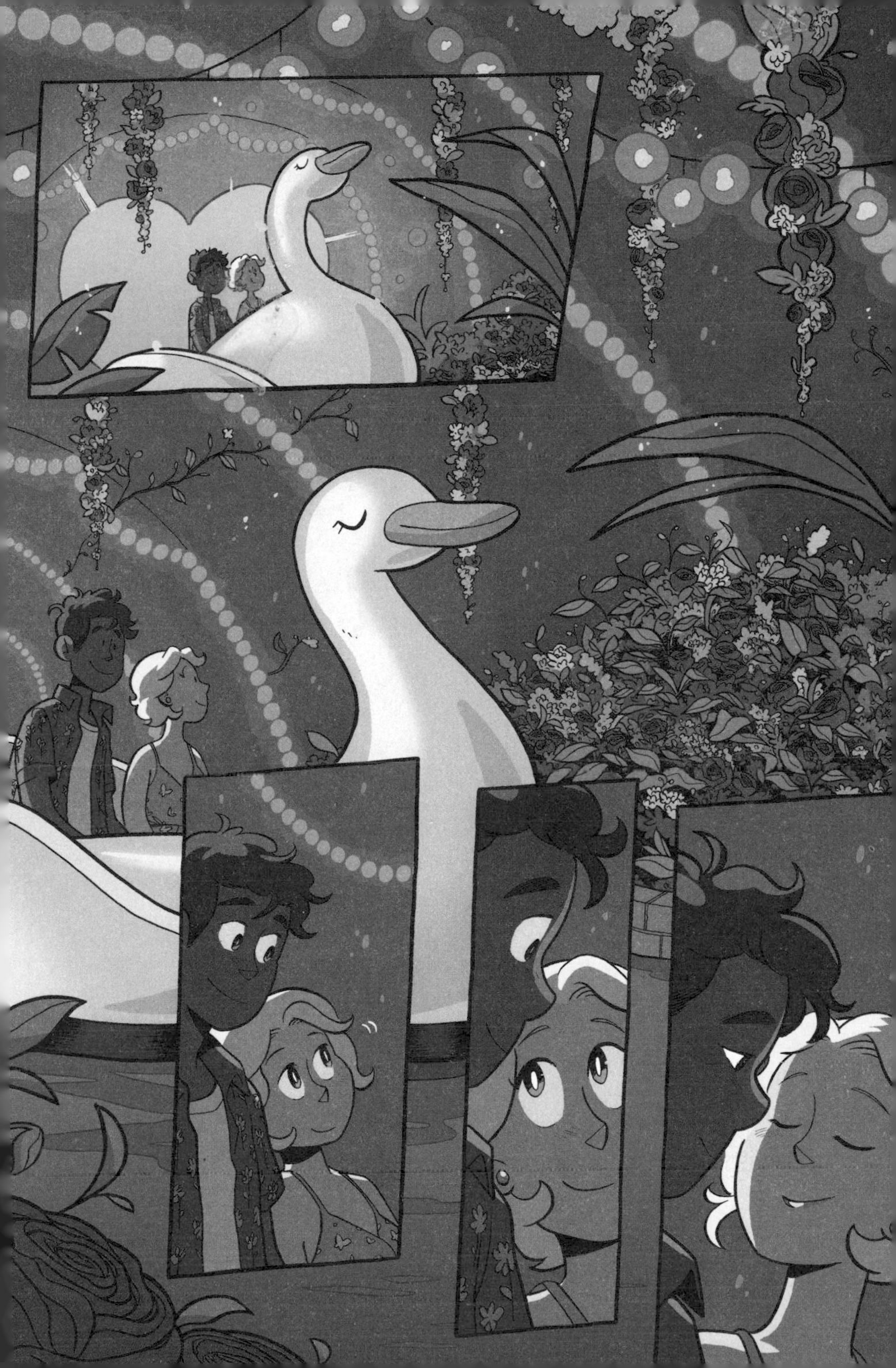

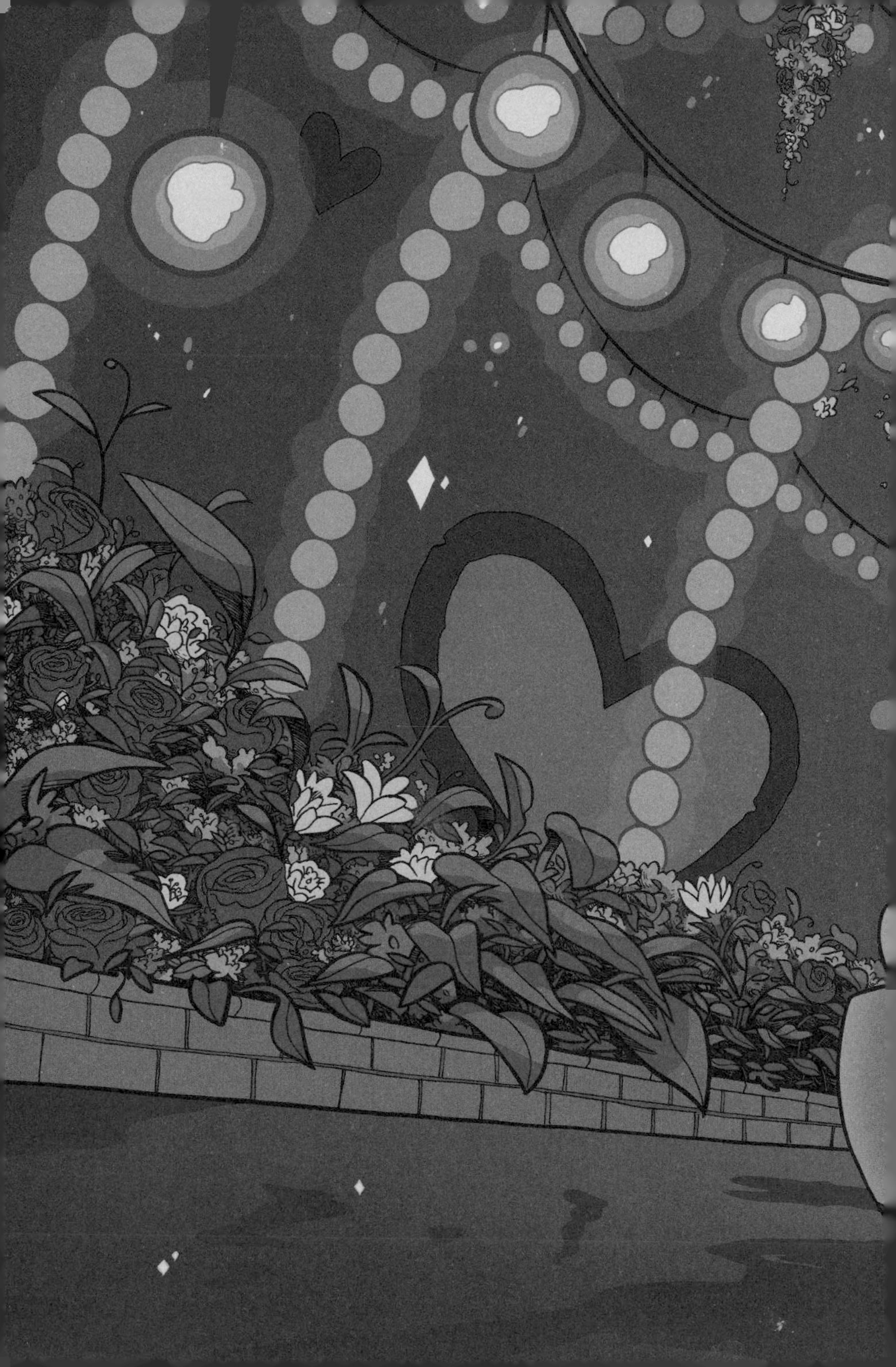

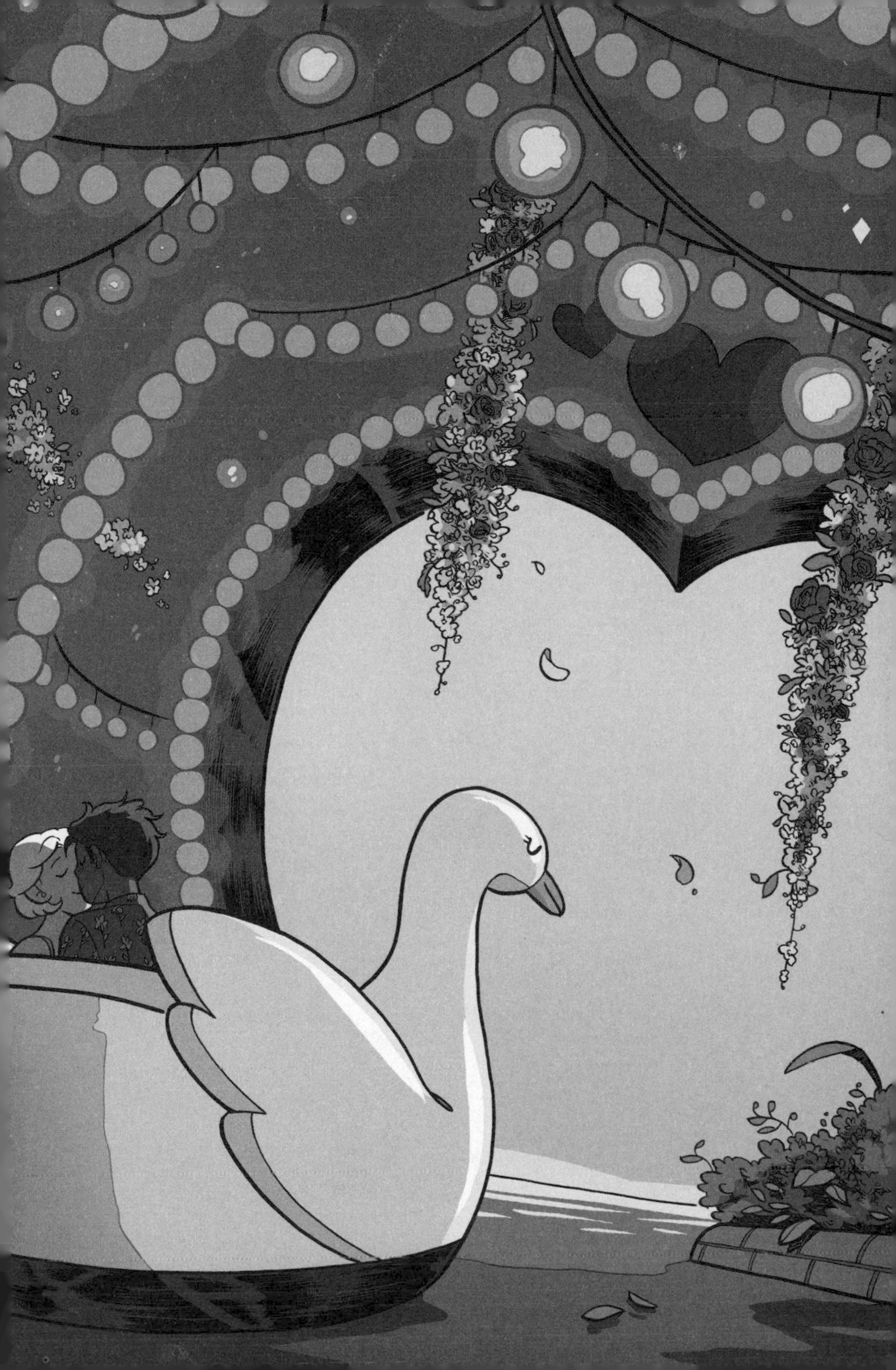

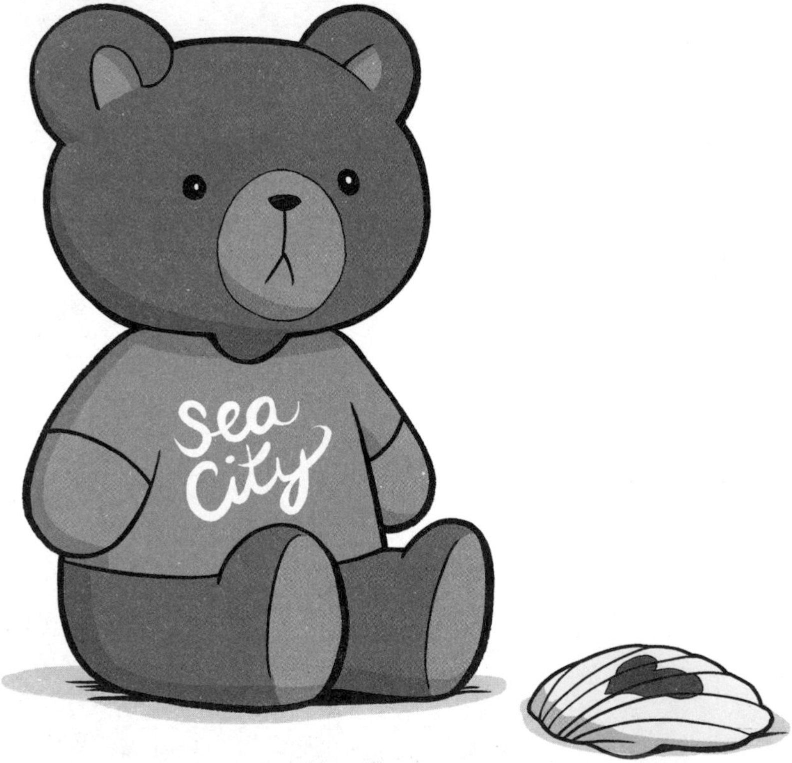
Sea
City

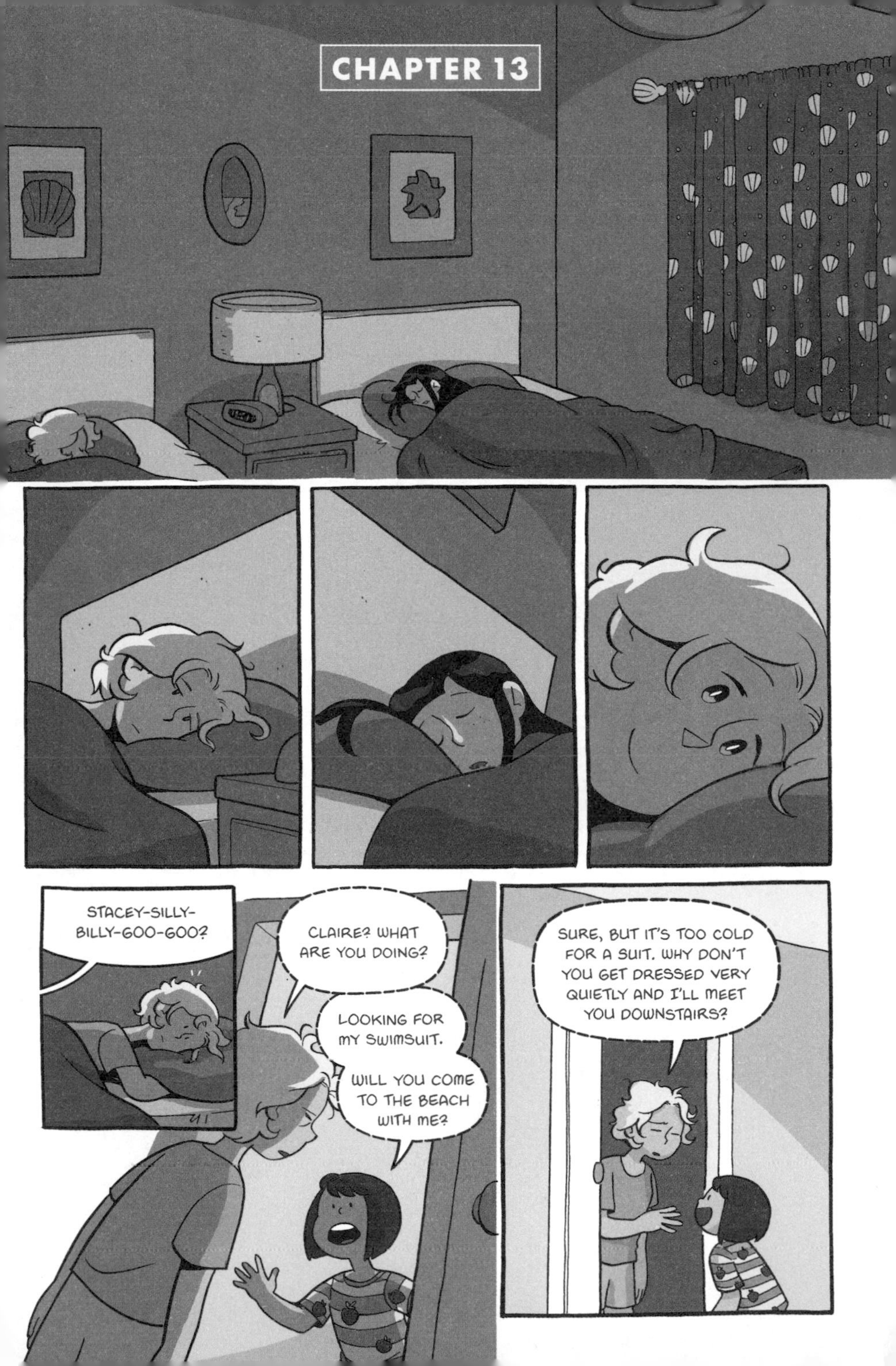
CHAPTER 13
STACEY-SILLY-BILLY-GOO-GOO?
CLAIRE? WHAT ARE YOU DOING?
LOOKING FOR MY SWIMSUIT.
WILL YOU COME TO THE BEACH WITH ME?
SURE, BUT IT'S TOO COLD FOR A SUIT. WHY DON'T YOU GET DRESSED VERY QUIETLY AND I'LL MEET YOU DOWNSTAIRS?

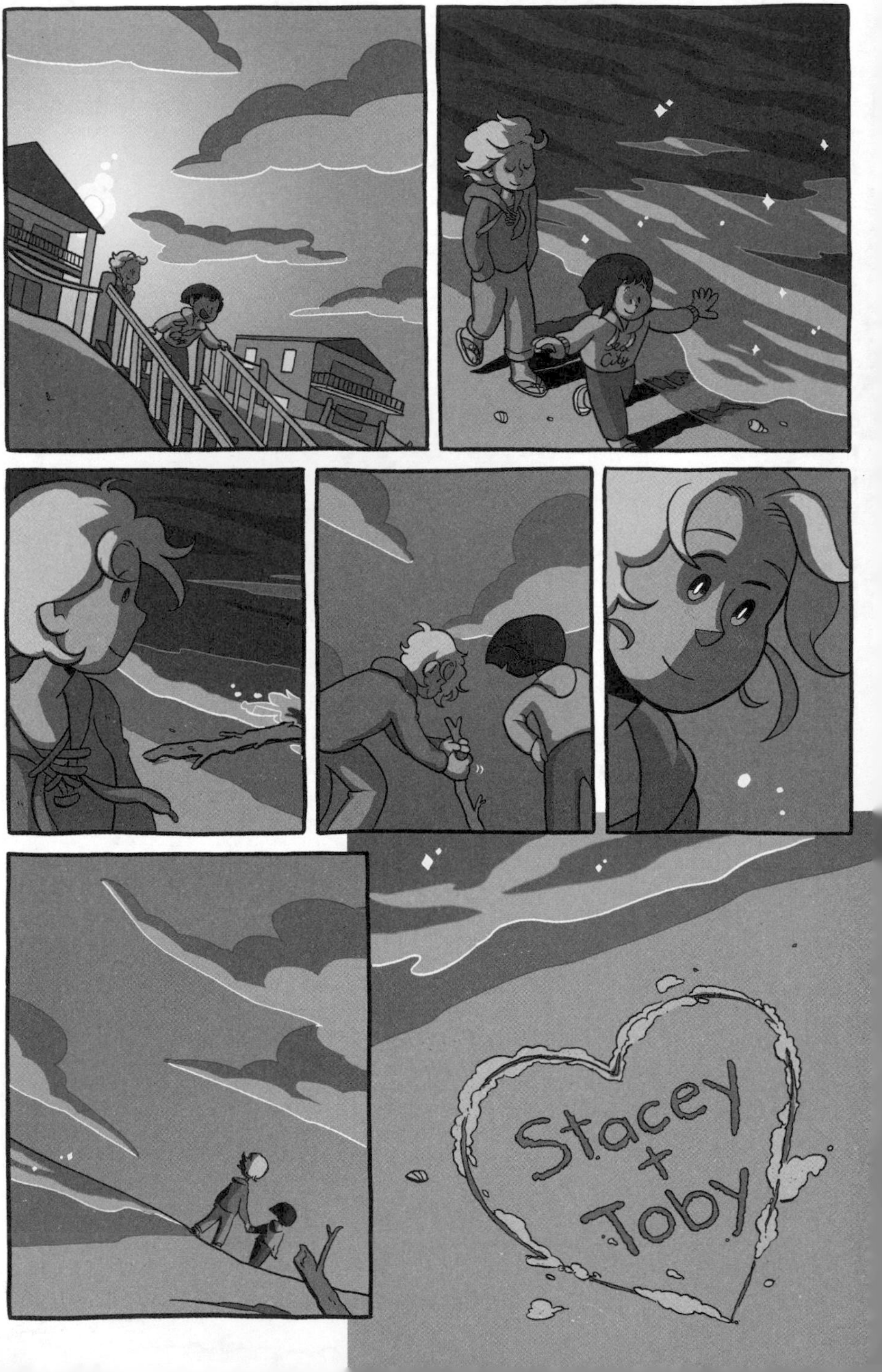
Stacey
+
Toby

149

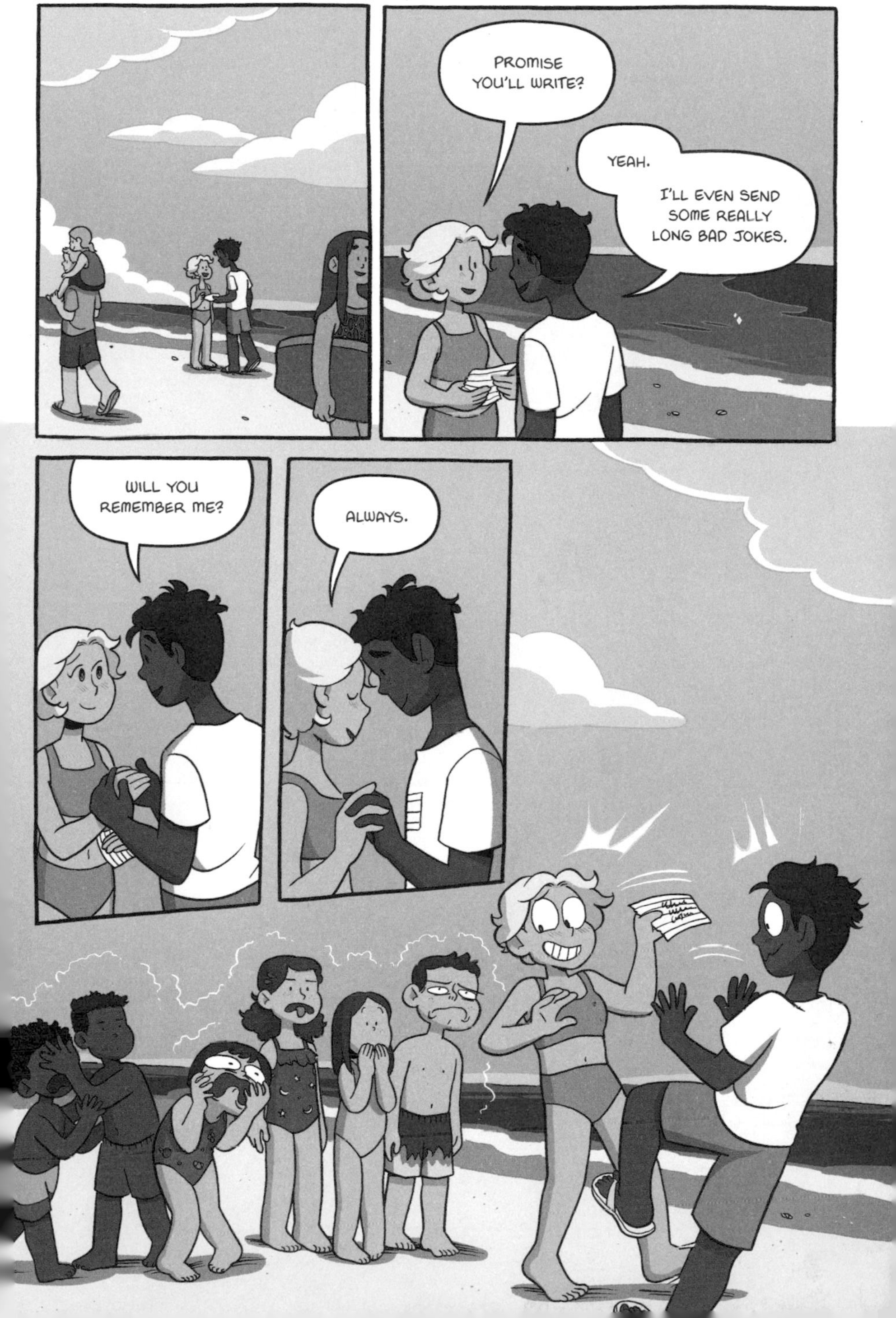
PROMISE YOU'LL WRITE?
YEAH.
I'LL EVEN SEND SOME REALLY LONG BAD JOKES.
WILL YOU REMEMBER ME?
ALWAYS.

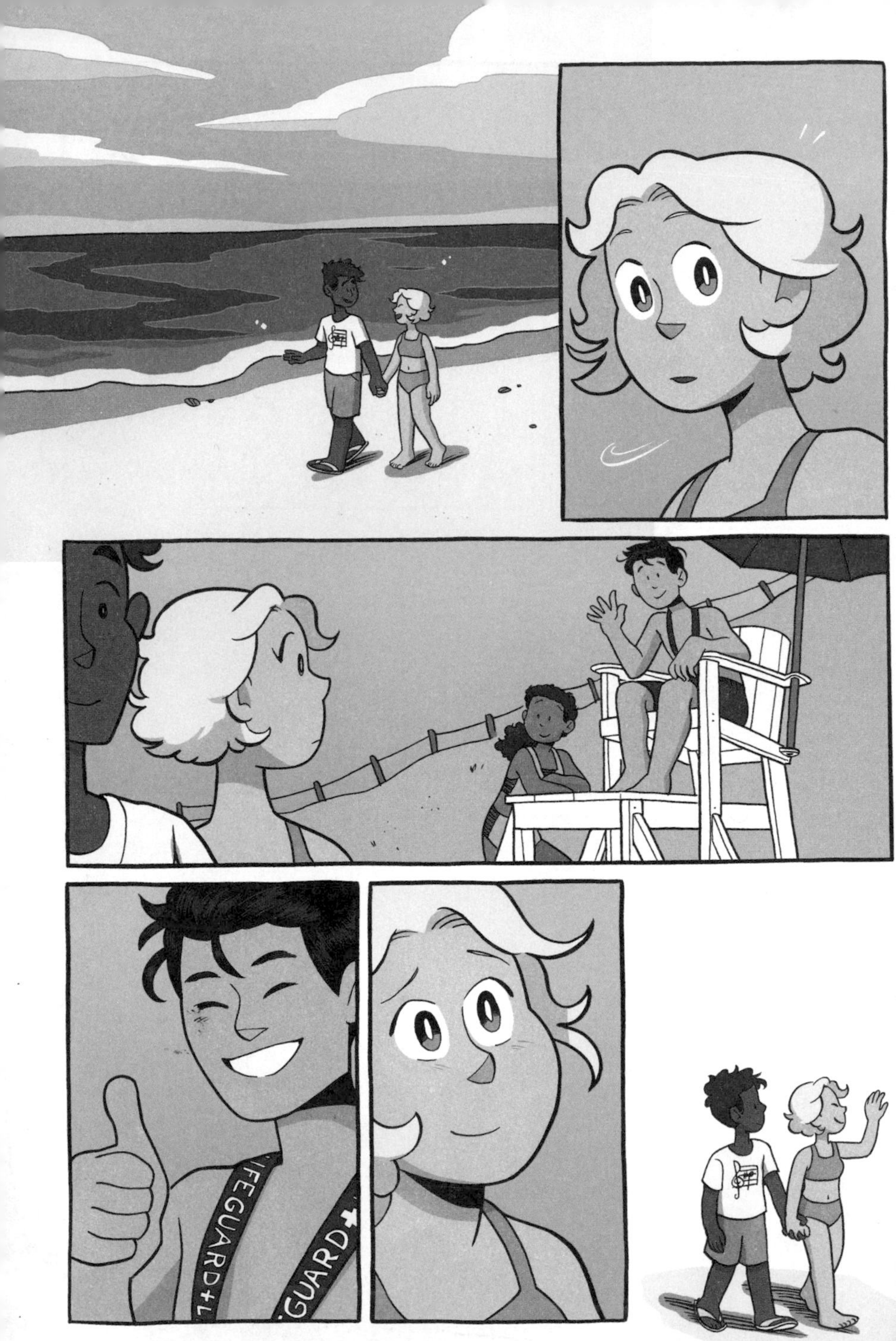
IFEGUARD+L
GUARD+

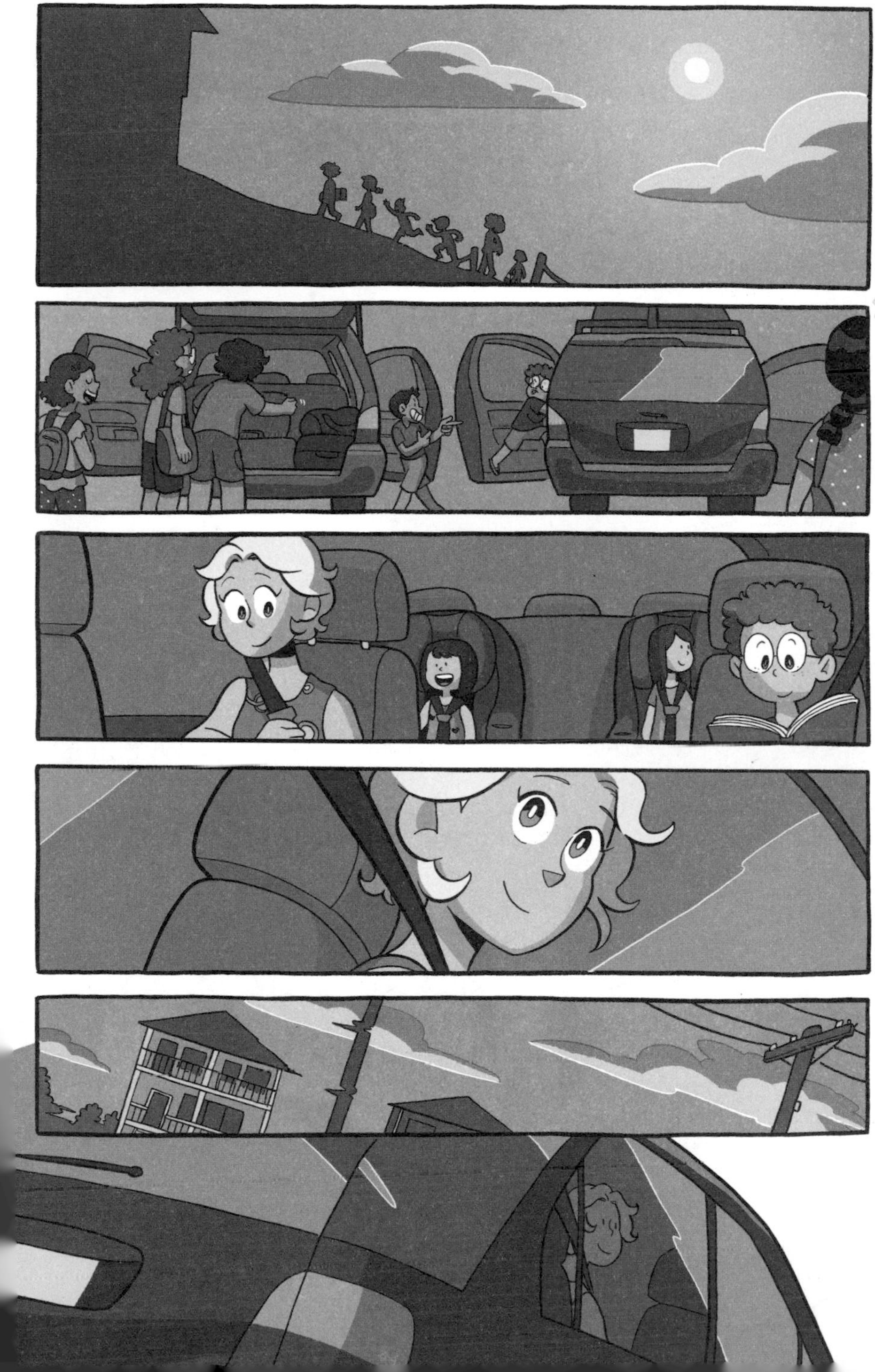

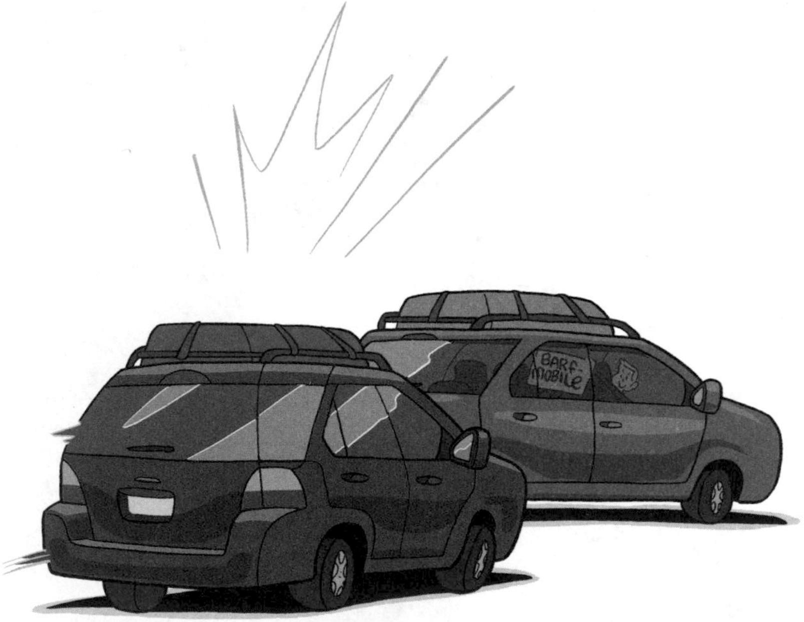
BARF-MOBILE

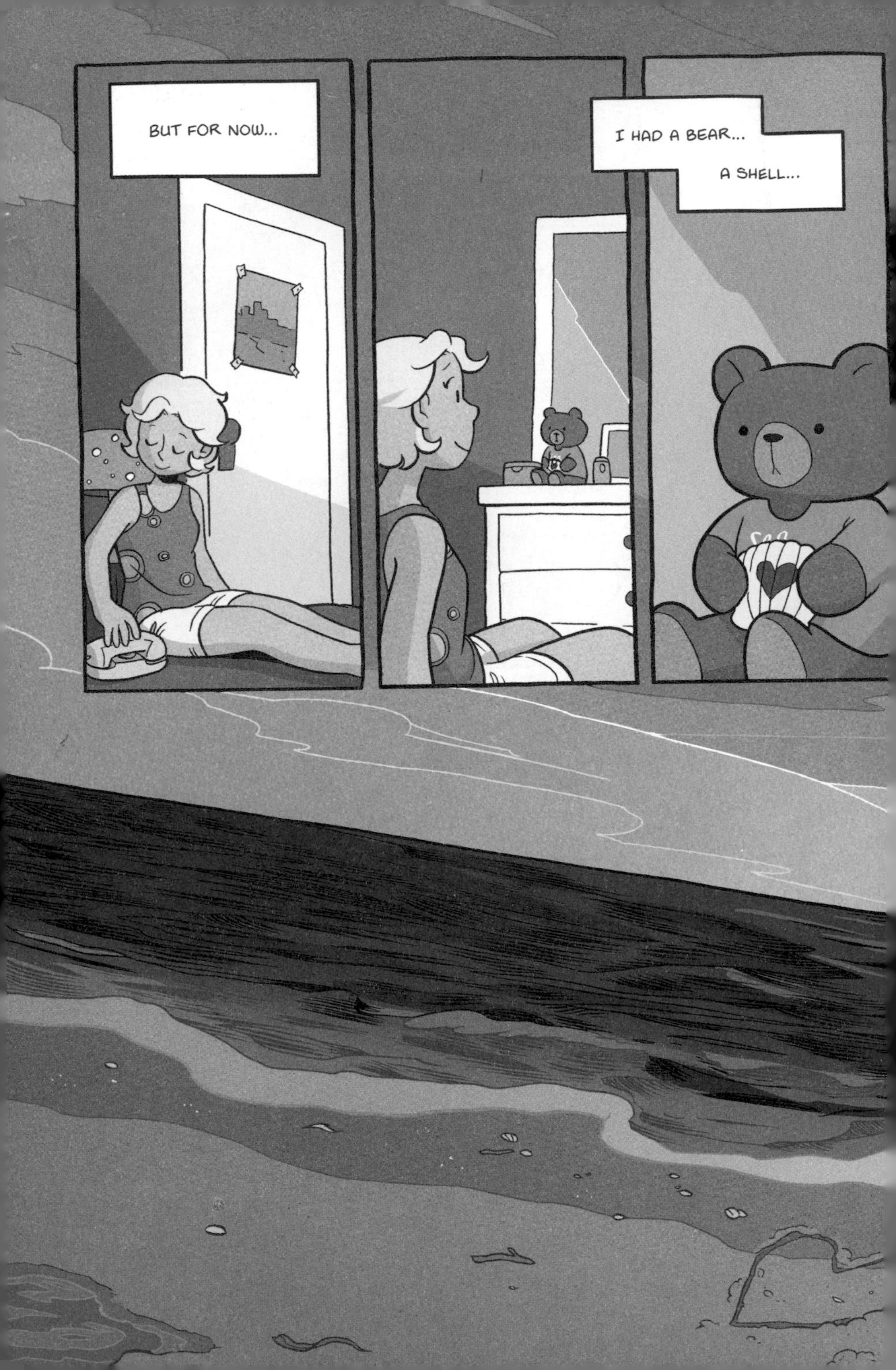
BUT FOR NOW...
I HAD A BEAR...
A SHELL...

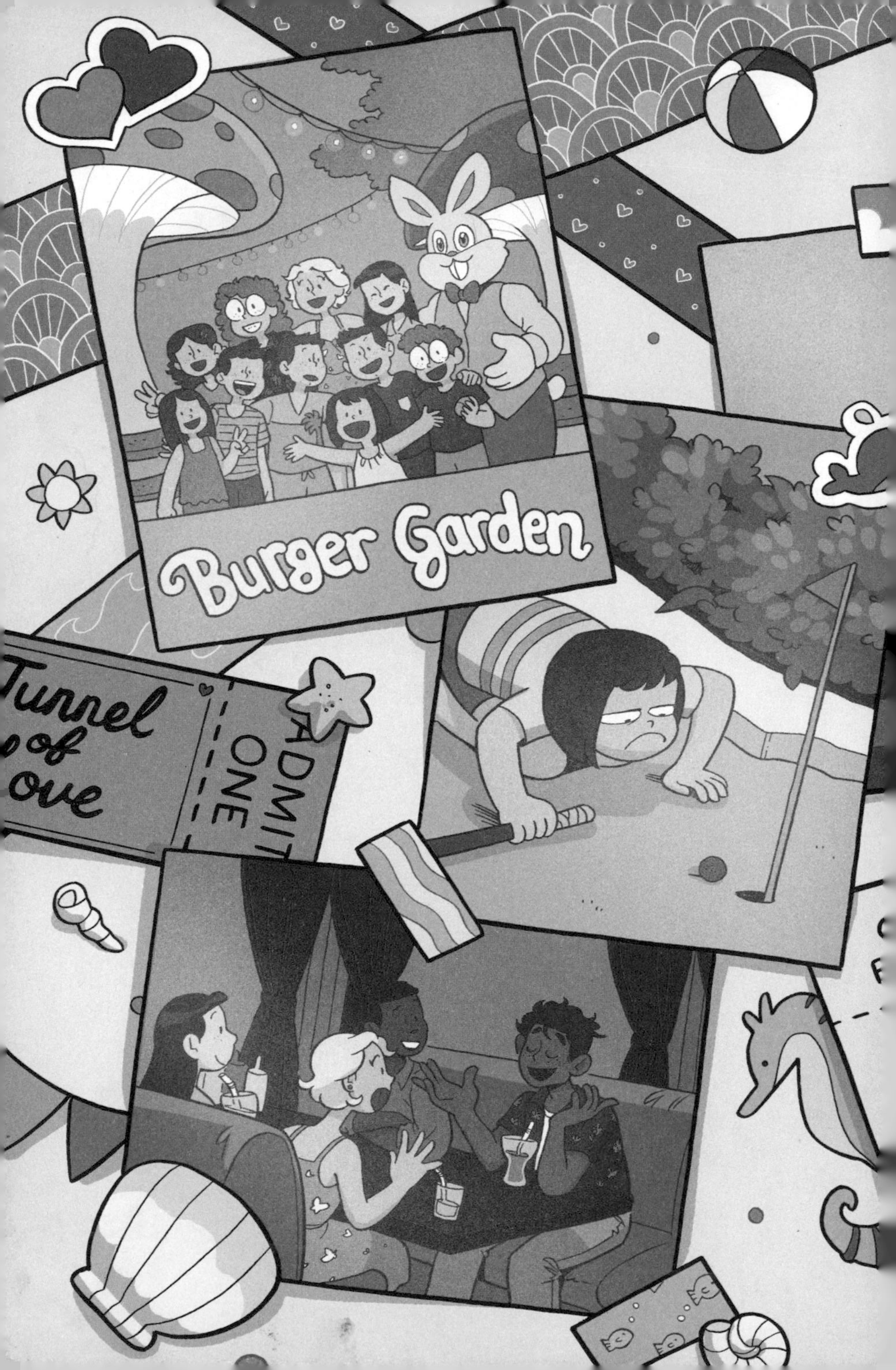
Burger Garden
Tunnel of Love
ADMIT ONE

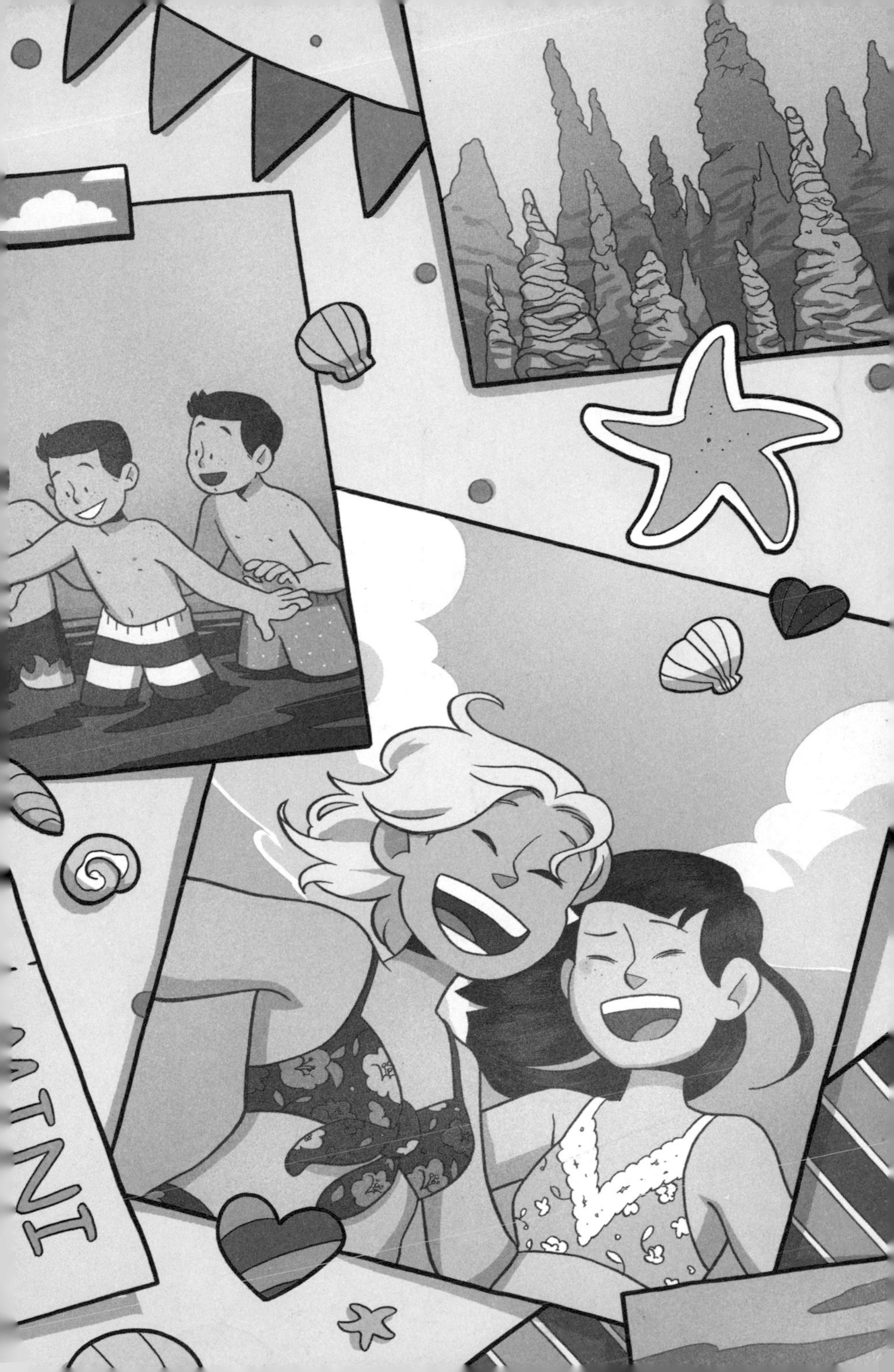

ANN M. MARTIN'S The Baby-sitters Club is one of the most popular series in the history of publishing — with more than 176 million books in print worldwide — and inspired a generation of young readers. Her novels include *Belle Teal, A Corner of the Universe* (a Newbery Honor book), *Here Today, A Dog's Life,* and *On Christmas Eve,* as well as the much-loved collaborations, *P.S. Longer Letter Later* and *Snail Mail No More,* with Paula Danziger, and *The Doll People* and *The Meanest Doll in the World,* written with Laura Godwin and illustrated by Brian Selznick. She lives in upstate New York.

GALE GALLIGAN is the creator of *New York Times* bestselling graphic novel adaptations of *Dawn and the Impossible Three* and *Kristy's Big Day* by Ann M. Martin. When Gale isn't making comics, she enjoys knitting, reading, and spending time with her adorable pet rabbits. She lives in Pleasantville, New York. Visit her online at galesaur.com.

DON'T MISS THE OTHER BABY-SITTERS CLUB GRAPHIC NOVELS!

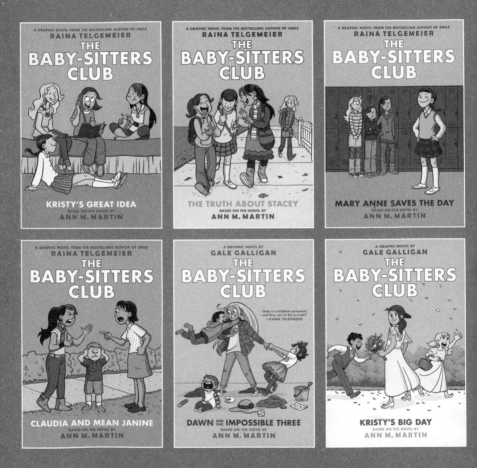

A GRAPHIC NOVEL FROM THE BESTSELLING AUTHOR OF *SMILE*
RAINA TELGEMEIER
THE BABY-SITTERS CLUB
KRISTY'S GREAT IDEA
BASED ON THE NOVEL BY
ANN M. MARTIN

A GRAPHIC NOVEL FROM THE BESTSELLING AUTHOR OF *SMILE*
RAINA TELGEMEIER
THE BABY-SITTERS CLUB
THE TRUTH ABOUT STACEY
BASED ON THE NOVEL BY
ANN M. MARTIN

A GRAPHIC NOVEL FROM THE BESTSELLING AUTHOR OF *SMILE*
RAINA TELGEMEIER
THE BABY-SITTERS CLUB
MARY ANNE SAVES THE DAY
BASED ON THE NOVEL BY
ANN M. MARTIN

A GRAPHIC NOVEL FROM THE BESTSELLING AUTHOR OF *SMILE*
RAINA TELGEMEIER
THE BABY-SITTERS CLUB
CLAUDIA AND MEAN JANINE
BASED ON THE NOVEL BY
ANN M. MARTIN

A GRAPHIC NOVEL BY
GALE GALLIGAN
THE BABY-SITTERS CLUB
"Gale is a brilliant cartoonist, and fans are in for a treat!"
~ RAINA TELGEMEIER
DAWN AND THE IMPOSSIBLE THREE
BASED ON THE NOVEL BY
ANN M. MARTIN

A GRAPHIC NOVEL BY
GALE GALLIGAN
THE BABY-SITTERS CLUB
KRISTY'S BIG DAY
BASED ON THE NOVEL BY
ANN M. MARTIN